GOLDEN

REUTS PUBLICATIONS

golden

MELINDA MICHAELS

Cover design by Ashley Ruggirello
Cover art Copyright 2015 speedofmyshutter/So-ghislaine/Sirius-sdz on DeviantArt.com

ISBN: 978-1-942111-15-3

This is a work of fiction. Names, characters, places and incidents are either the product of the author's imagination or are used fictitiously, and any resemblance to actual persons, living or dead, business establishments, events or locals is entirely coincidental.

REUTS Publications
www.REUTS.com

Dedicated to those who lived once upon a time.

CHAPTER ONE

*I*t happened again. Hanna couldn't believe that it happened again, and in homeroom. *Damn it,* she thought. *This is so embarrassing . . .*

Hanna Loch sat in the nurse's office, holding an ice bag to the side of her head that had hit the desk when she passed out—the new girl's desk, nonetheless. She groaned inwardly. This was the second time in a week it had happened, and it was mortifying. She hadn't had blackouts like these since she was eight years old. And now, after almost ten years of being blackout free, she'd had two in the same week. *Once upon a time, a weird girl kept passing out,* she thought sarcastically.

"Now, you say this happened Monday?" the nurse asked. She was a large, stocky woman with pale hair and dark eyes. She looked like one of those female opera singers who dressed like a Viking.

"Yes," Hanna answered, playing with her necklace. It was a comforting habit she usually fell into when she was thinking or nervous. "When I was at work. I'd just finished cleaning off this table when I bumped into this guy, and then this—" Hanna motioned her free hand to her head, "—this happened, I guess. I don't know. One minute I'm wiping down a table, the next I'm laying on the floor with a bunch of people standing around me." She shifted in her seat, flinching as she moved.

"Any headaches?"

The headaches that followed the blackouts were unlike any she'd ever experienced. She felt as though someone was banging a hammer squarely on her forehead, though that could have been from the fall. She'd had headaches before, but these were different, stronger, and this particular one had been followed by a wave of nausea.

"Yes, right after I black out. When I come to, I get the worst headache ever."

"Mmm," the nurse murmured, looking down at her chart. Hanna watched as she checked off a questionnaire dealing with head trauma. The nurse looked slightly confused. She probably never dealt with anything more serious than a few epidural needles and insulin shots. Her favorite diagnosis was postnasal drip for anyone who came through her doors, whether they actually had it or not.

"Well?" Hanna said after several minutes of silence. She wouldn't have been so pushy if this was any other day, but she was aggravated with herself for blacking out and she didn't have any patience left. The nurse looked up over her clipboard, her eyes telling Hanna that she hated impatient students more than anything in the world.

"As far as I can tell, Miss Loch, there's nothing wrong with you," the nurse said condescendingly. "But since you'll probably want a second opinion, I suggest you go see your family doctor." She bent over her desk and scribbled on a piece of paper. "Give this to your teacher when you get back to class."

Hanna just looked at her. "Class? Don't you think I should be sent home, so I can go see my doctor?"

"Miss Loch, you're not going to die between now and the end of the school day."

"I really think I should go—"

"Miss Loch," the nurse said in a stern tone. "Go back to class."

Witch, Hanna thought as she tossed the nurse the ice pack before leaving the room. She overheard her mumble something about respect as she left, but Hanna wasn't in her usual good mood. She was annoyed that she'd blacked out in front of her homeroom class and even though she wouldn't admit it to anyone, she was a little scared. *Why did I black out?*

As she walked down the hallway, Hanna tried to remember the first time it happened, which was easy. Everything about that day was vivid in her head, because it was the first memory she had. She'd been eight years old when she woke on the couch to see her parents and grandparents standing over her. Everything before that day was a blank. No matter how many times she tried or how hard she concentrated, she couldn't remember anything. It was as if she'd been born that day. What was even more frustrating than not having any memory of the first eight years of her life, though, was the fact that no one could ever explain *why*.

She'd had x-rays, CAT scans, and blood work, done just about every test science provided to determine what caused them, but nothing ever came back positive. A brief episode with a psychiatrist had gotten them nowhere. Apparently, Hanna's memories had disappeared, and her blackouts were a side effect. That was the only explanation she received.

She debated going back to class as she walked to homeroom. It was nearly second period, so she'd get back just in time to be questioned by everyone, or at least her best friend Carly. The rest would probably stare and wonder what was wrong with her.

Her steps slowed until she stopped completely. This was ridiculous. Just because the bitter nurse wouldn't send her home didn't mean she had to stay. *Screw it*, she thought. She was leaving, with or without a nurse's note. She normally didn't ditch school, but this wasn't a normal day.

People don't just black out, she told herself as she headed down the empty hall of New Hope High School. She doubted if the nurse had even read her medical history. Her blackouts hadn't happened since before she'd permanently moved in with her grandparents.

Making sure there wasn't anyone around, she pushed open the main door and hurried down the front steps as fast as she could, making a beeline for the parking lot. Taking her car keys out of her purse as she walked, she paused for a moment as her head throbbed. Maybe driving was a bad idea. What if she blacked out again? She'd cause an accident for sure, if not kill herself.

She looked toward the road and wondered if she should walk, shrinking inside her coat. It was early March and though Michigan had experienced a bizarrely warm winter this year, it was still only thirty-something degrees out. She shivered as the wind cut threw her. Town wasn't too far away. Sure, it was foggy and there was a very light, misty snowfall that gave the world around her an ethereal look, but she shouldn't drive. It was too dangerous. Besides, if she was going to drive her car to college at the end of the summer, she couldn't crash it now. She didn't have the time or money to fix it.

Decision to walk made, she put her keys away and made her way through the parking lot, over the grass barrier, and onto the quiet road that sat in front of the school.

I won't get into any trouble for this, she thought as she crossed the street. Her grandparents would agree with her.

For a moment, she thought of what her parents would say if they were in Michigan and not gallivanting around the world, studying the migration pattern of the great white shark. Or was it the Orca now? Every time she got an e-mail or phone call from them, all she heard about was how fantastic their new study was going. She'd been bitter toward her parents when she first moved in with her grandparents, but her resentment had dwindled over the years. Her grandparents were far more fit people to live with, and she was glad to have them.

Gram and Grandpa were much more relaxed than most of her friends' parents, probably because they had been through raising kids before. They let her have a little more freedom than most, and she was grateful. Her friends thought she was the luckiest person in the world to have such cool grandparents, but she always bristled when they said things like that. Even though she'd made peace with her parents being away, she was still a little bitter. In her opinion, her friends all had normal parents who didn't live on a boat thousands of miles away. They had siblings who stole their clothes and arguments with their parents. She constantly felt like there wasn't a place she belonged. Her grandparents had taken her in because she was their granddaughter—they sort of *had* to take her. Of course, that was the least of her problems today. She had to get home and call the doctor.

She rubbed her hand across her forehead, squeezing her temples with her thumb and index finger, soothing her subsiding headache. It was nearly gone now, but a feeling of uncertainty lingered. She inhaled deeply, trying to shake it off.

The snowy mix that fell around her began to lighten up. She tucked one of her pale, shoulder-length strands behind her ear. Her hair was slightly wet, and she grumbled at the thought of it frizzing as she watched the half-melted snowflakes disappear into the black pavement. She and the rest of New Hope were surprised at how mild the winter had been, and as she looked to the woods on either side of the road, she acknowledged the peacefulness of it all. The world was quiet and still and she couldn't help but think that it looked sort of *enchanting*.

She smiled to herself. She would have bet a week's worth of tips that no one had ever called New Hope enchanting. The mist hung dreamlike in the air, as if a cloud had settled to earth; the falling wet snow made her feel strangely calm. She shook her head . . . maybe that blackout had affected her more than she thought.

Hanna hardly recognized the sound of screeching tires on wet pavement. She looked up and saw an old truck speeding toward her through the fog. She'd begun crossing the road without even knowing.

She inhaled sharply, lifting her hands as everything around her went into slow-motion. She thought about how stupid she was for putting her hands up, as if they'd deter the speeding pile of metal about to kill her. She saw everything in that instant before her impending death: the driver's face, his eyes wide as he noticed her; the paper cup he held in front of his face, partially covering his expression; the cold wind that blew, and the falling mist that seemed suspended in mid air. She saw every detail as her thoughts were littered with inconsequential things instead of flashes of her life. She couldn't move, even if she'd had the sense to try and jump out of the way.

Why do people hold their breath when they're about to be injured? She closed her eyes and braced herself. Her heart felt like it stopped as the screeching of rubber on pavement echoed around her. Had her body decided to just cut out the middle man and quit on its own, knowing that her heart was going to stop beating anyway? It was a ridiculous thing to be thinking at the moment. *Are these my last thoughts?*

She felt the sudden rush of something big blow past her. She tried to match the sound of a speeding car and crunching metal to the image of the old truck running her over, but it didn't match. Why was there crunching metal, but no pain? Paralyzed with fear, she could barely move her legs. Opening her eyes, she saw something completely different from what she had expected a split second earlier.

She saw the old truck, only a foot from where she stood, and to her surprise, a brand new, light blue Ford F-150 was crunched up into the side of it. Smoke and vapors rose from the collision, and she could almost taste the gasoline coming from the wreck. The driver of the old truck climbed out, his face showing a million emotions.

"Shit," Hanna said quietly.

"Oh my God!" he said. "Oh my God, are you okay? Jeez, this guy came out of nowhere!"

Hanna was silent as she watched the man inspect his damaged vehicle. *I'm in shock*, she thought dumbly. If that blue truck hadn't crashed into the other one, she would have been dead. She tried to move, but couldn't. She was in awe of the scene in front of her, and she suddenly noticed that the world around her was slightly different. The air tasted sweeter; her vision felt sharper. Even the smell of the surrounding trees seemed overwhelming, as if she'd never experienced the smell of late winter before. She felt exhilarated and terrified all at once.

Her focus wandered to the Ford's passenger-side door to read a large magnetic sign: "Vann Construction; Offices in South Carolina and Michigan." A phone number was listed at the bottom. The driver's door opened and a pair of construction boots landed on the ground. She tried to see the man's face as he moved around to inspect his mangled truck, but was distracted by an old woman who'd come from somewhere to fuss over her.

"Are you all right, dear?" the old woman asked. It was Mrs. Watson, a senile woman who always walked around New Hope when her middle-aged son was at work. Hanna nodded mutely, more interested in the conversation a few feet away.

"Didn't you see me?" The old truck's owner was nearly yelling.

"I saw the girl in the road. I saw you," the Vann guy said in a lower voice, his back toward Hanna. "I didn't know what else to do. You were going pretty fast." He didn't sound angry that he'd just totaled his obviously new truck to save her life.

She sucked in her breath, only just fully registering that she wasn't dead, but had come seriously close. She tried to look away from the Vann guy and couldn't. He had saved her life, and his truck had been destroyed in the process. She felt a pang of guilt, though she'd have gladly chosen herself over a truck any day.

"I wouldn't have hit her," the other man lied, though it was obvious they were all aware that if things had gone differently, they'd be calling the morgue instead of their insurances.

"Do you want to sit down, dear? You look a little shaken up," Mrs. Watson said.

"No, I'm fine," Hanna insisted. "I better be going—"

"Hey, you! You saw it. He hit me, right?"

She tore her eyes away from the Vann guy's back as the other man called to her.

"What?"

"He *hit* me!" the man yelled. But then a sudden change came over his face. "Oh, you're that Loch girl."

Hanna bristled. She stared at him and recognized the man, but couldn't place his name. He suddenly looked uncomfortable. "Well, you saw it, didn't you?"

She couldn't believe he was actually trying to blame the Vann guy for damaging his car, even though he'd almost killed her because he was drinking his coffee instead of watching the road. Sure, she hadn't looked both ways before crossing the street and so she was partly guilty, but she wasn't thinking about that. All she could think of at that moment was the nerve of the guy who'd almost killed her.

"I didn't see anything besides your truck about to run me over," she answered coolly, giving him a nasty look. The clarity she had seen in the world only moments ago began to fade, and she suddenly felt low, like she had just been dropped off a cliff. She inhaled and was disappointed the air was no longer sweet. What was wrong with her?

"I have to go."

She turned to leave, ignoring the man's angry sputtering behind her, but jumped when a hand wrapped around her elbow in a surprisingly strong grip.

"Listen, I don't—" Her words faltered as she turned back and saw that it was the Vann guy.

"Are you sure you're okay?" he asked, concerned.

She was too taken by him to say anything at first. He was younger than she originally thought, maybe only a couple of years older than herself, and she was surprised at how attracted she was to him. His face was classic looking and strange; he could have been plucked right out of a gothic painting. For a second, she thought she saw a dark, purplish haze around him, just as if he actually were from a portrait.

11

His dark black hair was short on the sides and longer at the top, styled perfectly. The square jawline and Roman nose were enough to win him modeling jobs, and his eyes made her feel warm, despite their cool gray color. They were amazing, the most beautiful gray eyes she'd ever seen.

Beautiful, she thought. There wasn't a better word to describe him.

"Are you all right?" he asked again, worry clouding his face.

"I'm fine, thanks," she finally said as he let her go. "And thanks for, you know." Her words failed as she nodded toward the accident. Her heart was beating an insane rhythm inside her chest.

He smiled, relief plain on his face.

"Anytime," he said, and she believed him.

He was on the phone in a minute—talking to his boss, by the sounds of it—while the other man was cursing up a storm. She was already down the road when she saw cop lights. She decided to hurry her pace, not wanting to be seen by Owen. He wouldn't be too thrilled if he found her to be the cause of an accident while ditching school.

Owen was like her older brother. As her adopted cousin, they were basically related, though he still insisted on being addressed as "Officer Peirce" when he was in uniform. He came to New Hope six months ago, and they'd become close since then. She couldn't understand why he'd left the exciting world of New York City to come to rinky-dink New Hope and be a cop, but it was nice getting to know someone she hadn't known her entire life.

She wasn't as worried about Owen though. She was more preoccupied with the accident that had nearly killed her. Why had she been able to see so crystal clear in those few moments before the crash? The air had tasted so sweet; the pavement shone like polished coal. She heard every decibel of the tires screeching. Had her senses gone into overload because of the danger she'd been in? Her heart was still beating faster than normal, but her vision and sense of smell had settled back into place. Her heartbeat was the only remaining evidence of her near death experience. *It was terrifying,* she thought, *terrifying, and yet exhilarating at the same time.*

Hanna turned and looked at the empty road behind her. Was it completely crazy to want to feel like that again, just for a moment? What would it take? If she could be prepared, if she could anticipate the feeling, she bet she could experience it better.

Shaking her head, she walked as quickly as she could down the road and eventually got to town. What was she thinking, wanting to feel like that again? Focusing on her strides, she pushed all thoughts of it out of her mind.

She looked up at the buildings in front of her. It was a small town that hadn't ever had a large population, but especially in recent years. The crumbling infrastructure combined with the winter months made the atmosphere pretty depressing, but Hanna was used to it. It was still cold and gray, even with the warm winter, making New Hope feel like it was having one very long, very rainy day.

Passing the grocery store and the diner where she worked, she tried to look inconspicuous. Because New Hope was such a small town, Hanna expected to be stopped by someone every time she walked down the street. Usually, she didn't mind and welcomed a smile from a neighbor, but today was just turning into one of those days. She'd blacked out, ditched school, left her station wagon, and almost got hit by a truck . . . she just wanted to get home and call her doctor.

She'd been walking for twenty minutes when she saw red and blue lights reflecting off the wet pavement in front of her. She knew it was Owen without looking. He was going to give her hell for ditching.

She stopped, turning when she heard the car door open and close. Owen was walking toward her, his officer's face firmly in place.

He was a tall man, with light brown hair cut like a crew cut, but left a little longer. His eyes were strange—Hanna could never tell if they were green, hazel, or brown. He was handsome in his own way, but she thought that, despite coming from New York City, he didn't look very out-of-the-ordinary. Not like the Vann guy, with his black hair and surprisingly tan skin.

Just as she thought of him, she noticed movement in the back of Owen's cruiser. She squinted and saw the Vann guy in the back of the car.

"What are you doing?" she demanded as Owen stopped in front of her. "Are you arresting him?"

She actually felt upset. Is the Vann guy going to jail? And do I really have to keep referring to him as the "Vann guy?" How about, the guy who saved my life, or the guy who has beautiful eyes? She squared her shoulders.

"Hanna," Owen said in a surprised tone, though his face looked disapproving. "What are *you* doing is the question. You don't look surprised to see me."

"Well, are you arresting him?" she asked again, ignoring his question.

"What are you doing out of school? It's only . . ." he looked at his watch, agitating her more by not answering her question. ". . . 11:34 a.m. Skipping class?"

"I'm going to the doctor," she conceded.

"Oh. Well, all right . . . what do you know about a car accident over on Route 17?"

"Are you arresting him?" she asked for the third time.

Owen looked back at the car. "I could be. I could not be. Why are you so concerned about it?"

"I just know that you shouldn't arrest him. He ruined his truck to save my life."

That got Owen's attention. "What do you mean he saved your life?"

"I was crossing the street where Fetterman Road meets Route 17. It was foggy and this old, black truck was coming at me. I thought I was going to get hit, but next thing I know, his Ford had T-boned the other truck," she said, pointing to the cop car. "After he asked me if I was okay, I left."

"You left a crime scene?"

"Yes, I know, bad on my part," she said, fighting the urge to roll her eyes. "But that guy saved my life. You can't arrest him."

Owen was silent for a moment, and she regretted leaving the accident. He'd probably already charged the Vann guy, and if she hadn't left the scene, she would have been able to sort it out. Owen was a strict guy, especially when he wore his uniform, but besides being a stickler for the law, he was always fair.

"Jeez, Hanna." He shook his head, as if he was having an inner struggle. "Why'd you leave? I remember quite clearly telling you and your friends never to leave the scene of an accident at that prom safe driving thing you had at school a few weeks ago."

"I know," she said.

"Only guilty parties leave the scene," he said, sounding as if he'd rehearsed the line a thousand times. He might be a good guy, but he was a complete geek for law enforcement. He waved a hand at the car. "This guy's license is expired. I have to take him in."

"Do you really? Can't you just, you know, write him a ticket or something?"

"I can't. I already called it in." Owen looked back at his car again. "Why would you leave the scene?"

She really didn't want to tell him about her blackout, and certainly didn't want to mention that something about the guy in the back of his cruiser excited her. She felt her cheeks warm and hoped that Owen would think it was the wind instead of her blushing.

"I didn't want to make it a big thing," she said, looking over his shoulder.

"Well, now I have to take him to the station. You know, the other driver denies that you were even there," he said. "He said he was just driving the speed limit when, out of nowhere, he was hit."

"Well, he's lying," she defended. "He was speeding and couldn't see me through the coffee cup that was blocking his vision. He would have killed me if the Vann guy didn't hit him."

"The Vann guy?"

"I don't know his name," she shrugged, nodding at the cop car.

Owen sighed. "It's William Vann. I'm going to need your statement. Otherwise, it's just one word against the other. It seems everyone at the scene showed up after the incident, except Mrs. Watson, but she's practically senile." He shook his head. "Where's your car?"

"I left it at school."

"Why?"

"Owen, please," she said, rephrasing when she saw the look on his face. "Officer Peirce, can I just come to the station later? I've got a major headache, and I just want to get to the doctor."

Owen looked at her with concerned suspicion.

"What's up with you, kid?" he asked, his voice switching to his gentler, civilian tone. His "big brother voice," as she called it. "You don't seem like yourself."

She could see that he wasn't going to let her out of his sight until she'd convinced him she was fine.

"I blacked out in class today," she confessed, keeping her eyes on the cruiser. Did William Vann just sit up straighter as she spoke? He couldn't have heard her, could he? *I hope not,* she thought, uncomfortable with the idea of the handsome stranger knowing her strange affliction.

Owen noticed where she was staring and turned to look at the man in his back seat. "It's okay, he can't hear you," he said reassuringly. For some reason, she wasn't so sure. "Why'd you black out?"

"I don't know. I mean, I used to black out when I was younger, but I haven't done it in almost ten years. I just want to go see my doctor and make sure I don't have a tumor or something."

"Get in the car," Owen said, switching back to his police officer voice. "I'll take you to your doctor's."

She fought a smile. He was always so serious when it came to being a cop and even more so now that he viewed her as a younger sister. They'd connected in a weird way when he came to New Hope, and she'd always believed it was because they were both outcasts, her without her parents and him being new to the area. She couldn't pinpoint what else made Owen so different, but at the same time, he didn't seem to be able to figure her out either. Whatever it was, they were content with being a little odd, and they looked out for each other.

"No, that's okay. I'm fine, really, and I'm almost home. I'll have Gram drive me." She started walking backward, her eyes shifting from Owen to his cruiser. "I'll come down to the station after the doctor. I promise."

"Yes, you will," Owen said as he got back into his car. "Or I'll subpoena you."

She smiled at him and gave a little wave, to which he nodded. As the car pulled out into the street, Hanna's eyes wandered to William in the back seat. *There's something about people in the back of cop cars*, she thought. They seemed like caged animals whose faces became burned into memory simply because they could be dangerous. The mind just can't help but remember them.

She felt a shiver go down her spine when William caught her eye out the back window as the car drove away. She waited for the vehicle to disappear behind the corner, knowing she would never forget his face. There was something about his eyes that seemed hypnotic. He wasn't smiling like he had when they spoke briefly earlier. She wished he would.

Guilt washed over her. Why would he smile now? He'd been arrested and was going to be at the station longer than necessary because she was going to the doctor. First, he'd wrecked his truck to save her life; then he'd been arrested because she left the scene. Owen said his license was expired, but still. It was pretty much her fault.

"Damn it," she said aloud as she crossed the street. She'd go and give her statement to Owen first, and hopefully, they'd let William go. It was the least she could do for the man who'd saved her life. She cringed at what he would think of her once Owen told him that she'd had other things to do first.

She let out an aggravated half sigh, half grunt. This was turning into one of those horribly long days that seemed to never end. It was all the right kinds of wrong.

CHAPTER TWO

Hanna pulled open the heavy glass doors of the police station and walked into the small building. She looked to the front desk where the receptionist, Mrs. Hines, sat giving her a tentative smile. She returned the woman's greeting, not feeling much like smiling. Mrs. Hines was Gram's best friend, though, so she made the effort.

Hanna knew almost everyone here, from Mrs. Hines to the chief of police—Captain McCormack—who always used to stop by her house on Sundays to catch up with her grandfather. Then there was Officer Riley, who had just married one of the new teachers at her school, and Miss Thompson, who was the daughter of Mr. Thompson, who sold the diner where Hanna worked to Peter Olympia. She could just about connect everyone to someone in New Hope.

Of course, there were exceptions, like Owen. The only other person she couldn't connect was William Vann. For some reason, when she thought of the name "Vann," a little tune would play in her head, like a song or jingle. *Where have I heard that name before?* She'd never seen his truck driving around town; that was for sure. It was like he'd come out of nowhere, in the middle of nowhere.

As she tried to place his name to the song in her head, she shrugged off her coat and walked to the front desk, reminding herself that if he hadn't come out of nowhere she'd probably be dead. She grew slightly nervous about seeing him again. How do you act around someone who saved your life?

"Hello, Hanna. Odd seeing you here," Mrs. Hines smiled up at her, looking over the glasses that rested on the tip of her nose. Even though she was in her mid-sixties, Mrs. Hines was a beautiful lady, with short dark hair streaked with silver wisps and dark skin that seemed to never age. She was always smiling and was like a second grandmother to Hanna.

"Hi, Mrs. Hines. Can I see Officer Peirce?" she asked.

"Well, he's in interrogation," Mrs. Hines said. Her eyebrows rose. She seemed to be excited that there was actually someone to interrogate. Now that Hanna thought of it, the whole police station seemed to be buzzing with excitement.

"Sweetheart," Mrs. Hines said, her smile fading a fraction. "Why aren't you in school? Is everything all right?"

"Yes," she began. "Actually, no. Can you call Gram? I left my car at the school, and I want to go to the doctor. I've been having some serious headaches all day."

"Oh dear, of course I can call her. Just have a seat—"

"Hanna?" Captain McCormack asked, coming out of his office. "What are you doing here? Is everything okay?"

Hanna had to smile. Everything ran like such clockwork in this town that for her to be out of school before noon on a Tuesday was the most bizarre thing anyone had ever witnessed. On top of the car crash, they were practically thrown for a loop.

"I'm fine, Captain McCormack," she said. "I was just looking for Officer Peirce. He needed me for questioning."

Mrs. Hines looked up from dialing, surprised. Captain McCormack seemed equally interested.

"Questioning? For what?"

Her smile faded slightly. Was she going to have to explain to everyone what had happened to her and why?

"Hanna," Owen said, coming out of the interrogation room. "I thought you were coming after the doctor?"

"Doctor?" Captain McCormack repeated, looking worried.

"I'm fine, really," she said, walking past the captain. She walked down the hallway and straight into the room where Owen was holding the door open.

It was a plain, eggshell-colored room with a black table, a few wooden chairs, and William Vann. Her breath hitched when she saw him, his eyes looking just as bright and wild as they had before. They made her think of ice dripping down the side of a rock. He smiled, making Hanna think he'd been expecting to see her.

He sat with one hand wrapped around a paper cup and the other on his lap. Hands down, he was the best-looking guy she'd ever seen, but something about his smile made her uneasy. She ignored the little voice in her head warning her to stay away from him and smiled in return. He was a mystery, and she was attracted to him.

"Take a seat, Hanna," Owen said, irritated. Was he annoyed with her? Setting her coat aside, she sat and avoided looking at William. "This is William Vann," Owen continued. "Mr. Vann, this is Hanna Loch."

She nodded at him, barely letting her eyes linger.

"Hello," she said quickly.

"Hello," he said slowly.

She bit the inside of her cheek to stop herself from smiling at him again. Why in the world did she want to smile so much? Her cheeks heated up.

Owen hit the tape recorder that was sitting on the table.

"This is Officer Owen Peirce, at 11:53 a.m., Tuesday, March fifteenth. Continuing in the questioning of Mr. William Vann. Hanna?"

"Yes?"

"Please state your full name."

"Hanna Loch."

"No, middle name, too."

"Oh, Hanna Georgette Loch."

"And what were you doing today between the hours of ten and twelve?"

Hanna leaned over, not really sure how to talk to a recorder. She glanced at William and caught his subtle smile.

"I was walking home on Fetterman Road when I had to cross to get to Route 17."

"Why were you walking on Fetterman Road?"

"I already told you."

"Hanna," Owen said in a quick, matter-of-fact voice. "Just answer the question."

"Okay," she said, fiddling with her necklace. She noticed William watching and stopped. "I left school because I blacked out and wanted to go to the doctor. I didn't want to drive because I was worried that I might black out again, so I decided to walk."

She focused her attention on the recorder, cheeks hot, not wanting to look at either of them. William probably thought she was a weirdo. She could have strangled Owen.

"So, you were walking down Fetterman Road and decided to cross it to get to Route 17. Is that correct?"

"Yes, I have to walk up Route 17 to get home."

"You said you were going to the doctor."

She shot Owen a look.

"I can't walk to the doctor's office, Owen. I had to get a ride."

"It's Officer Peirce, Hanna," he said sternly.

She rolled her eyes. She was trying hard not to look immature, but Owen was riding her last nerve. She was cold and tired from walking in the wet snow, she just wanted the day to be over, and he was reprimanding her for using his first name.

"I was walking home so I could get a ride to the doctor, because I didn't want to cause an accident driving in case I blacked out again, Officer Peirce," she said pointedly. "It was foggy out. I was almost across the street when I heard a car. It didn't have its headlights on. Maybe that's why I didn't see it. When I looked up, it was close enough that I could see the guy finishing his coffee. I froze and shut my eyes."

"You didn't try to get out of the way?"

Hanna tried not to make any expression. She was starting to think there was a reason she hadn't moved, but it wasn't anyone's business. She didn't want to die, but it had felt like her body wanted to go against instinct and keep her rooted to the heart of danger. After the initial fear of the situation subsided, she'd felt her heart beating and everything had seemed different. The air was crisper, the colors were brighter. Maybe she was a little crazy.

"Hanna?"

"What?"

"I asked why you didn't try to get out of the way."

"Oh . . . well, I don't know. I was scared. I tried to move, but

I couldn't, so I just closed my eyes and braced myself." Neither William nor Owen spoke, so she continued. "Anyway, I heard a loud crash, and when I opened my eyes, I saw that his truck had T-boned the other one, right before it hit me. The other driver got out of the truck and seemed fine. William seemed fine. I was fine, so I left."

Owen nodded slowly and looked at William.

"Well, that's pretty much word for word what Mr. Vann said. Mr. Dinzki denies that you were there."

"Why?"

"Because," William spoke for the first time since saying hello, "it makes him the victim, and not the one who almost killed someone." William held her gaze and shrugged. "He just doesn't want his insurance going up."

"What about your insurance?" she asked before she could stop herself.

"What?" He looked confused.

"It's just, your truck looked pretty expensive . . ." She trailed off. This was just like her, bringing up the worst points to see how people would react.

"It's not a big deal," he said with a tiny shrug.

Hanna blushed, embarrassed that she'd asked. He'd smashed his truck into another just to save someone she didn't know—of course he didn't care about insurance rates. Her head started pounding.

"Can I go now?" she asked Owen, hoping to leave before she said any more foolish things.

"Yeah, that's all I needed you for. You're free to go too, Mr. Vann."

"Thanks," William said.

Hanna was out the door before William stood up from the table. She didn't want to walk out with him and could just imagine the questions he had for her: what kind of fool doesn't jump out of the way? Or worse, what if he told her that she should have more respect for law enforcement? He didn't seem like the type to lecture, but she wasn't going to stick around and find out. It was bad enough she had seemed like some silly high school girl; it'd be mortifying if he treated her like a kid. Besides, she didn't know him—would he think it weird if she waited for him? But then, why did she care what he thought?

She walked swiftly down the hallway, deep in her own thoughts, when she heard Mrs. Hines call her.

"Hanna!"

She stopped and turned, hoping she could still get out of the building before William exited the room. "Loretta said she couldn't get here for another hour or so. She went to Bay City this morning with your grandfather for his cardiologist appointment. She said you should make an appointment with the doctor for tomorrow."

"Thanks, Mrs. Hines," Hanna said half-heartedly, turning back toward the glass doors.

Maybe she'd overreacted and shouldn't have rushed out of school. It was probably better this way. She'd go home, shower, get into her pajamas, and just go straight to bed.

She'd forget this day ever happened. And who knew? Maybe she'd wake up tomorrow and find out this whole day had just been a bad dream.

She pushed her way through the glass doors and hurried down the sidewalk to cross the parking lot. She'd almost made it to the road before realizing she left her coat inside the police station.

"Damn it," she muttered. She turned to go back and almost ran right into William, his beautiful eyes looking straight at her. Her breath caught as her heart raced. She hadn't even heard him following her.

"You forgot your coat," he said, holding out her light yellow peacoat with its black buttons. "I'm surprised the guy didn't see it. It's pretty bright."

"It's not that bright," she said defensively, taking it. There was an awkward pause as she put it on. "I really am sorry about your truck," she said to fill the uncomfortable silence. "I'm guessing your dad is going to be pretty upset."

"My dad?"

She pointed at the logo on his shirt. "Vann Construction. Established 1991. I'm guessing it's the family business."

"Actually, my grandfather started it. My dad took it over in 1991. Why do you think he'll be upset?"

She shrugged. "It looked like a company car, so I imagine he'll be pretty pissed about it being totaled. Especially since you're from the South Carolina location."

William's eyes narrowed. "How do you know that?"

She smiled, getting uncomfortable. *Why didn't I just stop talking? Or, even better, never start.* "The sign on your truck. It said you have offices in South Carolina. Since I don't know you, I figured you were from there."

He watched her quietly for a moment.

"You're perceptive, aren't you?"

"Everyone is, they just don't remember things like I do."

"Why are you so good at remembering?"

She frowned and felt the color drain from her face. It was a simple question, but a loaded one.

"I just am," she said, hoping he didn't notice her expression change. "Anyway, thanks for grabbing my coat."

"No problem," he said, not making a move to leave.

She wondered if he was making her feel nervous on purpose. Why did he look so comfortable while she felt the opposite? She became aware of each beat of her racing heart, and suddenly, the air was sweeter. The mist seemed to float in place around them. Every detail was magnified, just like when the truck almost hit her.

She inhaled sharply and took a step back, surprised when William did the same. She stared at him warily, unsure of what had just happened. He looked equally suspicious of her. Why would he think he had to be cautious around her? She decided she didn't want to know.

"I have to go. Goodbye," she blurted, and left.

She looked both ways several times before crossing the street, not wanting a repeat of earlier. She walked briskly, not caring if he knew she was rushing to get away from him. For whatever reason, William made her feel the same heightened awareness as almost dying, and if she couldn't get out of the way of a speeding truck, at least she could walk away from a strange man. A strange man who had amazing eyes. And looks to die for.

Stop it! she scolded herself. She looked over her shoulder to catch one last glance of him, but he was gone. She took a deep breath. *Good. Just be gone, so my life can go back to normal.* Whatever "normal" was.

She was happy for the uneventful walk home. She didn't need any more brushes with death or odd strangers to fill her thoughts, but she couldn't get William out of her head, no matter how she tried. She plopped on her bed and pulled her favorite stuffed wolf up under her chin. He was her best comfort when she was out-of-sorts. She looked around her basement room. It was meant to be a second living room, but since Gram had trouble going down stairs, it became Hanna's bedroom when she began high school. She'd plastered the walls and filled her shelves with howling wolves, standing guard over her with their glowing eyes. She always felt safe and secure when she knew they were watching.

She heard the front door open a few hours later. "Hanna!" Gram called from the upstairs living room. "We're home!"

Hanna had showered and changed before trying to rest, but was unable to sleep. William's face burned in her mind, and she couldn't stop replaying the events of the day. He'd seemed so different, so out of place in New Hope, yet there was something familiar about him. He seemed a little quieter than other guys she knew. She was certain he wasn't in high school anymore. He had to be at least four years older, which didn't seem like a lot when she thought about how her grandparents were seven years apart.

A knock sounded at the top of the stairs.

"Hanna? Are you home?" Gram's voice carried down the staircase.

"Yes," she answered, shaking herself from her thoughts.

"Well, come upstairs."

She rolled off her bed and climbed the stairs. The basement door opened into the kitchen, which was a dated room in desperate need of a make-over, even though it was clean and comfortable. Gram kept her kitchen the same as when she'd first moved into the house in the mid-sixties. It was retro in the way that style repeats itself.

"Hey," Hanna said as she put the kettle on for tea. It was an old habit to make tea for her and Gram. "How was the cardiologist?"

"Great," Grandpa said as he took off his coat and hung it on the back of a chair. He curled his hand into a fist and tapped his chest. "Doc says I've got the heart of a man ten years younger."

Hanna smiled.

"With the mindset of a teenager," Gram said. "Your grandfather thinks he's going to bike across the state this summer."

"I am," he countered.

"We'll see about that," Gram said in a tone that suggested they would do no such thing. She took his coat, hung it up on the coat rack, and took a seat. "Now, Hanna, what happened today? I got a call from Mrs. Hines."

She took a deep breath and explained her day: the blackout, the nurse, the headaches, the car crash, and the interrogation. The only thing she left out was William's name. She didn't really know why, but she didn't want to tell them about him.

"Goodness," Gram said when she was done. "Did you call the doctor when you got home?"

"Yes, I've got an appointment to see him tomorrow."

Her grandparents were pretty old-fashioned, in the sense that if you wanted something done, you needed to do it yourself. She'd never had any problem with taking care of herself, and actually preferred their approach. They'd instilled in her at a young age an independence her friends didn't have, and she thought she was better off. She knew that when they were hard on her it was to prepare her. So when she got bad grades, they didn't scold or ground her, they gave her a list of colleges she wouldn't be able to attend with her GPA. It wasn't a scare tactic; it was just an honest demonstration of the importance of school, and she thought she was more level-headed than most girls her age because of it. She wasn't likely to argue with Gram over stupid things like curfew or grades. She was expected to act like an adult, because she was treated like one.

"Well, thankfully, you're all right," Grandpa said as he kissed the top of her head.

"Yeah," she said, her focus elsewhere. "Gram?"

"Yes, dear?" she answered as she stood up to fix her tea.

"When was the last time I had a blackout?"

The tension in the room grew thick. It was a heavy question and one that she always followed up with, "Why can't I remember anything before the third grade?"

"Hanna, we've been through this," Grandpa began. "You last blacked out when you were eight, the day you started school, I believe. Isn't that right, Loretta?"

Gram only nodded, keeping herself busy.

"Yeah, but why? What caused them?"

"We never found out, he said. "Your parents took you to the best doctors, and they ran so many tests with no results. After a while, it seemed pointless to keep you out of school and it had been over a year since your last blackout. We all decided that you'd gone through enough."

"But why can't I remember anything before starting the third grade?"

"Please, Hanna," Gram cut in.

"No, every time I ask about it, you both brush it off. I should be able to remember—"

"You know, I've always had a bad memory," Grandpa interrupted. "Isn't that right, Loretta?"

"See? You do that. You sidestep the question, and I never get a straight answer," she said loudly.

"Hanna, it's been a long day," Gram said. "Why don't you get some sleep? You seem tired."

Being tired has nothing to do with it, she thought as frustration began to fester inside her. Since the day she woke on the couch when she was eight years old, they had refused to answer her questions about why she couldn't remember. It was aggravating, and the only thing her grandparents wouldn't talk about with her. It seemed the harder she tried to focus, the darker the spot on her memory became.

She'd learned to live without knowing, had even accepted that she was just born different. It was why she tried so hard to remember every little detail, like William's shirt and the sign on the side of his ruined truck. She was perceptive, because she was always afraid that she might forget. To live and grow up without memory of nearly half your life was scary.

She looked back and forth between her grandparents, but neither said another word about it. It was always like this. She would question them, they would refuse to answer, and then they would go about their day like nothing had happened. She'd been furious when she first started asking them, but she was so used to their brush-offs on the subject that now it just annoyed her.

She went back downstairs, shutting the door behind her. As she got into bed, she ignored the lights of passing cars that shone through her little window at the top of her wall. She stared at one of the large wolves on her wall and tried to focus on her memories before she fell asleep, frightened that she wouldn't remember them in the morning.

CHAPTER THREE

After she got dressed the next morning, she grabbed the copy of *Of Mice and Men* she was reading for English class and went upstairs. Her class was expected to have a presentation ready by the following week on the social effects of the Great Depression. Hanna actually liked the book, despite it being a depressing story. She read it as she ate her usual breakfast, which consisted of a couple pieces of toast. She had almost finished the last chapter when she heard Grandpa call her from the living room.

"Hanna, I thought you said you left your car at school?"

"I did," she said, too engrossed in her novel to be bothered.

"Then why's it sitting in the driveway?"

Hanna looked up from her book, then stood and went into the living room. Grandpa was standing in front of the bay window, pulling back the curtain as he peered out.

Hanna looked out and there was her station wagon, parked in the driveway.

"What the . . ."

Grabbing her coat, she threw on a pair of boots and hurried outside. It was a cold morning, but the sun was rising in the blue, cloudless sky. She could see her breath, but hardly noticed the chill. She marched straight up to her car and opened the driver's side door.

There on the front seat were her keys and a note, neatly folded, with the letters *H. G. L.* written on it. Her initials.

She picked it up and opened it. The note read:

> Hanna,
> Your keys fell out of your pocket at the police station.
> but you had already left when I found them.
> Hope you don't mind.
> W. V.

Hanna read the note several times. William had taken her keys and drove her car home for her, and she wasn't sure how to feel about it. Flattered? Worried? How did he know where she lived? And why would he take time out of his day to do something like that for a stranger?

She went back inside, the note from William clutched in her hand. She wondered if she would ever see him again, because now, she couldn't think of anything or anyone else. It was unlikely, since he was only in town on business. She pushed him to the back of her mind, not yet willing to try and understand her feelings when she thought of him.

When her grandfather asked how her car turned up in the driveway, she told him Carly dropped it off.

Best not to worry him, she thought as she got ready for her doctor's appointment.

The ride to the doctor's office was more exciting than the actual visit. Dr. Martin did several tests and determined that there wasn't any real concern, giving her two extra strength ibuprofen for the headache she didn't have anymore.

"You can stand to put a few pounds on," the doctor said. "You're too thin."

The rest of the day was spent trying to avoid the mammoth amount of food Gram kept pressuring her to eat.

"You are staying home the rest of the week," Gram said firmly, spooning more mashed potatoes onto her plate. It was sweet on her part, but eating was the least of her worries. She'd received an in-school suspension notice for cutting out of class yesterday and would have to spend the following Monday in study hall.

By Friday morning, her mood finally changed and she felt like herself again, even though her dreams had been a bit strange. She couldn't remember them, but she woke up feeling like she was being hunted or stalked by something she couldn't see. It was strange because it had felt so real, and yet, she couldn't remember anything from it except how she felt.

That afternoon, she decided to try and call her parents, even though they were currently somewhere in the South Pacific. She was toying with her phone when her "Time after Time" ringtone went off.

"Hello?" she said into the phone.

"Is that all you have to say to me?" a girl's voice asked. "Where the hell have you been?"

"Oh, hey Carly," she said.

"'Oh, hey Carly?'" Carly mocked. "What happened to you? You ditch school Tuesday, don't even ask me if I want to go, apparently almost get creamed by a truck, and now you're not in school the rest of the week. Are you okay?"

"Yeah, I'm fine."

There was a pause and Hanna's grin grew. Carly hated waiting and was obviously eager to hear every detail.

"Oh my God," Carly said, her favorite phrase. "You're going to make me drag it out of you?"

"It's a long story." She plopped onto her bed. "What are you doing tonight?"

"Nothing really. A few of us are going to head over to Thurmont Mill. I was calling to see if you wanted to go—you know, because we're friends—but obviously, you're too busy doing what? Oh, that's right, you won't tell me."

Thurmont Mill was an old abandoned mill that sat near a train track in a deserted piece of forest about twenty minutes from Hanna's house. It was where most of the kids her age hung out, and it wasn't unusual for a party or a bonfire to be held there every few Fridays.

"I'll tell you tonight, all right?" Hanna said. "You're so dramatic."

"Oh my God, I hate when people call me dramatic."

"Bye, Carly."

"Byyye," she said sarcastically as Hanna hung up.

She pushed her phone into her pocket and tried to brush her thin, wavy hair. She hated her hair. It was freakishly light blonde due to her Swedish heritage, but the color wasn't so much the problem as the fact that it never wanted to grow past her shoulders. She always kept a shoulder-length bob cut that reminded her of those creepy porcelain dolls Carly's cousin, Morgan, collected.

After giving up on her hopeless hair, she put on a mustard colored knit hat and a black long-sleeve shirt over her gray Rolling Stones tee. She looked in the mirror and was as satisfied with her appearance as any eighteen-year-old could be. Not thrilled, but at least she didn't look like a freak.

She skipped every other step as she climbed the staircase, bursting into the kitchen and frightening her grandfather.

"Do you have to jump around like that?" he chided over his crossword book.

She grabbed an orange out of the fruit bowl on the kitchen counter and twirled out of the room.

"Sorry, Grandpa!" she said as she crossed the living room, her stocking feet sliding a bit on the hardwood. She leaned one hand against the front door as she bent down to grab her boots.

"Where are you going looking so lovely?" Gram teased from her armchair. She would always reminisce about how, when she was young, people dressed up to go out.

"To hang out with Carly. I don't need to wear a dress to do that," she smiled. "What are your plans for the night? Going to the Hines'?"

"No, we are not!" Grandpa yelled from the kitchen.

"He's angry because he lost a bet or something to Frank," Gram said. "We're heading over there in a little bit."

"No, we're not!"

"Hush up!" Gram snapped. Looking back at Hanna, she smiled. "When will you be home?"

"I don't know. Eleven? Twelve?" Hanna guessed. She knew midnight pushed their comfort zone, but it was Friday and after the week she'd had, she guessed they wouldn't argue with her.

"You have your phone?"

"Yes."

"And no drinking?"

"Gram, I don't drink."

"Of course not. What eighteen-year-old has ever drank?" she said sarcastically.

Hanna really didn't drink, but she knew kids that did. She knew her grandparents were just worried about her.

"No drinking, promise. Love you two!" she said as she grabbed her keys and jetted out the door.

She hurried across the lawn and hopped into her station wagon. It took a try or two for the engine to turn over, since it was an old car, but she wouldn't have traded it for anything.

She drove down Opossum Creek Road and took a right onto Route 209. Carly only lived a few minutes away, so when she pulled into her driveway, Carly was already standing there waiting.

"What took so long?" Carly asked as she jumped into the passenger's seat. "I'm freezing."

"You're wearing a tank-top," Hanna pointed out. "Here," she said, reaching behind her seat for a hoodie. "Put this on. Did you forget it was March in Michigan?"

"Well, it's been so warm lately," Carly said. "Plus, Troy is going to be there."

"Troy Denton?" Hanna made a face. "Why are you always trading in old boyfriends for new ones? What happened to Andy?"

"Ugh, don't even get me started on him," Carly said, sounding frustrated. "And if you actually liked anyone in school, you'd know that I'm not the weirdo for having boy troubles. You're the strange one, not me."

Hanna grinned and shook her head as she turned off Route 209 and headed down a dirt road. The sun was just setting behind the trees as Carly rolled down the passenger's side window. The faint smell of a bonfire drifted into the car as they drove. Carly pulled out a pack of cigarettes.

"Don't you dare smoke in my car," she warned. Carly made a face at her and put her smokes away. "And the reason why I don't like the guys in our school is because I don't see the point."

She didn't actually have a better reason than that. There were several guys who were cute enough, a few who were smart enough, but none really grabbed her attention. Not to mention that she had known all of them since elementary school and it was a little weird finding someone she used to finger paint with attractive.

"That is such a lame excuse," Carly dragged out.

"It's the only one I have. I guess I'm a weirdo," she admitted, slowing her speed to avoid the potholes in the road.

"I guess you're just into older men. Hot college guys who drive your car home for you," Carly said, grinning.

"Shut up," she replied, shaking her head and grinning back.

Apparently, everyone at school had heard of her little "incident," and she didn't want Carly to get all excited over something that was never going to amount to anything. However, Hanna knew that if she held back information on

William, she'd be endlessly teased about him and decided not to make it into a big deal.

"William Vann," she answered evenly. "He saved my life."

"Wait. He's hot *and* he saved your life?" Carly laughed. "How lucky are you?"

"He's not hot."

"What are you, blind? He looks like the guy in that movie."

"Oh, yeah? That guy?"

"You know what I mean."

"I have no clue what you're talking about," Hanna said, hoping to move off the topic of William.

"Whatever . . . I can't believe my dad wouldn't let me take the car, like that scratch I got on it was my fault."

"Carly," Hanna said in disbelief. "You rear-ended a guy at a stop sign."

"It wasn't a guy, it was Charlie Metzger, and I barely tapped him."

"His bumper almost fell off."

"You sound like my dad," Carly said.

They drove for ten more minutes before they reached an opening off the side of the dirt road where several cars were parked. Hanna pulled her car in between a Jeep and a Ford Focus and turned it off. Getting out, she smelled the bonfire and heard the vague chattering of people through the woods. Music played loudly in the distance as she walked around the front of her car.

"You're not a weirdo," Carly said, smiling and hooking her arm around Hanna's. "You're just living in a fairytale."

They walked through the woods and followed the path of glow sticks that had been left to light the way. It was only a short distance before they came to the clearing.

The area had once been used as a wheat field decades ago. An old, decrepit mill that had been falling apart for ages stood against the edge of the woods, looking eerie and haunted. There were several urban legends about the former owner, but ghost stories about this place had been told so many times, they'd lost their fright factor.

Some years ago, a train rail was placed on the edge of the property, which caused the rediscovery of the place by local teens whose parents had worked on building the rail. It had become a hangout for high school students ever since.

A crowd of people were hanging out around a raging bonfire in the middle of the field when they walked up. Laughter rang out like the music that played and everyone seemed to be smiling or telling a story. Hanna really only had one friend, but Carly was a social butterfly and often brought her out to parties. She felt the familiar uneasiness as they approached the crowd, especially when a short, redheaded girl made her way over to them.

"Oh no," Carly leaned over and whispered.

"Hey, guys!" the redhead said. "About time you got here."

"Hi, Melanie" she said. "Nice haircut."

"Thanks! You like?" she said, flattered. Almost instantly, her smiling face turned to one of shock. "Oh my God, Hanna! How are you?"

"I'm fine."

"Everyone's talking about the accident. I can't believe that you ditched school and almost got killed! That will teach you, right?"

Hanna gave her a fake smile, trying hard not to get annoyed. Melanie had a good heart, but she was the most annoying gossip in the whole school.

"And then that Vann guy came and drove your car off the lot after school. It was the most bizarre—"

"Wait, you know him?" Hanna interrupted.

Melanie looked surprised, as if she had never been cut off before. The eagerness in Hanna's voice wasn't lost on her and her surprise turned to excitement.

"Of course I know him. You don't?"

"Cut it, Melanie, who is he?" Carly said.

"William Vann of Vann Construction?" she said in a tone that expected the others to know the name. "They've had a commercial on TV for a few months now?"

Realization slammed into her as she thought of the commercial that played every time her grandparents watched the local news. That's where she had heard the name, and why Vann Construction sounded familiar. They'd been airing commercials for their company for months.

"Oh, that's right," Carly said. "Duh. I feel like an idiot."

"Yeah," Hanna agreed.

Melanie continued. "William's, like, the heir to the Vann fortune. Their original business is in South Carolina, but they do business all over the place. They're huge."

"How do you know so much about them?" Carly asked suspiciously.

"The internet," Melanie answered smartly.

As the three joined the rest of the party, Hanna's thoughts drifted to William. For whatever reason, she felt slightly let down now that he wasn't some tall, dark mystery who came out of nowhere and saved her life. He was just a regular guy—granted, a guy with a rich family—but that didn't add to his appeal. If anything, it repelled her. Money made her uncomfortable and people with money only made her weary. She wasn't from a rich town or a rich family. She was pretty average and liked it. While most people her age dreamed of being rich and famous, she liked to fly under the radar.

After an hour or so of mingling and trying not to think about William, she tried to focus on a group of guys in their grade playing a terribly inaccurate game of tackle football. Carly gushed over Troy, the athletic leader of the bunch. The screeching of a distant whistle echoed through the trees, interrupting Hanna's thoughts.

"Train!" Troy yelled. Carly looked crestfallen when he went running toward the tracks, her flirting put on hold.

"I hate that stupid train," Carly said as they followed everyone toward the tracks. "It's such a stupid game. Someone's going to get seriously hurt one day."

"Hurt isn't the word," Hanna said, her adrenaline kicking in. "You'd be killed instantly if that train hit you."

"Ugh, morbid much?"

"Come on," she said, pulling Carly along.

The game was chicken. The guys would line up on the track, wait, and listen. As the train came closer, they would see how long their nerves would keep them there, though most of the time, they all jumped off before the lights on the train could even be seen through the woods.

No one had ever been hurt, but that didn't mean there hadn't been some close calls. Everyone heard the story of a guy who graduated a few years ago whose shoelace got caught on a loose railroad screw. He almost lost his foot, but that didn't stop others. If anything, it just taught everyone to tie their shoelaces and tuck them into their sneakers before standing on the track.

Hanna wasn't wearing sneakers. She was wearing boots. She was almost on the tracks when Carly's voice brought her back to reality.

"What are you doing?" she asked.

"Huh?"

"Were you going to do it?"

Hanna grinned. "Yeah, why not?"

"What are you, crazy?" Carly asked in her "I-can't-believe-you're-going-to-be-this-stupid" voice. "This is completely stupid and dangerous."

"No one's ever been hurt," Hanna argued. "I'll be fine."

"You're acting like an idiot," Carly called after her as she climbed the incline to stand on the tracks.

The guys looked surprised as she took her place with them. Troy seemed particularly impressed, though she didn't want any of his attention. If Carly liked him, he was off limits, and he already wasn't her type. He looked like he could be her brother, with his light hair and greenish-blue eyes. Maybe if she was the narcissistic kind, she'd fall madly in love with him, but she preferred someone completely different. Someone tall, with black hair and gray eyes . . .

The whistle of the train blew again, this time much closer to the clearing. Everyone who wasn't on the tracks began to call out, whether they were words of encouragement to stay on the longest or commands to get off from worried friends or girlfriends.

Hanna didn't hear any of it. She was focused on her heartbeat as adrenaline began to pump through her veins. This was life at its best. Sure, standing on a train track waiting for a speeding train might be considered suicidal, but she figured people who jumped out of planes with parachutes were in far more danger than her. There were a million and a half "what ifs," but she couldn't focus on any of them now that her senses had opened up.

She could smell the scent of winter dying in the air, the bitter odor of unbloomed daffodils beneath the dead leaves. It was strong. She could even describe the taste of the steel that made the tracks. She felt superhuman. It was like being in a new world, everything bigger, brighter, and louder.

Why haven't I done this before? she wondered, excitement coursing through her.

"Hanna, this isn't funny!" Carly called. The only people left on the tracks were Hanna, Troy, and another guy she didn't know. "Get down!"

"It's not even close, Carly," she answered.

But it *was* close, and getting closer each second. The tracks began to vibrate, and her feet felt like they were buzzing. The whistle sounded again and a hush fell over the crowd. Maybe they were drowned out by the noise of the train.

Then, lights appeared, flickering between the trees. The other guy jumped off the tracks, leaving just her and Troy. Troy kept looking back at her and then down at his friends. She could tell he didn't want to stay on the tracks for much longer, but to feel like this, she would have stayed forever.

"Hanna, I'm serious! Get off!"

Hanna didn't listen. She watched the train round the bend and straighten out. It was beyond fast, beyond anything that she'd ever felt. It was powerful and raw, hurling toward her at full speed. The tracks were practically jumping under her feet and she was sure she would lose her balance if she didn't concentrate.

"HANNA!" Carly yelled again, but only Troy leapt off the tracks.

She was the only one left, looking death in the face. The train was sheer and flat, and two yellow windows looked at her, like the eyes of a demon. She could almost read the emblem on the front of the train car, but she wasn't concerned with what the writing said.

The train's whistle blew again and a few shrieks echoed from the crowd. It was going too fast for her to judge how many feet she still had, but the noise of the train and the screams from everyone were deafening. Her heart was racing and the excitement felt so electrifying that she almost missed her chance to jump.

Launching herself to the left at the last second, she rolled down the incline on the opposite side, just missing the train. She came to a stop, lying on her back; her breath was shallow and fast. A giddy smile spread across her face. She had almost died again, for the second time in one week. It felt *incredible*.

What the hell was wrong with her?

Sitting up from the cold ground, she waited for the train's passing. A feeling of guilt settled into her as she realized that Carly was probably freaking out.

"Damn," she muttered to herself. She'd probably scared everyone to death. She knew she shouldn't do things like that, but it was irresistible. She compared it to being a junkie, which was sort of true. She craved the excitement of walking that line between life and death, and the thrill had been too much to ignore. Of course, she was going to have to deal with Carly, but she couldn't help but think it was worth it.

She rolled over to her side and was about to stand when something in the distance caught her eye. The train cars continued to whizz by, so she couldn't hear anything, but she definitely saw something and hesitated to move.

Her heartbeat, which had barely settled back to normal, began to beat furiously. She felt almost nauseous now, as if having too much of the fear and thrill was making her sick. Hanna tried to crawl backward as slowly as she could. The moon was just coming out from behind a cloud when whatever it was moved again; it headed out of the brush of the forest and into the clearing.

Hanna inhaled sharply. A full-grown wolf, teeth bared and inching menacingly toward her. She had no place to run. The train was still passing and if she went left or right, it wouldn't matter. A gray wolf that size would tear her to pieces.

"It's okay, it's okay," she whispered, trying to soothe herself more than the wolf. "I'm okay."

A low, threatening growl began to rumble in its throat as it approached her. All she could do was tell herself that there was nothing to be afraid of, because it wasn't going to hurt her. As if it read her mind and wanted to challenge her, its head went back and it snapped its teeth. She jumped when its growl turned into a bark.

"Okay, okay," she tried again. "Easy. Easy. Just stay," she said, holding a shaking hand up.

The train finished passing and the wolf turned, disappearing into the forest. She sat frozen, staring at the spot in the woods where it had vanished. *What was a lone wolf doing here? Did they even have wolves here?*

Carly's voice tore her from her thoughts.

"YOU JERK!" Carly yelled, coming down the slope. "Are you out of your mind? We thought you were killed! Oh my God, Hanna. You gave everyone a heart attack!"

"I'm sorry, but—"

"But what? You wanted to scare everyone? Damn it, girl, you are the biggest idiot in the world—"

"Carly, I know. I'm sorry," Hanna said, suddenly feeling terribly drained. "I think I want to go home."

"Fine, let's go."

"I don't want to ruin your night," she said honestly as she stood up. "Stay."

"Well, it's too late for that. You scared the life out of me," Carly said. "I'm not staying—"

"Don't let me ruin your night. I just want to go home and go to bed." She saw that her friend was visibly upset, but she had an idea. "Hey, why not ask if Troy can take you home?"

The anger and fright that shadowed Carly's face melted away and a sly smile crossed her face.

"Don't think I'm going to stop being mad at you, just because you had a great idea," she said, her smile faltering for a moment. "Honestly, Hanna. You scared me."

"I know, Carly. I'm sorry," she said again. The two made their way up and over the train tracks, where a group of people looked greatly relieved to see that she was alive. Troy and a few of the football players met them half-way.

"Hell, Hanna, we thought you got clipped!" Troy said. "That was crazy!"

"Yeah, it was!" someone else agreed. "You're insane!"

Several other calls of encouragement rang out, and when she decided to leave, she ignored the protests for her to stay. Most of the guys were looking at her in awe, while most of the girls were feigning to be sad she was leaving. *Apparently, stupidity is a turn on for guys*, Hanna thought as she pulled her keys from her coat.

It was only ten thirty, but she could barely stay standing up. Seeing that wolf had been unexpected, and she felt like her energy had been zapped. All she wanted to do was go home.

She got into her car and drove, thankful that tomorrow was Saturday. Then, in the same thought, she cursed because she had to work. At least it was the early shift and she wouldn't have to be there all night, even if that meant waking up early.

Pulling into her driveway, she saw that her grandparents still weren't home. Feeling slightly silly that they had a better stamina for night-life than she did, Hanna opened the front door, turned on all the lights, and headed downstairs.

After taking a shower and getting into her pajamas, she thanked whomever was listening that she was still alive and curled beneath her covers. She thought about William and then decided to think of something else. She hardly knew him.

But, she argued internally, *he did save my life.*

Man, she thought, *I need to stop talking to myself.* The wolves on her wall stared at her, and just as she was about to fall asleep, she swore she heard a wolf howling.

CHAPTER FOUR

*H*anna tossed and turned. Dreams of wolves and dark shadows following her made for a restless night, and she forced herself back to sleep at least twice. When her alarm clock finally said six, she was wide awake and just about to get out of bed, but then she heard it again.

A wolf's howl.

It sounded mournful and close. After several minutes of listening to it, she got out of bed and threw on a sweatshirt. She was certain it had to be from the wolf she saw last night. If it was the same wolf, she was going to see why it was stalking her.

The house was quiet and still as she walked into the kitchen, closing the basement door behind her. The grayish light of morning dimly lit the kitchen, and she tried her best not to make any noise as she crossed the linoleum floor toward the sliding back door. She could still hear the howling, but with the sun just on the verge of shining over the treetops, the woods behind her house were hardly visible.

She slid open the glass door, walking out onto her porch and into the frigid morning. She scanned the woods from the edge of the deck, but she couldn't see anything. The howling was coming from straight ahead, or at least she thought it was. It sounded closer.

Her eyes strained as the moments stretched on. The howling would stop every few minutes, only to begin again. She leaned over the edge of the deck's banister, eager to see if the wolf would appear.

"Hanna?"

Startled, she spun around. Her grandfather stood in the doorway. "What are you doing?"

"Jeez," she said, putting a hand over her face. "You scared me."

"I scared you?" he said. "Look at your hands. How long have you been out here?"

She looked to find her fingers turning blue. *How long have I been out here?*

"Come inside before you freeze to death."

Hanna gave one last look over her shoulder, but the howling had stopped. The sun had finally reached the horizon, but there still wasn't any movement in the woods. The spell was broken. She turned and joined her grandfather inside.

Strange morning, she thought as she sat down at the kitchen table while Grandpa made coffee. She was acting like a lunatic. Wolves she liked, but real ones growling ten feet from her face? That wasn't normal and didn't belong in her life. She would be better off pretending that none of it happened.

She had started making her breakfast when Gram walked into the room.

"Morning," Hanna said, still lost in her thoughts.

"Good morning, dear," Gram said. "You were home early last night. Your grandfather and I were surprised to see your car in the driveway when we pulled in."

"Yeah, I wanted to take it easy," Hanna lied as she grabbed a mug from the cabinet. "You know, because of the headaches."

"I thought you haven't had one since the blackout?" Gram said, trying to sound indifferent, and failing miserably. Hanna knew she was worried, but was trying to pretend like it didn't bother her.

"I haven't, but I didn't want to cause one by staying out too late, what with work."

"Oh, you're working today?" She seemed eager to change the topic. Hanna poured coffee and reached for the sugar.

"Be careful driving. Your grandfather and I almost hit a dog or something last night on our way home. It looked rabid."

Hanna nodded absently.

"The owners probably haven't caught the poor thing yet. We were at a stop sign when it jumped out in front of us, teeth bared and everything."

She turned slowly to face her grandmother. "Did you say it was a dog?"

"Yes. It looked like a husky, or a malamute. Your grandfather thought it was a wolf, but wolves haven't been in this area for decades."

Hanna lifted her coffee and held it up to her lips. The steam warmed her face.

"Hanna, are you all right?" Grandpa asked.

"I'm fine," she insisted, but neither of her grandparents looked convinced.

She finished her coffee and returned to her room, deciding that she'd be out of mind if she was out of sight.

The last couple of days had been confusing. She didn't know what her problem was, but she'd felt off ever since her blackout. It didn't help that she thought she was being stalked by a wild animal.

Aggravated with herself, she dressed for work. By the time she left the house, she'd convinced herself she was the biggest idiot in the world. She usually wasn't hard on herself, but when she was, she was her own worst enemy. It was crazy to think a wolf was anything more than a wild dog, so she shouldn't be acting so strange. Her grandparents were already worried about her; she didn't need to freak them out more with her irrational thoughts and feelings.

As she pulled out of her driveway, her phone rang. She took it out of her coat and saw that it was Carly.

"Hello?" she said.

"Well, I hope you're happy," Carly's bitter voice yelled. "Ugh! You're like, the worst friend a girl could have!"

"Wow, calm down. What's wrong?"

"He likes you! That's all we talked about last night after you left," she said. "He thought you were so cool for almost getting killed. Honestly, Hanna, why do you have to be so fricking weird?"

"Easy, Carly. I don't care if Troy likes me or not."

"Ugh! He'll probably think that's awesome too, that you don't care what he thinks!"

Hanna rolled her eyes. "Carly, I don't like Troy, so we're not going to be dating and you can just calm down now. I don't like him like that."

A short pause followed.

"Really?"

"Yes, really, you idiot," she said gently. She loved Carly like a sister, but sometimes, she was just plain insane. "I don't even talk to him."

"Well, he still thinks you're the coolest chick ever. What were you thinking? You could have been killed."

"One, it doesn't matter what he thinks and two, I was just having some fun."

"Whatever." Carly seemed to be out of steam. "Can I get a ride to school on Monday?"

"Yeah, sure."

"Oh, and can we pick up Anne? I was talking to her last night after you left and she's really a cool person. I told her it wouldn't be a problem to grab her Monday morning. Is that cool?"

She groaned inwardly. Anne, the new girl whose desk she'd hit when she passed out. *What a fun car ride that will be.* She wondered for a moment if Carly had faked being angry with her so she could get her to pick up Anne, but it didn't matter.

"Sure, not a problem."

"Great."

Hanging up, she drove to the post office to drop off a few applications for the colleges that still refused to accept electronic ones, then headed to the diner for her lunch shift. She enjoyed working there, even though she often wished she was somewhere else while working. Her boss, George, was an older man who mostly spoke to her in Greek. George was always on the phone with his brother, who co-owned the diner and managed a second in a small town in Northeastern Pennsylvania.

The lunch rush was always busy on Saturdays, and it wasn't until four when George told Hanna to take her break.

Hanna was clearing her last customer's table when the door opened and the tiny hairs on the back of her neck stood up. She noticed the smell of the rice pudding being made back in the kitchen, and she paused. The sunlight bouncing off the remaining snowbanks outside seemed brighter. The music playing on the radio sounded clearer, and the warmth from the heating vent above her seemed to intensify.

Her heart beat faster. She knew this feeling well by now, but this time, there was something more. She also felt dread.

A sudden shooting pain split her forehead. *Again?* she thought, trying hard to concentrate on her work. She heard footsteps approaching, and when they stopped right behind her, she was scrubbing the table so hard she probably looked like a madwoman.

"What did that table do to you?" Troy's voice sounded.

Hanna stopped, disappointment filling her when she saw Troy standing there. She didn't feel like talking to him just as her headache deepened. She could have sworn she sensed something foreboding, but it was just Troy and an elderly man who came in after him. She put a hand to her forehead.

Great, she thought, *this headache isn't going away.* It felt like her head was splitting open. She leaned against the table.

"Hey Troy," she said, trying to sound as cold as possible. "Want a seat?"

"Sure, I'll sit at the counter," he said, taking a seat at the countertop where Angie, the other waitress, handed him a menu.

Hanna almost dropped a plate as she finished clearing her table. Her head hurt so much, she could barely focus on anything.

She moved to take the elderly man's order, who was joined by what looked to be a construction worker. Her head gave an extra painful throb after she took their order and put the ticket in the kitchen. Looking up, she saw there was another customer.

He looked to be in his late twenties, with long hair hanging out of his blue beanie hat. A shadow seemed to hang around him, as if he were sitting in a thin, black fog. He was staring at her like he wanted to rip her apart.

Surprised, she wondered why. She'd never seen him before. She closed her eyes tightly, blinking a few times before the shadow disappeared. He wasn't frowning, but there was something about his face that made him look angry. Thankfully, Angie was up, and he was her customer.

She forced a smile and turned back to the counter where Troy sat.

"So, how've you been, Hanna?" Troy asked pleasantly, smiling at her.

"Good," she said, not returning his smile. He was off limits, and besides, he wasn't her type. "You?"

"I'm good," he answered eagerly. "So, last night was pretty crazy, huh?"

Hanna looked at Angie, who raised her eyebrows. *Great*, she thought, turning back to Troy.

"It was stupid," she said. "That whole train game is completely immature."

"Oh yeah, I agree," Troy said, quickly adding, "except for when you did it." Hanna looked at him and he seemed flustered. "I mean, you're not immature."

"Right," she said, confused. Her order was called, and she left to grab it gratefully.

She overheard the construction worker and the older man talking as she brought their order over. She rarely eavesdropped on the patrons in the diner, not because she was so well mannered, but because no one really had anything important to say. She pretended not to listen as she set the burger and fries down, but her fingers slipped in surprise when the older man mentioned Vann Construction.

"I've never heard of him," the worker said, looking at her as she dropped the plate on the table. Thankfully, it was only a few centimeters. "What's the guy's name again?"

"William Vann, but it's his father I'm talking about. Jacob Vann," the old man corrected. "Remember? It was something like ten or fifteen years ago? They were up here building houses. Vann Homes."

The construction worker shook his head as Hanna slowly moved toward the coffee station behind their booth.

"Oh, wait . . . yeah, I do remember the name. But they were only up here for a few swanky buildings on Lake Michigan," he said. "They halted their homes division, remember?"

"I'm not talking about their business," the old man said. "I'm talking about those murders. Remember?"

Hanna racked her brain, trying to remember anything about a murder, let alone *murders* in or around New Hope, but she couldn't remember ever hearing about such a thing. There were murders in cities like Detroit and Ann Arbor, but New Hope wasn't a big city—it wasn't even a big town. A murder would have been something to remember, especially plural ones.

"Yeah, I do remember," the construction worker said, recognition sounding in his voice. "Wasn't that around the time of that kidnapping?"

"Hanna?"

"What?" she nearly shouted. She jumped as she turned around, completely immersed in the conversation she was overhearing. Troy was standing behind her, surprise on his face.

"Are you okay?" he asked.

"I'm fine," she breathed, though her headache was getting stronger. She moved away from the coffee station and back around the counter. Troy followed her.

"You can't come back here," she said pointedly.

"Oh, right," he said, moving out from behind the counter.

"What's up, Troy?" she finally asked. "Did you come here for a reason?"

He looked sheepish. He shifted his weight from one foot to the other, and she got a sinking feeling in the pit of her stomach as he forced himself to look her in the eye. "I was wondering if you wanted to-go-with-me-to-prom?"

He asked it so fast that she almost didn't understand. Or maybe she just didn't want to understand. She hated being asked out, especially when she wasn't interested in the boy asking. It had only happened once or twice before, but she couldn't stop herself from feeling like a complete monster when she turned them down.

"Oh," she said quietly. Uncomfortable tension hung in the air between them, and it must have been noticeable because Angie came out of the kitchen, arms folded as she leaned against the wall, completely unashamed that she was watching what should have been a private moment.

"Thanks," Hanna said awkwardly.

Troy's face lit up.

"So you'll go?" he asked excitedly.

"Oh, no," she said unevenly. "I can't. I'm busy."

Cringing as Troy's smile disappeared, she couldn't believe what she'd said. *I'm busy? What kind of an excuse is that?* Now she wouldn't be able to go to prom, just to avoid an awkward run-in with Troy.

"You're busy?" he repeated, unconvinced.

Fix it! she yelled at herself. *Tell him something else!*

"Yeah, I'm busy," she said, her inner self screaming at her. "I'm actually going away that week to see my parents," she lied, hoping that he believed her. "You know, because they're not here."

She could have killed Angie when she snickered. Troy looked like he was trying to grasp not only her decision, but also the fact that her parents weren't around.

"Oh, yeah," he said slowly. "You live with your grandparents, right?"

Hanna ignored the part of her that was annoyed he didn't remember. Why in the world would he want to take her to prom if he had no idea about her life? It was common knowledge that she lived with her grandparents.

"Yeah," she said. "So I can't really go to prom because I won't be around. But," she added, "thanks for the invite. I appreciate it."

"No problem," he said, turning to leave. She was relieved, until he stopped. "Wait," he said, turning back. "What about next Friday?"

She felt the color drain from her face, but the next thing she heard was Angie.

"Oh sweetie, you don't look so good," she said in her thick Michigan accent. Hanna looked at her as she addressed Troy. "Hun, why don't you come back later? Hanna's been feeling just awful all day, and I don't think you're making it any better," she said sweetly.

"Oh, right," Troy said dumbly. "See you later, Hanna."

He waved and left. She turned to Angie.

"Oh my God," she said. "Thank you, Angie. You saved me."

"Oh sweetie, it was nothing," Angie said, smiling and chewing her gum like it was going out of style. Angie always reminded her of one of those waitresses from the fifties. She was sweet, sassy and had her badly bleached hair pulled back in a messy bun while her dark roots stretched over her head. Still, Angie always seemed concerned about Hanna. "Are you all right? You seem a little flustered."

"I'm fine."

"You sure?" Angie pressed, a quizzical expression on her face. "You scared the beJeezus out of me and George after that blackout the other day."

Hanna nodded.

"Oh, if you say so." She nodded her head toward the door. "That poor thing, though. He was cute. Why didn't you say yes?"

"He's not my type," Hanna said, ignoring the sudden image of William that flashed in her mind. "Plus, he's off limits. Carly likes him."

"That's too bad," Angie said, looking out the window. Hanna followed her stare and saw Troy walking toward his car. "He's a looker."

"He's the lacrosse captain," Hanna said.

"I bet," Angie said, laughing out loud, as she usually did when she found something she said funny.

Hanna couldn't help laughing too, and soon George came out, chiding them in Greek.

Her headache lasted for the rest of her shift, though it faded significantly as the diner cleared. The construction worker and the old man left, and she regretted not hearing the rest of their conversation, though they'd both looked at her strangely after Troy startled her. They'd spoken in low voices after that and left without leaving much of a tip.

Angie grumbled at the poor tip she received from the angry-looking man. Hanna was oddly glad when he left. Something about him made her uncomfortable. He'd kept giving her hateful looks that she didn't understand, and she hoped he never returned to the diner, at least while she was working.

When her shift finally ended, she hung up her apron and left through the side door of the kitchen. She agreed to pick up Angie's shift that Tuesday, since she had a date and needed someone to cover for her. Hanna agreed mostly to return Angie's favor of getting rid of Troy.

Troy, she thought with agony as she stepped out into the cold air. He was probably on his way back. Hanna looked carefully left to right before running to her car, hoping not to be spotted. She paused with her key in the door as she saw someone near the plaza across the street.

Hanna ducked behind her car. The person looked around, peering through storefront windows.

"William?" Her eyes narrowed. Something about his movements made her suspicious and when he disappeared behind the sporting goods store, curiosity got the better of her. She crossed the street quickly, hoping she hadn't lost him.

The early spring sun was just beginning to set; the long shadows of the trees stretched across the road and up the few buildings that lined the street. She didn't know why she was so determined to follow him, but she blamed it on the construction worker and the old man with their talk of old murders. Something about the Vann family didn't sit well with some, and she wanted to know what they were about.

She hurried down the sidewalk, slowing to a stop when she reached the sporting goods store. Peeking around the corner, she didn't see any sign of William. She moved along the side of the building and saw nothing but an empty parking lot, edged by the woods. She felt let down. Suddenly, a hand covered her mouth and panic set in as she tried to fight free. She was pulled backward; whoever had a hold of her was strong. Within seconds, he was in front of her, pressing her against the brick wall of the sporting goods store.

William's eyes looked menacing, his hand still covering her mouth.

"Hanna?" he said in a rough whisper, surprise lighting his face as he recognized her. His hand dropped. "What are you doing?"

"What are you doing?" she countered, breathing heavily. She shoved him away, then wished she hadn't. He'd been awfully close . . . she pushed the thought away and went on the defensive. She didn't want to admit that she'd been following him. "You're the one snooping around."

"I wasn't snooping," he corrected.

"Then what were you doing?" she asked. "Do you know Garret Simpson or something?"

"Who?"

"The guy who owns this place," she said, nodding at the store. When he didn't seem to know, she tilted her head, hoping silently that she hadn't interrupted a robbery. "What were you doing back here then?"

"I was taking a short cut," he said reluctantly.

"Through the woods?" she asked, unconvinced. "The only thing through those woods is the quarry and the police station." He looked guilty, and she was even more intrigued. "Were you headed to the station?"

"You should get out of here," he said, avoiding the question. She felt a flash of annoyance that he brushed her questions aside, just like everyone else did.

"What were you doing?" she repeated, trying to make her voice hard.

"None of your business," he snapped.

"Fine," she said coldly, setting her jacket right and turning away.

"I don't want you involved," he said to her retreating back.

"Whatever," she muttered, doing her best to ignore her curiosity.

Without another look, she walked back down the alley and headed toward her car. She felt like a moron. What had she been trying to learn by following him? It was obvious he didn't want her around. He probably thought she was just some annoying high-schooler and really, she hadn't helped her case.

But why had he been headed toward the police station through the woods? Did he not want to be seen? *Obviously,* she thought as she reached her car. Otherwise, he wouldn't have attacked her. She heard howling off in the distance and glanced back across the street at the now dark alley. She felt a flash of alarm at the idea of William wandering the woods with that wolf out there, but she shook her head and climbed into her car. He didn't "want her involved," so he could do just fine by himself.

Her thoughts reeled as she drove home. She wanted to talk to someone about William, but Carly wouldn't understand. She would chalk it up to her having a crush on the new guy in town. No, she needed to talk to someone who had a different perspective, not her best friend.

Hanna found herself on the road to Owen's house instead of her own. She had to tell all of this to someone, and Owen was the best person she could think of.

CHAPTER FIVE

*W*illiam pulled his black, double-breasted coat tight around his shoulders as he walked down the road after his confrontation with Hanna. The cold weather was harsh and though it helped him clear his mind, he missed the warmth of South Carolina. *Why would anyone willingly live in such a harsh climate?* he wondered as the sun went down.

And why did I snap at Hanna like that?

Don't think about her, he chided himself. *You're supposed to be thinking about work.* He had been having trouble focusing on the blueprints his father sent him and decided a walk would clear his head. When he recognized the road he was on as the one Peirce took to the police station, he wondered if he could ask to see a police file, but decided against it when Hanna surprised him out of nowhere.

For what felt like the hundredth time, he replayed the first time he saw her, crossing the road without so much as a glance as to where she was going. He'd only wanted to see her, to know who she was and what she looked like, but he hadn't expected to see her in the middle of the road the day he arrived.

William kicked a rock in the road. The morning he arrived in New Hope, he was more concerned with finding a bite to eat than seeking out Hanna Loch. He'd pulled off Fetterman Road to find a map on his phone. Service kept cutting out, so he thought if he stayed put, it would help. Of course, it hadn't, and he was about to pull back onto the road when he saw her.

She'd walked across the street, glowing faintly as people like them did, a fine golden hue surrounding her as she moved slowly into the path of danger. She'd looked lost in thought, and for a split second, he had been too, until he heard the engine of another truck roaring down the street. He'd barely even looked back to see her reaction when he'd slammed on the gas, hoping to cut in front of it before it hit her. But he'd T-boned it instead. Either way, it had saved her, and that's what mattered.

He frowned. The thought still confused him. Why had he saved her?

A crude thought, but he couldn't stop wondering. It was as if all logical thought had gone out the window when he saw that oncoming truck. No idea for his own safety; no thought about anything except to save her. He wondered if Annabelle had felt the same way.

No, he thought. *Don't think about that.* Yet, wasn't that the reason he'd volunteered to come here and work on the housing project? He'd wanted to know who she was for years. What about her made Annabelle give her own life?

Looking up from the wet pavement, he saw a wolf approach him, trotting down the side of the road.

"Good boy, Wyatt," he said, patting the wolf on the head. He was getting close to the family lake house.

The coolness in the air soothed him as much as he'd let it. Regardless of everything, he had an almost primal urge to go to her house and figure out all the personal queries he had about her, but he wouldn't. It wasn't his place to just show up out of nowhere, introduce himself, and assume she'd even be open to wanting to know him, especially after what Peirce had told him.

He'd known who William was the moment he got to the accident site.

"Vann," Peirce said as he stepped out of his cruiser. He didn't need to look at his expired license to know him. "What are you doing in these parts?"

"Oh great, you know this guy?" the demolished truck owner said sarcastically. "Then I guess I'm screwed."

To his credit, Peirce hadn't even reacted to the man. He waited with calculating eyes locked on William. They'd known of each other for years, though this was only the second time they'd actually seen each other. William hadn't been in the position to speak freely the first time they met, since he had been wearing a ski mask at the time. He wondered if Peirce even knew this was the second time they were meeting, but judging by the way he looked at him, he guessed that Peirce did.

"Work brings me here," William said evenly. "Nothing else."

Peirce seemed satisfied with that answer, though he still looked at his license with speculation. In fact, he seemed positively overjoyed that it was expired and that he had to sit him in the back of his cruiser when he took him to the station.

"Listen, Vann, I don't want any trouble while you're up this way, you understand?" Peirce had said as they drove to the station. "I've got enough on my plate without having to deal with some folklore bullshit."

His wording had surprised William. *Folklore bullshit? This, coming from the guy whose family prided themselves on that very "bullshit?"* What was he about now? And what the hell was he doing in New Hope, Michigan?

Of course, that question was answered after he pulled over to check on Hanna, who'd been walking down the road. William knew whatever cover he'd had was blown.

"What did you say to her?" Peirce asked when he got back in the car.

"I didn't say anything. Why?"

"She wasn't happy about me arresting you."

"But I'm guessing you're thrilled about it?"

Peirce didn't speak.

"What are you doing here, Peirce?" William asked after they pulled away from Hanna. He watched her eyes follow the car until it turned out of view. "This is a long way from New York."

"Normally, I'd tell you go to Hell," Peirce answered, a bit more aggressively than before. "But I have some more important things to deal with right now, so just listen. That girl you saved? Stay away from her. She's none of your concern, you got me?"

"None of my concern? She's one of us. Doesn't she already know to stay away from *me?*"

"She doesn't . . . she's not aware of it."

"Not aware? Are you telling me she doesn't know who she is?"

"She knows who she is. She's Hanna Loch. She doesn't have any idea about this messed up little world, and she doesn't need to know—"

"Of course she needs to know. What the hell does she think happened to her? What happens when they come back? What about Annabelle—"

"She doesn't know about any of it. She's blocked it out. Her past is a black hole to her, and she doesn't need to know anything about what happened. She's better off this way. Hell, she gets to be normal." There was envy in Peirce's voice. "So stay away from her."

William glared back at him through the rearview mirror before grinning.

"So, that's why you're here. You got called in to what, protect her? Keep it from happening a second time?" William let out a bitter laugh. "You good guys never cease to amaze me. Don't you know that it's going to happen, whether you want it to or not? It's her story, and it can't be changed. Annabelle tried to alter it, remember? And she got herself killed."

"Annabelle was the only decent one in your entire family," Peirce bit out. "And us good guys know the one fact your kind can never seem to grasp."

"Which is?"

"Good will overcome."

Of course Peirce would say that, it was his damn family's motto. It was easy to believe in good, everyone did. Or at least, they wanted to. There wasn't much challenge in wanting to see the good in everyone and hope that everything would turn out for the best, but William knew differently. Good guys always got the happily ever after. They would crumble if they knew that everyone in the world was much darker than they appeared. He knew it well enough. It was the curse of being a Vann.

He'd been able to see the evil in everyone his entire life. He knew what people were capable of, and it always irritated him that people like Peirce assumed being good was such an easy choice. Annabelle had made the choice, despite her family, and it killed her. He remembered what his father said at her funeral, that one "should never try to prove to the world that they are something they're not." Annabelle would still be alive if she'd just accepted it.

William accepted it.

He finally reached the lake that sat behind his family's home. He was furious that Peirce thought he would be able to do what Annabelle couldn't. *He thinks he can save the Loch girl for good this time? Doesn't he realize that you can't change fate?* Peirce would wind up dead along with Hanna, especially if he thought that keeping her in the dark about everything was a good idea. If she didn't know what was coming after her, what chance did she have?

None, he thought, surprised that he was so annoyed by that fact. He tried to shake the feeling of hopelessness. If it were up to him, he'd be telling her everything he could, but it wasn't his business. He knew better than to mess around with someone like Hanna, especially after what happened with Annabelle, but he couldn't help but feel like he needed to at least tell her, warn her in some way.

A sour smile spread across his face. *Wouldn't that be something, if the big bad wolf helped out an innocent?* As if he didn't know that he'd get himself killed in the process. It would be easy, just to let her know that she should be on the lookout. Peirce said that she didn't know about their twisted little world, so she would have no objections talking to someone like him. It would be easy to casually run into her somewhere, start a conversation, and then just let it slip.

He shook his head and cursed. Even when he wanted to help her, he thought about it as if he were stalking prey. Guilt washed over him as he let the idea go. He couldn't get involved; it would just cause more chaos. It would be best to just do his work and let her go about her life . . . not expecting a thing . . . just like prey . . .

Cursing again, he turned down the driveway of his family home and climbed the stairs to the wrap-around porch.

"Come on, Wyatt," William called. The wolf nuzzled against his hands. "I'm debating something."

Wyatt tilted his head, as if he understood the words.

If only you could talk, he thought. *Then I'd have a second opinion.*

"That girl is going to get killed if she isn't careful," he whispered. "And I don't know what to do about it." Wyatt made a strange, throaty noise, and William pretended he'd asked the question that had bugged him all night. "I don't know how I feel about her. I don't even really know her." He paused, nodding after a moment. "But I don't hate her. I thought I would, but there's something about her, something I can't explain . . ."

He always assumed that he would hate her, if not feel a strong dislike, since his family often blamed her for Annabelle's death, but he hadn't felt it when he saw her or when she spoke. He didn't feel it when he saw the locket hanging around her neck, though he had been more than surprised to see it. William thought he'd never see it again and yet, it hadn't bothered him seeing it on her.

Even though he knew he came off rather cold when she crept up on him earlier, he hadn't felt any of the negative feelings he thought he would. If anything, he was intrigued. She was a bit brave, a bit naive to follow him, but he saw strangeness in her eyes. A mixture of strength and pain and mystery that he had never witnessed before. He wanted to know her, to talk with her, to learn things that she could undoubtedly teach him.

After all, she wasn't exactly the good guy in her story. If anything, she was a criminal—theft was a crime. He smiled as he stood and walked back into the house. He hadn't thought of Hanna that way before and for whatever reason, he found it comforting to see her in such a light—a bit of a villain in the good.

CHAPTER SIX

Turning down Quail Trail, Hanna tried to avoid the potholes that seemed to multiply every time she went to see Owen. He lived in an old vacation cabin that he'd been trying to renovate for a few months, and even though it was a slow process, it was coming along. She hoped he was home and not working the night shift. She pulled into his driveway and saw the cop cruiser.

On break, she thought as she got out of her car and headed up the few stairs to the porch. Knocking quickly, she saw his shadow move behind the curtains he'd hung to shield his windows from paint splatter.

"Hold on," his muffled voice said. She could tell he was surprised to see her as he pushed open the screen door. "Hanna? What are you doing here?"

"I need to talk to you," she said.

As Hanna walked into Owen's house, the scent of paint and turpentine slammed into her, causing her eyes to water. The kitchen and living room were covered with old bed sheets and paint cans, while the wooden walls of the cabin were a dark mahogany color and looked as though they'd just been covered in wood cleaner. She coughed.

"God, Owen, what are you doing in here without a mask?" she chastised him, covering her mouth and nose with her hand. "You're going to pass out."

"My bedroom is sealed off," he said in his "I-know-what-I'm-doing" voice. He was dressed in his cop uniform. "What are you doing here, kid? I've got to get back to work soon."

"I have to ask you a few questions," she said, getting down to business. "It won't take long, but can I ask you on the porch? *I'm* going to pass out in here."

"Yeah, sure," he said as he grabbed his coat off of an old wooden chair. On her way out, Hanna noticed a few pictures laid out over the unfinished dining table he'd taken from her grandparents' basement. She paused and leaned over the chair. There was a new picture in the bunch—of Owen and an older woman who looked like she could have been his mother, or maybe grandmother. Hanna smiled, but it turned to a frown.

Owen was adopted by her aunt and uncle years ago, and this woman wasn't her aunt. She looked incredibly like Owen.

"Hanna," he said from outside the door. "Can we hurry this up?"

Forgetting the photo, she followed him out onto the porch, closing the door behind her.

"Owen, there's something weird going on." She started to pace. "I don't know what it is, but ever since my blackout, there's just been bizarre things happening, and I don't know who to talk to about it."

Chancing a look at him, Hanna was relieved to see he looked genuinely concerned as he leaned on the railing.

"What's going on?" he asked.

"Well, after leaving work today, that guy William—"

"Is that guy bothering you?" Owen interrupted, standing up. "I told him not to bother you—"

"No, no," she said. "Wait, what? You told him not to bother me?" Looking half annoyed and half sheepish, he leaned back against the railing. "Why would you tell him not to bother me?"

"He isn't for you, Hanna," Owen tried in a gentler voice. "He's just no good."

"What is that supposed to mean?" *Is it that obvious that I can't stop thinking about him?*

"I don't have the time to get into it now," he said. "Just steer clear of William Vann, okay? I'd appreciate it if you listened just this once."

"Why?" she asked, now unsure if she should tell Owen about what happened. Though everything seemed to point to William being a suspicious guy, she couldn't bring herself to believe it. Owen obviously did. "What's wrong with him?"

He seemed reluctant to talk, which only made her more curious. She folded her arms and waited for him to speak, hoping that he wouldn't brush her off. She didn't have any patience left to be brushed off again today.

"You're not going to like what I have to say," he cautioned.

"Tell me," she insisted.

"Listen, kid," he began. "I know these types of guys. They come from wealthy families with no worries in their lives, and when they're out on their own for the first time and see a pretty girl from a lower tax bracket, they think it'll be fun to mess around, but nothing ever comes from it."

She stared at him, stunned. "Uh, Owen, this doesn't have to be the 'your boyfriend's no good' speech. Trust me, William is definitely not interested." She was surprised that it hurt to say it, but he hadn't given her any other impression, especially not today. Saving her life obviously didn't mean he was smitten. "I just want to be his friend. He saved my life. I think the least I can do is be his friend."

"You're too nice, Hanna," he said with a slight grin. "But you don't owe that guy anything, and I'm sure he's got a friend or two in the area."

"How do you know that?"

"His family has a house over near the lake," he said, his smile flickering. *He really doesn't like this guy,* she thought. "They've been coming here for years. They were here when . . ." he trailed off, looking like he'd just stopped himself from revealing something.

"When what?" she asked.

"Why are you so interested?" he snapped, suddenly aggravated. "I'm telling you to steer clear of the guy. Why can't that be enough?"

"Because I need a good reason," she retorted loudly. "My entire life, everyone in this town has been careful not to mention things around me. Gram and Grandpa, teachers, neighbors, even Carly's mom! For the longest time, I thought I was paranoid, that I was making this stuff up."

She couldn't stop the words once she started. She always feared she was a little crazy, and it was because everyone she'd ever met in New Hope always seemed to be friendly enough, but not very sincere. When Owen moved here, he hadn't minced words around her, and she'd felt like he was the only honest person in her life. Now, he was acting like everyone else, and she couldn't take it.

"You've always been straight with me, Owen, and now it's like you're trying to hide something and I don't know why everyone is so freaking uptight around me." She paused, then added something she'd always been afraid to ask. "Is it because of my blackouts? Am I some kind of freak to everyone?"

"No, you're not a freak, and those blackouts aren't your fault," he said firmly. He shook his head and took a seat on one of the two battered lawn chairs that sat on his deck. "Sit down."

She did.

"Listen, it isn't my place to tell you everything, or anything for that matter, but I'm going to try something, okay?"

"Yeah, sure," she agreed, completely puzzled on the change of pace.

"Try and pull up your first memory."

"That's easy," she said automatically. "It was the first day of third grade. Mom, Dad, Gram, and Grandpa dropped me off and a teacher came out, took my hand, and walked me into elementary school." She smiled. "I sat next to Carly, and we've been friends ever since." She looked over at Owen, who wasn't smiling. "What?"

"That's your first memory?" he asked gently. "Third grade?"

"Yes," she answered, her smile fading.

"You were eight?"

"Yes."

"You know that's not normal, right?" he said as softly as he could. "You should have other memories way before eight years of age."

"I know that," she said defensively. "But you asked me what my first memory was and that's it. You don't think I've tried to remember further back?" She let out a bitter laugh and shook her head. "I try every single night to remember something, anything from before that day, but it's blank. Nothing, not even an inkling. There's no color, no scent, no feeling. It's as if I was just plopped in New Hope."

Owen looked like many different things were running through his head. Confusion, understanding, even empathy.

"You weren't just plopped here," he said. "You were born in Michigan and raised here."

"I know," she said uncertainly. "It's just that, I've always had to be told that. I can't remember it." She shook her head. "But what does this have to do with anything? I've made peace with it. I just don't have memories from before that day."

"You do, though," Owen tried to explain. He looked like he was deciding how to phrase his words so that they revealed only just enough. *What is he hiding?* "You have memories, Hanna. They're just locked up."

She fidgeted with the golden locket that hung around her neck, trying to be calm.

"Why? And how do you know that?"

"Hanna, it's really not my place."

"Please, Owen," she asked, her voice desperate. "Tell me something. Anything."

He was silent for a moment as his hands slowly rubbed together, weighing his options. He looked up.

"You witnessed a crime when you were a kid, Hanna. A crime you wanted or needed to forget."

"What crime?"

Owen looked positively torn.

He inhaled and exhaled slowly. "I really don't have the time to be telling you this," he said, sitting back as he put his hands to his eyes. "I'm pulling a double shift tonight, and you shouldn't be left alone."

"Who's going tell me the truth besides you, Owen?" she began to plead. "Gram and Grandpa still think of me as that eight-year-old girl, Mom and Dad are who knows where, and everyone in this town has treated me like a disease since I was little." She paused, taking a deep breath. "You're the only person who will tell me what happened."

"I'm not the only one," he said quietly, and she noticed worry in his eyes.

"Who else?" she asked.

That inquiry earned her a suspicious look. "No," he said, apparently deciding he had already said too much. "No, Hanna, it isn't my place, and don't go looking for answers, all right?"

Deflated, she sat back. "This is completely unfair," she said in her least mature voice. "Whose place is it to tell me my own memories?"

"Your grandparents," Owen said, as if it were obvious.

"They're not going to tell me anything," she said as he stood up. "I've tried for years to get them to talk to me."

"Try again," he said.

"Why are you being so difficult?" she asked, standing with him. "Just tell me—"

"No," he said loudly. He walked off the porch. Frustrated beyond belief, she followed.

"Fine, I'll find someone else to tell me."

"Good luck," he said, clearly not worried.

Then, something clicked. "Hold on. How did we get here? We were talking about William Vann." Owen avoided her eye. "He can tell me something, can't he?" She felt a thrill of excitement.

His face changed, becoming angry and, at the same time, afraid. He towered over her, his voice hard.

"Stay away from William Vann, Hanna," he warned. "I'm serious."

Owen rarely intimidated her, but at that moment, she was actually a little scared.

"What if I don't?" she pressed, growing angry herself. "What the hell happened that no one wants me to know about?"

"Just do what I say," Owen said sharply, ignoring her question yet again. "He's dangerous."

That caught her attention. "Dangerous how?"

He shook his head, looking annoyed that he'd said something else to interest her. "You're impossible," he said. "I can't keep talking about this—I've got to go."

Owen gave her a half-hearted wave and jumped into his cruiser. She waited for him to pull out of the driveway before she got into her own car. She didn't leave right away, too deep in her thoughts to drive.

Owen couldn't have meant what he said about her witnessing a crime. *He just wanted to get me out of his hair. He's wrong about this, just like he's wrong about William.*

She could never ask William about any of it either. *What am I supposed to say? "Oh hi, you never met me before saving my life, but do you know why I have blackouts and can't remember anything before I was eight years old?"* She'd look completely crazy if she did that, and she did *not* want to give him any other excuse to look at her strangely.

She nearly peeled out reversing the car onto the dirt road. It'd been ten years of her asking questions and getting no answers, ten years of being avoided by most people, while the people who actually spoke to her were either extremely cautious or completely self involved. She was so frustrated with the whole thing. It was like pulling teeth to get any information. For a brief moment, Hanna thought of herself as an evil dentist. She shook the image from her mind. Her imagination was just plain strange.

When she got home, she didn't speak to her grandparents and went straight downstairs to her room. She was too engrossed in what Owen had told her, and when she realized she was playing with her necklace, she laid down on her bed.

She inspected the round, gold locket that she had worn every day for as long as she could remember. *Which apparently isn't long enough*, she thought bitterly. It was another thing that she didn't remember receiving. It had always just been there, around her neck.

She rolled over and once again tried to remember anything before her first memory, but only came up with an empty picture.

CHAPTER SEVEN

*M*onday felt like one of the longest days of Hanna's life. In-school suspension dragged on so slowly that by the time school let out, she swore she'd aged a hundred years. After watching the clock on the wall for the last half hour, she was eager to get out and meet up with Carly. They had decided that morning, after the uncomfortable ride to school with Anne, that they would go dress shopping for prom, even though Hanna wasn't going anymore. They had waited until after the car ride to discuss it, since neither wanted Anne to come along.

Anne had asked Hanna about her blackout, which Hanna avoided talking about with anyone who wasn't family. It wouldn't have bothered her, except Anne kept bringing it up, even after it was obvious that she didn't want to talk about it. Hanna didn't know if it was because of Anne's questions or if another blackout was looming, but she had a wicked headache for the rest of the morning. Thankfully, it had vanished by the time school was over.

"Sorry!" Hanna yelled as she hurried to her car across the almost empty parking lot. She was glad that Carly was the only one waiting for her. "I had to rush around classrooms to grab my homework."

"No problem," Carly said nonchalantly. She opened the passenger door. "How was suspension?"

"Magical," she said sarcastically, getting into the driver's seat. "Anything happen in school?"

"Not really, except that Anne kept asking a bunch of questions about you in homeroom."

Hanna looked at Carly, a little surprised.

"Well, maybe not a bunch, but a few. Sorry about the ride this morning. I thought she was going to be a lot less . . . awkward."

"Yeah," she said, instantly feeling guilty when Carly voiced her thoughts. She tried to avoid talking about people behind their backs, though she was curious why Anne was so interested in her. "What sort of things was she asking?"

"Oh, you know," Carly began, appearing uncomfortable. "The usual—who are you dating, who are your friends—just things like that." She paused, looking out the passenger side window as they drove. "Why you black out."

"She asked that?"

Carly nodded.

"And what'd you say?"

"I said I didn't know," she answered. "I don't know. You never told me—"

"Because I don't know, Carly. It isn't like I'm keeping some big secret from you."

"Listen," Carly said quickly. "Can we just focus on something else? Like prom? I don't want to argue over nothing."

Hanna began to counter, but realized Carly was right. They weren't arguing over anything important, and she didn't want to ruin their shopping spree, which she'd been looking forward to all day. For the rest of the ride, they talked about what dress styles they liked and which famous person they each wanted to look like.

After getting to the mall and trying on dresses at a few stores, but finding nothing that satisfied Carly, they headed to the food court. Carly seemed more anxious about eating than finding a dress for prom, but Hanna welcomed the change of pace. Carly kept badgering her about going to prom, emphasizing the importance of attending such a monumental occasion in their young lives every time she stepped out of the dressing room.

Of course, Hanna realized why Carly was so preoccupied after they bought their food and sat down. Troy and his friends were by the Wendy's at the opposite end of the court, twirling their lacrosse sticks and laughing as two in the group pretended to wrestle. She looked at Carly, who was watching them as if they were the most interesting thing she had ever seen.

"Oh, please don't tell me that's why we came here," Hanna said, making a face as she bit into her chicken teriyaki.

"Don't start with me, Loch," Carly said, pointing her chopsticks at Hanna. "This is what normal teenagers do, okay?"

"What? Stalk people?"

Carly looked at her, unabashed.

"Why is it that I always feel like I'm trying to teach you about the norms of adolescent life, Hanna? Shouldn't you just know?" She tapped her index finger on Hanna's head. "Isn't it wired somewhere beneath that pretty mop of blonde hair you have?"

Hanna swatted her hand away and smiled.

"I just don't get it, that's all. Why waste your time on some guy in high school when, in less than six months, you'll be at college, surrounded by a whole new environment?"

"Who lives their life like that? Not living today because of what's going to happen tomorrow? It hasn't even happened yet," Carly answered, turning back to watch Troy laugh as one of the lacrosse players told a story. "Besides, what if Troy is my soul mate?"

"You believe in soul mates?"

"I don't know, but it's romantic to think about. Two souls, put on opposite ends of the world, only to reconnect and find each other?" she sighed dreamily.

Hanna rolled her eyes. "Opposite ends of the world? More like opposite ends of town."

"Which is even more romantic," Carly insisted. "Because now, we have to ignore all the social stigmas in our hometown."

"Social stigmas?" Hanna laughed. "Carly, I can honestly say you are the craziest person I know."

Carly laughed too, which attracted the lacrosse team's attention. Realizing that Troy was giving her googly eyes, Hanna stopped. She didn't want to divert any of his attention away from Carly.

"Uh, I just remembered, I have to grab some new seat covers," she said, quickly standing up. "I'll be right back."

"What?" Carly said, distracted by the guys headed their way. "But they're coming over!"

"They're for Grandpa. He wanted me to pick some up while we were here," she lied. "You know my grandpa. He's a lunatic when it comes to his car. I'll be right back."

"Okay," Carly said slowly as Troy reached the table.

"Hey, where are you going?" he asked.

"Got to grab something!" she said, leaving as quickly as she could.

She turned out of the food court and made a beeline for the escalators.

You're such a weirdo, she thought as she made her escape. *Why do you always do things like that?* It was as if she purposely tried not to have any other friends but Carly.

She walked through the crowded mall, wondering why she always tried to keep people at a distance. Troy was a nice guy, and even though Carly had called dibs on him, she didn't need to avoid him and the entire lacrosse team. They were a pretty good group of guys, so why did she avoid them, and everyone else, like the plague?

Because there's something wrong with you, a tiny voice in her head said.

She nodded, agreeing with herself. There was something wrong with her, and the less people around her, the better.

Then another thought danced into her mind. Carly had mentioned *soul mates*, and she couldn't help but feel a little disappointed in her friend. The term had always struck Hanna as a pretty idea better used in song lyrics than in the real world. There were no such things as soul mates. With seven billion people in the world, what were the chances that a person's soul would recognize another?

She was so deep in her thoughts, she wasn't watching where she was going and her shoulder bumped into someone.

"Sorry," she said offhandedly, not looking up.

"Hanna?" a familiar voice sounded.

Looking up and turning slightly, she saw William, looking at her with friendly recognition. She swallowed hard, surprised at how easily her thoughts went out the window, and how her mind suddenly focused on how incredibly handsome he looked. She thought that maybe she had just imagined how attractive he was, but even looking at him in the unforgiving fluorescent lighting of the mall, he looked just as she remembered.

Perfect, she thought.

"William," she said, a little out of breath. "Hi."

"Hi," he replied, smiling. "How are you?"

"Good. I'm good. How are you?"

"Good. Just grabbing some jeans," he said, lifting up a navy blue bag. "Funny, I keep running into you."

Hanna remembered their last encounter and was disappointed with herself for not acting a little more cold. He'd been lurking around like a criminal and snapped at her. Apparently, her face gave away her thoughts.

"Listen, about the other day, I didn't mean to be such a jerk. I just have some trouble thinking sometimes and walking actually helps, and . . ." He paused and looked down before looking her in the eye, his grin widening. "And I don't know why I'm telling you any of this." He laughed, sounding unsure.

"It's fine," she said, quick to accept his apology. "It's none of my business."

"Right," he said, though she didn't think he meant it. "Listen, I was just about to grab a coffee. Want to come?"

Unintentionally, she compared William's invitation to Troy's and couldn't help but notice the unwavering confidence in William. He seemed so sure of himself that she bet if she said no, he wouldn't have batted an eye. Of course, this wasn't a date, this was just coffee.

"Yeah," she said, nodding. "Sounds good."

He smiled as he turned to walk next to her.

"How's the car?" he asked as they wove through the hoards of mall-goers. "I hope you didn't mind that I drove it to your house that night, but you dropped your keys and I figured it would just be easier to drop it off."

"No, that was nice, actually, thank you. I should have thanked you the other day, but I forgot."

"It's all right. I was distracted." He paused.

"Why were you walking at night?" she asked, a little suspicious.

"It's easier to focus at night. Just alone with my thoughts."

"I know how that is," she said absently. "I always feel like it's just me and my thoughts, going a million miles a minute. I can't hold on to one idea."

"That's exactly how I feel most of the time," he agreed.

"You know, you should probably be careful, walking around here at night," she said, suddenly reminded by their conversation. "There's been a wolf hanging around, and it almost attacked me the other night."

William stopped walking, and Hanna almost tripped to stop as well. He had the tiniest hint of a smile on his face.

"Really?"

"Yeah, at a party at Thurmont Mill. Luckily, the train scared him away, but I'd be careful if I were you."

"The train? Wouldn't a group of people be more likely to scare him off?"

"Yeah, but I wasn't with a group of people. I'd just jumped off the tracks and was on the other side of the train when I saw him—"

"You jumped from the tracks?" he asked, obviously confused.

"It's this stupid game," she began, feeling her cheeks heating up. *Why am I telling him all this?* She began to fidget with her locket. "You try and see how long you can stand in front of an oncoming train. It's dumb and dangerous, but that's where I saw that wolf."

Hanna wanted to laugh at how stupid she must have sounded. When she realized that he was looking at her necklace, she dropped it.

"I'll remember that," he said, his eyes still on her necklace. Hanna covered it with her hand and he looked up. They continued walking. "But I think playing chicken with a train is a little more dangerous than walking around at night. Sounds like you might have a bit of a death wish."

"No, it's just . . . I don't know actually," she confessed, shaking her head. "It was dumb."

"Maybe . . . but then again, maybe not."

The tone of his voice sounded flirtatious, though it could have been her imagination. *I'm such an idiot*, she thought. *Of course he'd just been going for a walk. Why had I been so quick to assume that he was up to no good?*

Then she remembered the customers talking about the Vann family before she saw him that night.

"I hear your family has a place up here," she said, trying to sound nonchalant. "Is that where you're staying?"

"Yeah, but only for a few months. Then it's back to South Carolina. I'm only up here doing a few estimates and getting a base started for a few houses. A couple of clients have been bugging us to build some houses on Lake Michigan, even though our housing department hasn't really been up and running for a while."

"No? I thought you were in construction. Wouldn't building houses be up your alley?"

"They would, but we've sort of gone the other way with the business. Restoring historical buildings, building elaborate hotels. Houses aren't really our thing anymore."

"Then why build?"

"The price is right, I guess," he said. "We've been kind of slow with work lately and are scouting for new projects, mostly in New Orleans. Building houses is sort of our fall back when work isn't busy."

"But your company has built houses up here before, right?"

William looked at her.

"Yeah, we have."

"Sorry," she said, feeling embarrassed. "I just heard that somewhere. I try to remember things as best I can."

He smiled. "Why is that?"

Without thinking, she answered.

"I can't remember a lot about my past, so I try to memorize details about everything I can so I don't forget."

"You have a bad memory?" he asked, frowning.

"No, I remember most things. I've actually tracked almost everything I do in a journal for years. I just have a big hole in my memory from when I was younger, and ever since then, I've tried to make it a point to remember."

She was surprised she was confessing such a private fact about herself, but she didn't feel wrong in doing so. He nodded thoughtfully, as if he understood and continued to walk quietly next to her.

They stopped at a kiosk at the end of the mall called the "Fat Cat" and ordered two coffees. She noticed he drank his black with a single packet of sugar and marked it off in her "things to remember about William Vann" file. When she pulled out money to pay for it, he refused and instead pulled out his wallet. She saw he had a business card for Vann Construction and when he noticed her looking at it, he gave it to her.

"Just in case you ever want something built," he joked as he put his wallet back in his pocket. "My number's on the bottom."

"Thanks," she said. "I don't have a card to give you."

"That's fine." He smiled. "I'll just have to find you then."

Definitely flirting, she thought, grabbing a pen from a cup that sat on the counter. She wrote her number on a cardboard coffee jacket and handed it to him, smiling back.

They continued to walk, up the stairs and back toward the way they came on the upper level.

"So, are you enjoying New Hope?" she asked, taking a sip of her coffee.

"It's cold, but I like it. South Carolina can be brutal in the summer. And there isn't much to do here, which is a nice change of pace from Charleston. Can't get into too much trouble."

"Trouble in New Hope? There's never been trouble here," she said, before remembering yet again what her customers had said. For some reason, she kept forgetting that she should be trying to find out things about him and his family, instead of getting to know him. She shook her head. "I mean, I don't *think* there has ever been trouble around here."

William's steps slowed and she wondered if she'd hit a nerve.

"Wouldn't know," was all he said before changing the subject. "That Officer Peirce doesn't like me much."

Feeling her cheeks redden again, she recalled that Owen had told him to stay away from her.

"Sorry about him, he's my cousin and kind of a stuffed shirt. He didn't mean anything by it."

"I think he did," he said. "But it doesn't bother me."

"Why would he say something like that to you?" she asked, more to herself than to him.

"Probably because I'm new in town, and he's worried about you."

"But why would he be worried about anything?"

William didn't answer right away, but she noticed his brow furrowed a little.

"I don't know," he said finally.

She pursed her lips, somehow knowing he wasn't telling the truth. "Hmm," she said, looking toward the floor.

"'Hmm' what?" he asked.

"Nothing," she shrugged, biting her lip as she thought. He raised a quizzical brow and she sighed. "You're lying, but I don't know why or how I know."

His smile had faded. The intensity of his eyes seemed magnified when he wasn't smiling and for the briefest moment, she could have sworn she saw something surrounding him—a hazy aura, just like the other day, when she first saw him.

"Sorry," she said, shaking her head. "I just called you a liar to your face."

"I'd rather you say it to my face than behind my back." He grinned again and she felt at ease once more. "But you're right. I was lying."

And just like that, her ease vanished.

"Why?"

He was quiet a moment before answering.

"Because I don't want to frighten you," he said slowly. "And if Officer Peirce had his way, he'd tell you some pretty frightening things about me."

I bet he would, she thought as her stomach began to do somersaults.

"You seemed so familiar that day I met you," he continued. "Like a piece of me recognizes you from somewhere, but I can't put my finger on it."

His words made her stop in her tracks, one in particular ringing in her ears. Hadn't she just been thinking about this?

He paused. "Sounds a bit crazy, huh?"

She stared at him. "Recognize how?"

His expression was complex. She got the feeling she was supposed to know what he was talking about, but she didn't have a clue what he meant. After another few moments of silence, William spoke.

"You don't know what I mean by that?"

"Should I?"

If possible, he looked more confused.

"Yes," he said confidently. Her eyebrows rose. "You should know what I mean, so I don't have to say it out loud."

She tilted her head to the side, wondering what the look on his face meant.

"Are you embarrassed?" she asked, amusement coating her voice.

"Forget it," he said as he looked up and away from her, smiling as if he was holding back a secret. "But that's why Officer Peirce has a problem with me. I told him as much, and he didn't like it. I don't think he finds my family acceptable either."

"Family?" she repeated. "What do you mean?"

"Hanna! There you are!" Carly's voice sounded from ahead. She looked up and saw that Melanie had joined up with Carly and the lacrosse team. "Where have you been?"

She held up her coffee cup. They were still a few yards away and since the mall had filtered out a bit, Carly's yell was louder than it needed to be.

"Well, I guess that's my cue," William said quietly, so only she could hear. "It was nice talking to you."

"Yeah, you too," she replied, disappointed that it had to end. "Thanks for the coffee."

"Anytime," he said, just like after he'd saved her life. She couldn't wipe the grin off her face as he waved at Carly and left.

The look on Carly's face was priceless as she came bounding over, while the look on Troy's was somewhere between disappointment and bitterness. Refusing to talk about her conversation with William in front of everyone, she feigned a headache. It was a completely believable excuse since everyone knew she always got headaches, but it was the furthest thing from the truth. She'd never felt so good. She felt just like she did when she stood in front the train at Thurmont Mill. Everything was bright and brilliant.

"You look like you're on cloud nine," Carly said as they got into her car after leaving the mall.

"What does that even mean?" Hanna asked cheerfully, though she agreed wholeheartedly.

"It means you like him," she said in the most exaggerated way.

"I don't like him," she lied, smiling like a fool as she started her car. "I just think he's nice."

"Oh please, you're already picking out a white dress . . ."

"Shut up!" Hanna said, grinning as they drove home.

They talked about her conversation with William, even though she left out certain parts, like confessing that she couldn't remember anything before she was eight. She knew Carly would be offended that she'd told a complete stranger, when she hadn't even told her best friend.

Carly rambled about the lacrosse guys and how obvious it was that Melanie liked Troy. She went on and on about how she thought Troy liked her more than Melanie, and Hanna had to stop her after she started to compare herself to the gossip queen.

After she dropped her off, Hanna went home, still trying to understand what William had meant about her being familiar. *And why did he seem so sure of himself, and of how Owen felt about his family?*

She didn't bother trying to hide her excitement over seeing William when she got home, and her grandparents seemed happy that she was in such a good mood, though she didn't tell them why. If Owen had a problem with William, she bet her grandparents would too.

After dinner, she went downstairs and changed into her pajamas. She lay on her bed for a few hours, doing homework until her eyes became heavy. Her alarm clock blinked 11:01 p.m. and she grabbed her coat, looking for her phone to plug it in for the night.

Pulling her phone out of her pocket, she also found the card William gave her. She stared at it for a few minutes before quickly tapping his number into her phone, just in case she needed it. She placed his card in the mouth of a little wolf figurine that stood on her nightstand and fell asleep looking at it, wondering for the first time in a long time why she loved wolves so much.

CHAPTER EIGHT

*T*he following Saturday, Hanna promised Gram to help with the spring cleaning. It was a yearly tradition. Mrs. Hines would come over and the two older ladies would gossip, pulling everything out of the closets just to dust them off and put them back in place. Hanna never understood the point, since Gram always kept a clean house, but she offered to help anyway.

"How's the diner, Hanna?" Mrs. Hines asked as she sat at the kitchen table, dusting a pile of picture frames. Gram had just put on another pot of coffee and was sorting through a pile of clothes, placing some in a box labeled "Salvation Army."

"Good," she answered, tiptoeing around the kitchen to get to the sink. She started polishing Gram's copper pots. "How's the station?"

"Oh, not much excitement since you came in," she answered, smiling. "Although, there was a call the other day about a supposed break-in."

"Really?" Gram asked, curiosity in her voice. "Who?"

"Well, I don't think there was much to it. That Florence Baker, do you remember her? From that water aerobics class last year?" Gram nodded. "Well, she called in saying that she saw a couple of men trying to break into her neighbor's house. By the time the cops got there, there didn't seem to be much of a disturbance."

"That Florence is such a worry-wart," Gram said. "She always thinks something is going on. Why, I remember when Owen first moved to town. She was convinced that he was an FBI agent sent from Washington to deal with the supposed drug dealing 'infecting the town's youth.'" Gram laughed, while Mrs. Hines snickered. "As if New Hope were some bustling hot spot for such things."

"Ridiculous," Mrs. Hines said.

"Well, I don't know," Hanna chimed in, feeling the need to stick up for poor Florence. "I heard something about a drug bust that might be going down in a few weeks. Owen mentioned something about it, I think. It's scheduled for prom."

Silence. When neither of them spoke, Hanna looked up and realized that she had frightened the two. "I mean, it's not a big deal. I think they found a few joints behind the school at the winter formal, so they're planning to keep an eye on prom."

"Joints?" Gram repeated, unfamiliar with the term.

"Yeah, pot," she said, looking at them. "It happens. I know a few kids who smoke weed, it's no big deal."

"No big deal?" Gram repeated, her cheeks paling slightly.

"Gram, calm down. You know I don't do drugs. I just know some people who do."

"Not Carly?" Gram sounded horrified.

Hanna sighed. "No, Gram."

"Then how do you know so much about it?"

"Because I'm a teenager?"

"Goodness," Mrs. Hines said. "Drugs in New Hope? Who would have known."

"It's just a couple of potheads. Every high school in the country has them."

"In my day, doing drugs was considered a bad thing," Gram said with conviction. "I didn't know anyone who did, and if I had, I would have steered clear of them. I would think you would do the same, Hanna."

Hanna doubted that Gram never knew anyone who smoked pot, but then again, she had grown up in a time where there was some serious negative propaganda going on. It didn't surprise her that the two of them seemed terrified at the idea of a group of teenagers doing it.

"I promise, it's not that big of a deal," Hanna said, finishing up with the copper pots. She poured herself some coffee. "And you can stop looking so worried. I'm not into it. It just makes you extremely tired. I'd rather be doing other things than laying around getting high."

"How do you know it makes you tired?" Gram asked suspiciously.

"Because that's what people tell me," she answered without missing a beat. She was fine talking about things like this with Gram, but she didn't want to go into it with her and the conversation was getting uncomfortable. "Is there anything in the attic you want me to bring down for the Salvation Army?"

Gram eyed her a little before nodding.

"There are a couple of boxes up there that I couldn't carry down. I was waiting for Owen to come over tomorrow, but do you think you can manage?"

"Sure, not a problem," Hanna said, grabbing her mug of coffee.

She headed into the hallway between the kitchen and the living room where a long string hung from a door in the ceiling. She pulled down the ladder and did her best to balance her coffee as she climbed.

The attic wasn't really an attic so much as it was a crawl space. She clicked on the light and looked around. Grandpa had laid down thin sheets of particle board so they could store things up there, but every few feet showed the pink insulation beneath. It was warm and surprisingly organized, considering it was on the spring cleaning list.

Placing her coffee gently next to her, she sat with her legs crossed and pulled over a box that had "books" written on it in black lettering. If Gram was going to donate them to the Salvation Army, Hanna thought she'd take a look to make sure there weren't any books that might grab her attention.

She sifted through a few boxes, finding mostly cookbooks, her parents' marine life magazines, and a few do-it-yourself books before realizing there wasn't much that interested her. Still, she wanted to sit and finish her coffee before lugging the heavy boxes down, so she moved all the boxes that were going as close to the opening as possible, after which she sat and looked around.

A few boxes marked "Christmas" and "Baby Things" were scattered around. Hanna sipped her coffee, pushing a few out of the way with her foot as she noticed a box labeled "Family History."

Interesting, she thought as she put down her mug. She scooted over to it, making sure not to misstep and touch the insulation. It was an old box, with the flaps folded in. Pulling it open, she reached down for the first thing that caught her eye—a wedding album made from leather and covered in dust. Brushing it clean, she opened to the first page and saw a very unfriendly-looking couple in black and white. The woman, who wore a formal white dress, or maybe some other pale color, was sitting in a chair. Her light hair was draped over her shoulders, covered by a veil that went down as far as Hanna could see. Her expression was stone-like, without a hint of a smile. The man looked just as unpleasant, with pale eyes and some darker shade of hair.

"They look thrilled," she muttered to herself as she held the album up to the light.

Listed faintly on an elegant piece of paper beneath the picture were the words, "Gustave Quist and Iona Garther, married 1905." *They could be Gram's parents or grandparents*, Hanna thought. Flipping through the pages, she spotted another wedding photo. This time, the couple stood in front of an iconic landscape painting, the man dressed in a kilt, while the woman wore a more flowy and angelic gown than the tight, structured one Iona wore. Beneath their picture was scribbled, "Kevin Loch and Sarah Ruddick, married 1930."

After looking through a dozen or so photos of people long forgotten, she closed the album and put it aside, reaching into the box and grabbing a leather cylinder. She didn't know what it was at first, but then realized there was a rounded piece of glass at one end. It was a kaleidoscope. Holding it up to the light, she looked through and saw a brilliant display of golden stars dancing and twirling against a bluish background. It was beautiful and by the look of it, really old. Putting it down gently, she reached for the next thing her fingers found, which was a book.

The book didn't have a title or any words anywhere on the cover, but it looked far older than anything she had ever seen. The spine was wood and the ties that held it together were thin, frayed strands of string. As delicately as possible, she opened to the first page. There, on the front page was a list of names, though she could only make out a few. Ingrid was at the top of the list, followed by three crossed out names, then Alva and Gertrude. Four more names looked as though they had been smudged out, while the second to last, Loretta, showed only faintly. Loretta was Gram's name. The name below caught her attention. In the thickest, darkest lettering was her own: Hanna.

Confused and intrigued, she gently turned to the next page and saw a beautiful, hand drawn picture of a girl with long, curly hair and a look of deep sadness on her face. There was lettering beneath it in a language that didn't look at all familiar. Hanna took French, and it certainly wasn't French, or any Latin language. It looked older and odder than anything she had ever seen.

She turned to the next page and saw more of the strange writing. It was a story, she guessed, impressed that the entire thing was hand written. She imagined that something like this probably would fetch a fortune nowadays, but something in her heart tensed at the idea. This wasn't the sort of thing that one could just sell. It was more important than that, but she didn't know why.

She flipped through the pages, noticing that little pictures had been drawn here and there. There would be the girl again, with the same sad expression walking through the forest, and every now and then, a black square and what looked to be three sets of eyes stared out at her through the shade drawn around them. A shadow of a memory passed through her mind as she stared at the tiny drawings.

"Hanna!" Gram's voice called.

Slamming the book shut, she jumped and let out an uneven, "Yes?"

"What's taking you so long? I thought you were getting those boxes down for me."

"Yeah, of course. I'm coming right now."

"I hope you're not going through Grandpa's old war things. You know he doesn't like people handling those."

"I'm not."

After a slight pause, Gram added, "Or anything else up there. It's really not safe, what with the insulation."

"I'm coming," she said, slightly agitated.

Fighting off a sudden headache, Hanna put back everything she'd taken out of the box, including the little title-less book. This was something that would need her full attention, not while her Gram was bugging her.

She moved toward the opening and began pulling down the boxes full of books into the hallway. Gram was staring at her when she finally pulled the last one down.

"What?" Hanna asked, looking confused.

"What were you doing up there?" Gram asked suspiciously.

"I was just looking through some things," she said, squinting her eyes. "I got a massive headache all of a sudden."

"Oh dear," Gram said, slightly worried. "Why don't you go lie down? It was probably the insulation that gave you a headache."

"Yeah, probably," she agreed.

After helping Gram move the boxes into the living room, she went down to her room, laid on her bed, and closed her eyes. Her headache hadn't disappeared, and she hoped that a nap might help it pass, but she couldn't sleep. Her thoughts were still on the book in the attic.

What in the world is it, and why does it have my name in it? It seemed too old and delicate to be in a cardboard box, surrounded by a bunch of other family trinkets. It should be under glass, protected. She closed her eyes, trying to force her headache to subside.

By the time night fell, she couldn't help it anymore. After they ate and her grandparents went to sleep, she opened the attic door as quietly as she could. She held up her little flashlight from her keychain, not daring to turn on the attic light, in case Gram and Grandpa woke up. She climbed up the stairs and crawled over the particle boards toward the box. Without making much noise, she pulled back the flaps and began searching for the book.

It wasn't there.

Hanna frowned. She had put it back in last, so it should have been at the very top. She began pulling out all the items, just as before. After several minutes, everything in the box surrounded her instead. She looked through it all, hoping that she'd picked it up without noticing, but after several searches, she couldn't find it. Puzzled, she shook her head and put everything back, wondering if she had put it somewhere else.

No, she thought. She put it right back into that same box. It wasn't as if it could just disappear. She had held it, read it—well, read as much as she could—but she was sure it was real. She hadn't imagined it.

Tired and annoyed, she crept back down the ladder as silently as the old wooden steps would allow. She pushed the door up and was grateful that it was on a pulley system, which didn't make much noise.

She turned around to head for her door, stopping short when the light beneath the door of her grandparents' room suddenly went off. *Had that been on before? Had one of them come out to see what the noise was all about?*

Baffled by it all, she shook her head and headed back down to her room. If she weren't so sure she'd held that book, she would've guessed she was going crazy.

CHAPTER NINE

By the time Friday rolled around, Hanna couldn't take it anymore—she had to find out more about that book. She decided to ask her grandparents about their family history, claiming that she had a report to do for school.

They were happy to reminisce about their parents and grandparents, indulging in recipes and stories Hanna had heard here and there growing up. Grandpa went on and on about his proud Scottish heritage, even imitating the accent he claimed his grandfather had when he was young. Gram shared warm memories regarding St. Lucia Day and how she always regretted not making more of an effort to keep that tradition alive. Hanna suggested they celebrate it in December, which pleased Gram, but then Hanna started asking about specific names, like Ingrid, and Gram shut down completely. She muttered something about food shopping and left abruptly, leaving Hanna listening to Grandpa sing some old Scottish song.

"Grandpa," she began after Gram left. "Did Gram ever mention an Ingrid to you?"

"Sure," he said. "She was the first in her family to—"

Grandpa closed his mouth suddenly and gazed at Hanna sheepishly, like he'd just let something important slip.

"What?" Hanna asked.

"How do you know that name?"

"Owen," she said quickly, desperate not to sound like she knew about the little leather-bound book. "He mentioned it. Told me to ask you two about it."

"Owen told you that name?"

Hanna nodded, hoping he bought it.

"Listen, Hanna, it hurts your grandmother to remember certain things. You don't want to upset her anymore, do you?"

"No, of course not. I just don't understand why no one will tell me."

"Tell you what?"

She didn't know what she wanted to hear. She knew there was something about the book no one was willing to tell her, just like her blackouts and missing memories.

She wanted to grill Owen again about what he'd told her, but he had pissed her off by not answering her questions. *How could he just leave me hanging like that, with only bits and pieces of information, and then refuse to tell me anything else?* Even though she wasn't the type to hold a grudge, as far as she was concerned, she had every right to be mad at him. It was beyond frustrating. It felt like everyone around her was lying to her now.

Except William. She hadn't seen or heard from William since talking to him at the mall, even though she'd thought about calling him a million times. She still thought it was strange that he'd seemed to be aware of something, but now she felt nervous asking him about her past and didn't want to bring it up.

By the time she got to work that afternoon, she had decided to call Owen and meet with him, since it was his day off. She cursed herself for flip-flopping, but Owen looked to be her best option for getting information, if she could lock him down in one place long enough.

She sighed as she cleared a newly vacated table. There was still an hour left of her shift when Owen showed up at the diner. She ignored him at first. He turned Angie away, insisting he wanted to wait for Hanna, and it was only after George scolded her for making a customer wait forty-five minutes that Hanna gave in.

"What'll it be?" she asked coolly.

"Come on, Hanna," he said. "You aren't still mad at me, are you?"

"Why would I be mad? Because you drop little hints about my past and then refuse to tell me anything of substance?" she asked sarcastically. "I could see how that might be frustrating."

"Hanna . . ."

"Or maybe I'd be mad because you told a complete stranger to stay away from me, like I was some sort of disease. Maybe I'd be mad because everyone always thinks that I can't handle whatever it is that I don't know."

"Hanna, stop."

"No, you stop," she said, sitting in the booth across from him. "Stop treating me like I'm some little kid, Owen. You tell me I have memories, but they're locked up. You tell me William Vann's a bad guy, but you don't tell me why."

She picked up her necklace without a thought and looked at him, her anger having dissipated.

"I'm missing pieces from my past, Owen. How do you expect me to be?"

Owen seemed less authoritative in his civilian clothes as he stared at her from his side of the booth. She thought he almost looked sorry.

"You do have memories," he began after a long pause. "And they are locked up. It happens more than you think actually, but not with eight-year-old girls, as in your case. Something in your mind is blocking them, so you can't recall them. What that something is, well, it probably has to do with the fact that you witnessed something when you were younger, something no one should ever have to see."

Hanna felt the room grow still, and the lights suddenly seemed brighter. He was finally going to tell her something about her past.

"What?"

"About ten years ago, there was a detective killed in the line of duty. I think you witnessed it."

A chill crawled down Hanna's spine as the tiny hairs on the nape of her neck stood on end.

"You don't know?"

"To be honest, kid, I don't know what you saw." He paused for a moment before adding, "But whatever it was, you obviously don't want to remember it."

Hanna sat back in the booth, stunned by Owen's admission. *I witnessed a murder? I watched someone die?* Even as she repeated the words in her mind, she couldn't see it. It was like she had been handed a puzzle piece that didn't quite fit.

"Now, as for William Vann," he continued, shaking Hanna out of her thoughts. "I'm telling you to steer clear of him because the Vann family isn't the most respectable bunch. They're . . . different."

"Different how?"

"Different in a way that you and I are different." He paused, unsure of his words. "Have you ever noticed? How you and I aren't anything special, and yet not quite the same as everyone else?"

She constantly thought her memory loss had made her different, for as long as she could remember, but then she thought of when she'd first met Owen—there had been something familiar, and yet completely foreign about him. It was like they had been friends their entire lives, despite only meeting a few months ago. There had always been a bit of a spark between them, though not romantically. It was almost . . . otherworldly.

Secretly, she'd been feeling guilty that she felt the same when she first saw William.

"Yes," she said softly. "Yes, I've thought that."

"Yeah, well, the Vann family is like that. Different, but not like us."

"I'm confused," she said, shaking her head. "They're different from everyone else—like us, but not like us? What makes us so different?"

Owen sighed, shaking his head.

"It's hard to explain," he said, letting out a frustrated laugh. "You see, Hanna, there are people in this world that try very hard not to be judged by their pasts—pasts that last generations. Do you understand?"

She nodded, even though she didn't know where he was going.

"You and me, we're similar in the sense that we don't have to live down anything our family has done in the past. We don't have terrible secrets that we have to keep from people. We're the good guys, if you will."

"The good guys? Like in a movie?" she asked, hesitantly. "This isn't a movie though, Owen."

"Not movies, kid, stories. Like, folk stories."

"Folk stories?"

"Yeah. You, me, your grandmother—although I don't think she really believes in it. We're descendents of people who were used as characters in folk stories."

Hanna frowned, starting to doubt this conversation.

"So, what? You're saying we're related to fairy tale characters?"

"Don't," he said quickly, looking anxious. "Don't say the F-word, okay?"

"The F-word? Fairy tale?" Hanna laughed. "You're joking, right?"

"See? This is why," he said, sitting back and lifting his hand as if to put her on display. "This is why I didn't want to tell you. You're a smartass."

"You've got to be kidding me," she said in disbelief. She leaned over the table, her voice hushed. "You want me to believe that we're related to characters in fairy tales? You cannot be serious—"

"I am serious," he said quickly, leaning in. "But you're not looking at it the right way. When you hear *fairy tale*," he said with disgust, "you think of pretty princesses and magic and Disney movies. I'm not talking about that. I'm talking about where all that came from, where those stories were first heard and written down. I'm talking about the people who inspired those tales. Our people. Our ancestors."

Hanna could see how serious he was being. So, instead of making fun, she decided to just shut up and listen.

"I don't know when or where the stories got screwed up, and they started adding talking bears and fairies, but I do know that all of them were based off actual events, actual people."

"People like us?" Hanna asked.

"Yes," he said, sighing with relief that she finally seemed to be understanding. "But the stories you've heard your entire life, the ones Hollywood dreamed up, they're not the real stories. The real ones are far more disturbing than anything you could imagine."

She suddenly felt cold as her mind began to turn.

"What does this have to do with William? Or us, for that matter? So what if we're related to some people who inspired a couple of folk writers?"

"It's bigger than you think, Hanna, and it has everything to do with us and William Vann. You see, every few generations, the story that was based on one of our ancestors tends to repeat itself. I don't know why or how, but it does, and it's a general rule that families like ours understand for future generations. We tend to be drawn to others like us, but we need to be careful. Just how I said that you and I are good, there are those out there who are bad. Real bad."

Hanna shivered as what he said sank in.

"So, you're saying there are people out there who are descendents of the bad guys, just like we're descendents of the good guys?"

"Yes."

"Just plain and simple, no twists or anything, just good."

Owen eyed her, almost as if he knew she was testing him.

"And so you're also saying that the Vanns are bad? No ounce of goodness in them at all?"

"I'm not trying to pass judgment on the son for the father's sins or anything like that, but the Vann family hasn't always been high society. In fact, that's a recent occurrence. Like, only the last fifty years—"

"Fifty years?" she laughed again, though she was anything but humored. "Owen, you sound like a snob."

"The Vanns aren't good people, Hanna. Everyone in that family has a record, or had much longer ones before they were able to buy their way out of trouble. But I'm not talking about recent history. I'm talking about their heritage. Who they really are."

"Who are they?"

"Just take my word for it. William Vann is a bad guy, and he comes from a long line of bad guys. On top of that, his family and your family haven't ever been connected. You're not from the same story."

"Well, if that's true, I don't see the harm in being his friend."

Owen rocked back in his seat.

"You're too good, kid. Don't you think it's odd that you blacked out the same day he came to town?"

She shook her head.

"I blacked out earlier that week. It wasn't him."

"How do you know? How do you know it wasn't your body warning you?" Owen glared at her. "You can't trust him. You can't trust any of them."

The seriousness of his tone frightened her. For whatever reason, she could see that Owen had an honest dislike and distrust for William and his entire family.

"But he saved my life," she said numbly. "How bad can he be?"

Owen didn't have an answer for her. Their conversation ended there, since it was closing time and George was eager to leave.

She forgave Owen for his previous vagueness and thanked him for answering some of her questions as they walked to her car, though now she felt more confused. William was a bad guy, and there wasn't any way around it—at least to Owen. *What does his heritage have to do with any of it?*

"Good night, kid," he said as she opened her car door. He began to walk away. "Get home safe."

"Good night," she said, before adding, "Wait, Owen."

He paused and turned back to look at her.

"You know how you said our family never did anything to be ashamed?"

"Yeah."

"What did the Vann family do? Or what are they, like, famous for, I guess?"

He stared at her thoughtfully and at first, she didn't think he was going to answer.

"Murders," he said finally, eyes unblinking. "They come from a long line of murderers."

Hanna swallowed hard, surprised that he was so forthcoming. It was the second time in a matter of weeks that she had heard about the Vanns and murder while working at the diner. Maybe Owen was deliberately trying to scare her now.

"Oh," she said quietly, nodding. She had prepared herself to hear something more indistinguishable and wondered what fairy tale had a family of murderers in it. *Could they have had something to do with the murder I witnessed, yet can't remember?* "What about us?"

Owen looked down at the ground and shook his head. When he looked up, Hanna could have sworn there was a twinkle in his eye and a hint of a grin pulled at the corner of his mouth. Then, for the first time, she saw it: the same hazy aura that William had around him, except this time, it was brighter, and silver in color. It was so hard to explain that by the time she tried to put it into words, it vanished.

"We're famous for happily ever after, kid. Even you."

There's his famous elusiveness, she thought as he walked away. *What the hell is that supposed to mean?*

She got in her car and sat in the dark for a few minutes. She watched Owen's Jeep pull away and waited for the lights to go off in the diner. *So that's what William meant. He knew that I was like him, and that's why I seemed so familiar to him, just like he said.*

It was a lot to take in, but Hanna found everything that Owen said easy to believe. Of course, if it was true, she wondered why she hadn't ever heard about it from her grandparents. She also wondered why Owen knew so much about it. *He's adopted. How can he be such a barrel of information about my family history?*

She turned on her car, still absorbed in her thoughts when she noticed that she was nearly out of gas.

Just what I need, she thought as she pulled out of the parking lot. She was going to have to drive to the gas station on Route 209, since nothing in town was open at this hour. Usually, she hated driving so far late at night, but tonight she didn't mind it, since she had so much on her mind.

She drove without any music playing, too consumed in her own thoughts to listen. *It certainly seems plausible,* she decided by the time she reached the gas station. *Inspiration for stories can come from anywhere, especially real life, so is it really that hard to believe that I'm related to someone who inspired a story?*

She frowned as she got out of the car. Which storybook character was she related to? She tried to match something in her life that sounded like a fairy tale, but nothing seemed to connect. The gaping hole in her memory probably had something to do with that.

As she pumped her gas, lost in thought, a sound reverberated through the night, catching her attention. A wolf's howl. She stared in the direction from which it originated. Maybe it was the chill in the air, but she shivered and simply stood there, letting the cry sink in as she listened.

CHAPTER TEN

"Please pass up your reports on *Of Mice and Men* and open your books to page one hundred and three," Mr. Marks, Hanna's English teacher, said during third period on Wednesday.

Even though Hanna hadn't spoken to Owen again over the weekend, she'd decided to take his advice and stay away from William. Owen was like her brother—she trusted him, even though he was a little uptight. *He could be right,* she kept reminding herself. *I really don't know anything about William.*

"Miss Loch," Mr. Marks said, startling her from her thoughts. "Papers?"

"Yes, Mr. Marks."

She collected the reports from the students behind her and passed them up to Carly, who was seated in front of her.

"Thinking about someone?" Carly asked, smiling knowingly.

"No," Hanna whispered to her as she handed over the papers. She hadn't told Carly about her sudden change of heart with William. She wasn't sure if she could even call it a change of heart, since she hadn't actually wanted to stop seeing him. Carly was still looking at her, wiggling her eyebrows up and down. She decided to change the subject. "Did you finish the report?"

"Just finished it last period," Carly winked at her as she turned back around.

"We're starting our last unit today and for the majority of you, this will be the last English unit of your high school careers," Mr. Marks said, none too enthusiastically. Someone in the class called out "woohoo." "For a select few of you, this won't be your first attempt, but let's try to make a successful go of it this time.

"Now—fittingly, in my opinion—your last unit is based on the very stories that helped the majority of you learn to read. This is Classic Folklore from the fall of Rome to Medieval Europe." Several groans echoed throughout the class, but Hanna perked up, interested. "Settle down, settle down. Now, read chapters eight through twelve and do the questions at the end of each chapter. We'll review these at the end of class and for those of you eager overachievers, chapters fifteen to twenty will be homework for tonight and due tomorrow morning."

"Jeez," Carly said under her breath as she turned back to Hanna. "We'll be done with this stupid book by the end of the week. Six chapters for homework? Excessive, don't you think?"

"Ladies," Mr. Marks said. "Quiet."

Carly rolled her eyes and turned back, while Hanna opened up her book and began to read, glad for the work. This was one English assignment that she was actually excited for.

As she read about the foundation myth of Rome, she couldn't help but think about William for the thousandth time. She stared at the page, trying to concentrate. Rome's foundation myth was of Romulus and Remus; it had apparently been the inspiration of the wolf folklores of the Gothic period.

Wolves, she thought. She wondered if the wolf she'd seen was still in the area, or if he'd just been passing through. She hadn't heard his howling the past few nights, but she had been exhausted from making up all her extra school work and had passed out as soon as her head hit the pillow. *William is kind of like a lone wolf.* She smiled to herself. *Rugged, handsome, possibly dangerous, definitely like my wolves.*

"Miss Loch," Mr. Marks said in his monotone voice. She jumped. "Are you finished with the questions?"

Hanna realized she'd been staring into space.

"No, sir," she said.

"Then please continue with the assignment," he said, not even looking up from his desk as he graded papers.

She picked up her reading again, continuing to a series of stories where wolves were the pinnacle bad guy, including "The Three Little Pigs" and "Little Red Riding Hood."

The big bad wolf, she thought, still entertaining the thought of William as her lone wolf. *Owen had said murderers, not wild animals.* Although, Red Riding Hood was almost killed before the woodsman came into the picture. She had been warned about wandering off the path and hadn't listened. *I'm not anything like Little Red Riding Hood.* She wasn't on a journey anywhere, and William hadn't distracted her from her path. He'd saved her.

Flipping through the pages, she couldn't find a single story with a wolf that applied to her situation. Wolves were never the heroes, and she wasn't like any of the heroines.

A page titled "Godmothers: The Rule of Three and William Makepeace Thackeray" caught Hanna's interest for a moment. She skimmed the section, briefly reading a few lines about a story involving three sisters and the birth of the fairy godmother, but she flipped the page. *Who has ever believed in fairy godmothers?*

Her eyes scanned over a beautiful picture by Arthur Rackham, one of her favorite illustrators. A girl with wavy blonde hair stared up at her from the page, wearing a dated dress and holding her hands behind her back. She looked like should could have been a relative. She read the caption beneath the picture. It read simply, "Goldilocks."

She was surprised there weren't any bears in the background. *Isn't it "Goldilocks and the Three Bears?"* It seemed more like a portrait the artist had painted of a real person, as if he personally knew Goldilocks. She could almost imagine the rest of her story, after the incident with the bears.

She must have stared at the portrait for nearly half an hour, because before she knew it, the bell was ringing and they were off to fourth period.

"What a boring assignment," Carly said as they left. "I didn't even finish the work we were supposed to do in class. Now I have to finish that on top of my homework because Marks pushed going over everything until tomorrow." Carly sighed loudly. "This is such crap."

She barely responded. Her mind was still deep in folklore and ideas of wolves.

"Hanna!" Carly yelled.

"What?" she asked, looking at Carly.

"What's with you lately?" she asked. Hanna could see that she was honestly concerned. "You're not yourself."

"I've just been thinking," she confessed, turning down the hallway. They walked to Carly's locker. "I know, I've been out of the loop."

"It's that William Vann guy, isn't it?" Carly asked, giving her a sly smile. She batted her eyes and made a ridiculous voice. "Oh my God! Are you in love?"

"Shut up," she said, rolling her eyes, leaning her back against the lockers. She looked up and down the hallway. Students were rushing to get to their next class while others were hanging around until the last minute. She spotted a couple kissing like their life depended on it and made a face. "Gross."

Carly looked up. "Please, you're just jealous," she said as she switched her books and closed her locker.

"Hardly," she retorted, and they continued to walk. "Why would anyone do that? Put all of their personal business out there like that?"

"I would," Carly said, smiling. "If it were Troy. And you would too, if it were *William*," she said, putting emphasis on William's name.

"If I were going to kiss anyone," Hanna said, "it would be done in privacy. Not out on display for everyone to see."

"Still think you're jealous," Carly said as the bell rang. "I'll see you after class."

"See you," she said as she turned right into the Vo-Tech part of school. She had her art elective—Jewelry—with her favorite teacher, Mrs. Banta. She wasn't the strictest teacher, so Hanna took her time walking to class as the hallways cleared. She tried very hard not to picture William and fought the urge to smile. Anne stepped out of one of the Vo-Tech rooms. When she saw Hanna, the color drained from her face.

Hanna remembered giving Anne a ride to school, when Anne had started to question her about her blackouts. Hanna forced a smile.

"Hey, Anne."

The girl looked at her oddly before saying a quick, "Hi." She walked past her swiftly, looking down.

At least I'm not the only weird one at this school, she thought, staring at Anne's back. *It was as if she purposely tried make every encounter uncomfortable.* She remembered that Anne was still new, though, and then felt a little guilty for mentally picking on her.

A sweet smell suddenly caught her attention. The scent was strong, almost sickening. She'd smelled it a thousand times before, but smelling it now, in the school, was all wrong. She dropped her books and grabbed her head as a slicing pain blurred her vision. She tried to wait for the headache to subside, but a loud boom suddenly echoed through the hall, the vibrations humming through the floor. The fire alarm sounded. She tried to move quickly, but between her pounding head and the students flooding the hallways, it wasn't easy.

At first, the evacuation was orderly, but the smell of smoke caused a panic. Chaos ensued in the halls as people began to scream—the fire doors had malfunctioned and had shut the Vo-Tech wing off from the rest of the school. The only other way out was to go through the auto club room and open the garage doors to the parking lot.

Hanna switched directions several times before she got her bearings and headed toward the end of the hallway. When she got there, a wall of students blocked her. Thick, dark smoke seeped out from the cracks of the auto club's door. Most of the students behind her had already turned away, looking for another exit.

"How are we going to get out?" someone shouted.

"The Home Ec room," another voice answered. "Through the emergency door!"

The crowd shifted as everyone headed in the opposite direction, toward the Home Ec room. The smoke quickly filled the hallway and students struggled to breathe. Hanna forced herself to keep a level head. Fighting against the crowd, she headed to the art room across from the auto club; its windows were always open to help ventilate the room while students painted.

Hanna shouted over the noise as she pushed through the wall of people going the other way. "The windows in the art room should be open!"

A few heads turned to look her way and a couple of people even followed. She felt bodies push past her as she ran back into the smoke. She had reached the door to the art room when she felt the cold crawl up the back of her neck. Her vision blurred, and she couldn't catch her breath.

No, no, no! She was blacking out, and she couldn't stop it.

Hanna wasn't herself, or at least, she felt like she wasn't in her own body when her eyes opened. It was dark. She felt like she was swimming in jelly. Her arms and legs wouldn't move the way she wanted them to. She was sitting in a chair in a room that she'd never been in before, yet it was vaguely familiar.

Her chest ached, and she realized she wasn't breathing.

"Hanna!" a voice called, though it seemed to call through a million walls.

Part of her wanted to find the voice, take a gulp of fresh air, but another part of her wanted to stay in this room. She could see the dim light of morning shining through two windows on her right. Looking down, she saw her legs, smaller than they should be and dressed in purple corduroy pants. She hadn't worn corduroy pants since she was a little girl.

"HANNA!" the voice called again, louder.

Her lungs filled forcibly with air, and she coughed painfully.

She felt as if she was on the end of a tape measure, being snapped back. The room, the windows, and the corduroy pants vanished, and the next thing she knew, her eyes opened to reality.

The sunlight was blinding, and the air she breathed was fresh, but it hurt to suck in. She coughed violently as someone held her around the shoulders. Sirens and horns honked somewhere in the distance.

"Hanna," the voice said again, this time gently. Her eyes focused on the silhouette looking down at her. William's voice was tense. "Are you okay?"

She tried to answer, but all she could do was cough. She realized that her head was resting on his legs, while the rest of her body lay on the cold ground. His arms were wrapped beneath her shoulders, holding her up in an awkward half-hold. She felt dizzy and confused. What was William doing here?

"God, Hanna," William said, one hand coming to the back of her neck. "What the hell were you thinking?"

"What?" she finally coughed out. Her throat felt charred. She wondered how smokers dealt with it on a daily basis. "What are you talking about?"

"Listen, I know you get a kick out of almost being killed, but this—"

"I don't—" she tried to say, before coughing again. When she had it under control she said, "I don't get a kick out of almost dying."

"Really? Then what was that?" he snapped. She saw anger written all over his face, though his eyes were filled with some other emotion she couldn't understand. It reminded her of an expression Owen sometimes wore. She tried to think of why he would be so upset, but her head was spinning. "The train was one thing, but standing in a burning building until you pass out? Damn it, Hanna, you do have a death wish."

Hanna moved away from him, unable to think straight. He resisted at first, but then let go. It could have been the carbon monoxide she'd inhaled, or it could have been the way he touched her, but he acted as if he cared about her.

You're crazy, she told herself.

"This is ridiculous," he said quietly, looking away. "Don't you know how precious your life is?"

Stunned at his choice of words, she watched the change in William. Anger gave way to pain, and then confusion. He seemed lost, as if he didn't know anything for certain. How had she shaken his world so much? They hardly knew each other.

"I didn't do *this* on purpose," she said, motioning toward the school. He seemed to think she'd purposely stayed in a burning building, when she'd actually been fighting to get out. "I was going to the art room to climb out the windows, but there were all these people and I blacked out before I could get in the room."

Tears welled in her eyes and even though she was mortified, she continued before William could say anything. "I don't know why it happened again. I don't want to die, and yeah, I like the feeling I get when I'm surrounded by danger, but this was different. I didn't try to stay in there. I *was* trying to get out. Everything just went dark, and I almost—"

William's hand gently covered her mouth and she looked at him, willing herself to be steady. He seemed just as confused as she was, but she was glad, because for the first time, she didn't feel so alone.

"It's okay," he said, the pad of his thumb brushing at her tears. "Don't cry."

She reached for his hand, shocked by the warmth that spread through her when she touched him. She felt connected to him, as though a part of her that had been missing could only be found by him.

"Who are you?" she whispered, clutching his hand. "Owen mentioned something about you, but I don't believe him."

He locked eyes with her, and she was surprised when he answered.

"What did he say?"

She shook her head. "He said that you're a bad guy."

"What do *you* think?" he asked, his voice a little hesitant.

"I don't think you belong in a column marked one or the other," she said. Maybe it was because she had almost died, or maybe it was because he'd saved her, again, but she felt increasingly drawn to him. "I don't know what to think after that, though."

She leaned closer, but was stopped by his hand on her shoulder. The way he held her back made her wonder if he thought she was trying to kiss him.

His brow furrowed. "No. You're from a different story than I am," he said as he pulled away.

She tried to look indifferent, but she was emotionally exposed and exhausted. What did it matter if she was from a different story? And why did she suddenly feel small when he said it?

"I wasn't trying to . . ." she said adamantly, looking away.

"I didn't mean it like that," he replied, but she wasn't interested.

"No, William, it's okay. I get it."

She started coughing again and she wrapped her arms around bended knees. He leaned toward her.

"Hanna, listen to me. Owen's right. I don't come from good people, and I don't want to involve you in things that you were never meant to be a part of, but dammit, if trouble doesn't try and find you . . ." He sighed. "We weren't even supposed to meet."

She rolled her eyes, imitating Carly. "Oh, really? Why not? Because you're the descendant of a murderer?" The startled look on his face told her that she'd hit a nerve. "That's right. Owen told me. You have some messed up family, apparently, but it doesn't mean you are."

His voice was cold and determined. "You're not safe around me."

"Apparently, I'm not safe without you," she said bitterly. "You're a bad guy, William? Then why have you saved me, twice?"

William stared at her, speechless. She couldn't stop herself from reaching for his hand again. He jumped a little, but accepted her touch.

"I don't want to hurt you," he said quietly.

"You haven't so far," she said. "Quite the opposite, actually."

She should have been shaking from nerves, but the smoke inhalation had dulled her senses, making her too weak to realize that he was closer now. His face was only inches from hers. Her insides flipped like pancakes, but on the surface she was still. He was so beautiful, with ash smudged on his cheek, his hair messed up, and his shirt wrinkled. When he suddenly leaned in and kissed her, her mind went blank and her senses exploded. All the rush she'd felt in front of the train magnified in this moment. It was like kissing death himself.

She moved into him, hungry for something she had never craved before, but he broke away too soon, breathing unevenly. They stared at each other as they regained their composure. Hanna had kissed guys before, but never like this. It was like William was the very thing she had been searching for, and he didn't think they were supposed to be together. She thought very differently about that.

"William," she began, but he stopped her.

"You see? This shouldn't be happening. I shouldn't even know you."

"Why? Why are you so bent on that?"

"It's not that simple to explain, Hanna. There are rules that we have to follow, otherwise people get hurt. People have gotten hurt."

"I don't understand. If you're so concerned about these rules, why do you care about my well-being?" she asked, exasperated.

"I don't know," he said, the look on his face severe. "And to be honest, that's a little frightening to me. I've always known where I've stood with people, but around you, I don't know." His bluntness shocked her. "Just believe me. You don't want anything to do with me."

"I think I know myself better than you do," she argued.

"You'd think that," he countered. "But I know more about *you* than *you* think." His eyes shone darkly. For the first time since meeting him, she believed that he might very well be dangerous.

"So you're a villain, William?" she said bravely, ignoring the voice in her head that said to get away from him. "Well, just in case you didn't know, villains don't save lives. And they definitely don't stick around to make sure someone's okay."

Looking conflicted, William stood up and stared down at her. He was strong and dangerous looking enough to be a villain.

"Go around the front. There's an ambulance there. You need to be checked out by paramedics."

"I'm fine," she said.

"No, you're not. You're stubborn, and if you're not careful, it'll kill you."

He walked away from her. What could she say to make him stay?

"You're not evil, William," she called, making him pause. "I don't care who wrote you off as being a villain, because you're not."

It wasn't until he was gone from her sight that she thought again, *What was he doing in the school?*

CHAPTER ELEVEN

The scene in the front of the school could have been from a movie. Staggered, Hanna walked toward the parking lot where the entire student body had gathered as volunteer firefighters fought to contain the roaring flames. Medics tended to shaken teachers and students; frantic parents congregated in the overcrowded parking lot while the principal and his staff tried to instigate order. Ambulances held coughing students, who were all wrapped in shiny space blankets. Lines of people waited to get oxygen and water while others hugged and called out names.

She tried to spot William, but he was gone. It felt like he'd taken a piece of her with him.

She continued through the crowd, unsure of where to go or who to look for. She wished something would drown out the noise and fear that strangled the air. She passed students she knew and even nodded at a few that looked back at her, their faces anxious.

Like a movie, she thought again. *A terrible movie.*

Rumors circulated through the crowd, with some blaming it on a science explosion or on the auto students. No one seemed to know the truth. When she found herself standing next to her car, she figured she wouldn't be able to get out of the parking lot for a few hours and walking home was not an option. Not after last time.

She opened her car door and reached into the glove compartment to get her phone. She was going to call her grandparents, but when she saw a dozen missed calls from Carly, she dialed her instead.

"Hanna!" Carly all but yelled, sounding relieved. "Where are you? Are you okay?"

"I'm by my car," she said, tears starting to fall. She'd been walking in a haze since William left and hearing her best friend's voice brought her back to reality. "Are you all right?"

"I'm almost at your car, hold on."

Carly hung up, and Hanna turned around, trying to spot her in the sea of people. After a few moments, she saw Carly pushing through a group of people, followed closely by Troy. She went to meet her and the two hugged.

"Oh my God," Carly said, crying. "I thought you were dead! What kind of person doesn't answer their phone?"

"I left it in my car," she said, wiping away her own tears. "I'm so glad you're okay. Was anyone hurt?"

"A few kids passed out from the smoke, but the only one who really got hurt was Anne."

"Oh no," Hanna said. "I saw her a few minutes before it happened. Is she okay?"

"Her arm got burned pretty bad, but the paramedic said she'd be all right. They took her to the hospital."

She just shook her head and leaned against her car. "How did this happen?"

"I don't know," Carly said, looking back at Troy. "There are a few rumors going around that a teacher did it. Others said there was a gas leak in Vo-Tech. I think it happened in auto class."

Hanna thought of the smell that had been in the air moments before the explosion. Gasoline. It would make sense then if the explosion happened in the auto lab. She looked back at the school. The firefighters had contained the flames, but half of the building was completely black, charred and smoking. How long had she been unconscious?

"The school just went up, like a match," she said, shaking her head in awe.

"Yeah, now they'll need to build a whole new Vo-Tech," Troy said. "Wonder who they're going to get to do that."

Troy seemed to be more aware of Hanna than she was of him. His tone was sarcastic, but she was too mixed up to care why.

"How'd you get out?" Carly asked. "You were going to art, weren't you? The Vo-Tech was shut off because of the fire doors. I was so worried. I knew you were in there."

"Yeah," Hanna said. "I was walking to class when I heard the explosion. Then the alarms went off and everyone came out of their classes, and the crowd just kept moving . . ." She didn't want to tell them that she blacked out.

Troy fell into a long and epic tale of how he'd saved his entire gym class because he heard the fire alarm. Carly pointed out that they'd trained for fire drills since kindergarten and was thankful that only one person was hurt. They talked for a few more minutes, until Owen stepped out of the crowd, coming toward them.

"Hanna. Carly. Troy," he said, as welcoming as a cop could be. "Everyone all right?"

They nodded in agreement.

"Good. Carly, I believe your mother is looking for you." He pointed to a woman with curly brown hair and a pale, worried expression. Her arms were wrapped protectively around Carly's younger brother and sister as she called out.

"Oh, Jeez," Carly said. "She brought the twins? I better go."

"Troy, you should probably go with her," Owen suggested, his eyes locked on Hanna. "I have to ask Hanna a few questions."

Troy followed Carly reluctantly. Hanna looked up at Owen.

"What's going on?"

"Have you spoken to William Vann since last week?" he asked, flipping open a notepad to read his notes.

The question hit her out of nowhere. She couldn't lie to him, but she didn't want to answer. He took her silence as a confirmation.

"Did he tell you anything about himself? Anything about his family or his family's business?"

"No," she snapped, her temper rising. William had just saved her life, and now Owen seemed to be accusing him of something. It pissed her off. "As I recall, you were the only one telling me his family was a bunch of murderers. Now, what the hell is going on?"

Owen flipped his notepad closed.

"Hanna, this is a serious matter," he said. "I don't have the time or the patience to explain. Just answer my questions."

"No," she said, glaring at him. "I'm not just going to listen to you blindly, though I doubt you have much to worry about."

"Why is that?"

She shook her head, refusing to tell him about being saved by William again.

"Why are you even asking about William?" she asked hotly. "You think he had something to do with this?"

Owen's expression answered her. Apparently, it was exactly what he thought.

"William was seen on Route 17, about fifteen minutes ago. He was climbing into his car, which has been parked on the side of the road for more than an hour. What was he doing there?"

A sinking feeling hit her in the stomach as she reluctantly connected the dots. She had no idea what he was doing leaving another vehicle on the side of the road after the last one got totaled. The walk from the school to Route 17 was only ten minutes through the woods, and was much closer to the school than Route 209. If William had parked his car there for more than an hour, then he'd been around before the fire started.

"Why would he start the fire?" she asked herself out loud, though Owen answered.

"His family's in construction, aren't they?"

She stared at him.

"I'm not saying anything yet, but the fact that the district will need to hire a construction crew to rebuild half the school—"

"That's not fair," she argued. "You can't honestly think that he would do something like that."

"Hanna—"

"No, Owen. You have no right to say something like that. How could you even think it?" she asked, trying to control her anger. "You think he would put a bunch of people's lives in danger just to get his family some business? How could you accuse him of something like that after he saved my life?"

Owen looked slightly ashamed, but he held his stance. "He's only been in this town for a little while and I've already gotten two complaints about him."

"From who?"

"That's privileged information."

Furious, she stood up from leaning on her car and opened her driver's side door. "You know, Owen, you act as though you weren't ever the new guy before. You've only been here six months."

"I'm a cop."

"You're a jerk," she snapped, crossing her arms as she sat behind the wheel.

They'd always gotten along pretty well, but she was starting to wonder if they ever really were friends.

"How did you get out?" he asked, deciding to change the subject. She glanced up at him. He looked unaffected by her words, but the clench in his jaw suggested otherwise. She felt sorry for calling him a jerk.

"I walked out," she lied. "I was in the crowd."

"A few students said they saw you come from around the back of the school."

"Yeah," she admitted. "I came from around the back. I saw an emergency exit, by the janitor's closet in the Vo-Tech wing."

"So what was it? You came out with the crowd or you went out of the emergency exit?"

All of her regret for calling him a jerk evaporated. His tone made her feel cold.

"Are you accusing me of something, Owen?"

"It's Officer Peirce. Now, answer the question."

"You don't answer any of mine," she said coldly, slamming the car door shut. She refused to answer him, not because she was guilty of anything, but because she wanted to annoy him. She was furious with him, yet at the same time, she couldn't help but be angry with herself. William had told her he was a bad guy and almost all the indications pointed to him. But why did she feel, in the pit of her stomach, that something wasn't adding up?

She couldn't believe that William would burn down half the school, endangering people's lives, just for a job. Yet, hadn't he mentioned that his family's business needed new projects? That's why they'd resorted to building houses again, even though they hadn't for some years. Owen watched her for a few moments before walking away. She ignored him, but he was probably thinking the same thing she was: why was she so quick to defend a guy she'd only known for a few days?

There were too many questions for her to answer. She waited in her car as police officers eventually started to let cars leave. Before her car was directed out of the lot, she realized she didn't want to go home yet. She needed more time to think.

Without distractions.

Taking a right, she drove around the outskirts of New Hope until she crossed into the next township. She didn't know where she was going, but she needed to get away for a few hours. Life had gotten too complicated too quickly.

A week ago, she'd been living as a normal teenager, an average student with good grades, looking at colleges to escape her hometown as so many others her age tried to do. She was cleared of medical vices years ago and was considered about as normal as any girl her age could be. Sure, she'd just discovered that she had a slightly unhealthy attraction to dangerous things, but she wasn't like a thrill seeker or an adrenaline junkie. Was she? Would she end up becoming one of those people who had to jump from planes or dive with sharks every few months just to maintain normalcy?

To complicate things further, tall, dark, and mysterious walks into her hometown and everything starts going to hell. Why?

She needed to not think of William. Why did she find him so damn interesting? And why did he have to save her life? There were smarter girls, prettier girls, girls who didn't have strange blackouts. Girls who thought the bad boy image was the hottest thing in the world—so why did he have to come here, to her?

She never thought of "bad boys" as being particularly attractive. They drove fast, talked faster, and rarely cared what people thought, which was generally a good quality, until they started doing unsavory things. That's what bad guys did.

Morons, she thought as she drove. Sometimes, she felt like she was the only normal one around, despite her odd past

. . . but she knew she wasn't normal. Wasn't that the reason she had headed for the less likely way out of the school—through the art window—instead of staying with everyone else?

No, she thought firmly. *It was the best option.*

She turned around in some roadside gas station. The sun had set while she drove.

By the time she made it back to New Hope, she had decided she would never talk to William Vann again, not even if he talked to her, called her, begged her, or threatened her. Not that she thought he'd ever do any of those things, but she was serious. She was falling for him too fast and too hard, and if she wasn't careful . . . well, she wasn't eager to find out what would happen. *Maybe everything will be clearer in the morning,* she thought as she pulled into her driveway. Maybe if she slept on everything that happened today, all the answers she was looking for would be waiting for her by the time she woke up tomorrow.

Fat chance, she thought, climbing the stairs of the porch. She was half way up the steps when she heard the wolf's howl. In a strange way, she felt like it was the voice of a friend, agreeing with every thought she had.

CHAPTER TWELVE

William sat in the rented truck parked in his driveway, his knuckles turning white as his fingers gripped the steering wheel. He had all but sped home after several passersby slowed to watch him walk out of the woods, looking like he'd just crawled out of a fireplace. Black soot clung to nearly every inch of him. Someone was bound to have called in his suspicious behavior to the cops. He wouldn't be surprised if Peirce was on his way to arrest him.

But none of that bothered him at the moment. All he could think about was Hanna's limp body lying on the floor in the smoke-filled hallway. It shook him to the core, and he couldn't understand it.

Earlier that morning, he had been meeting with a local lumber yard boss at the diner when he noticed a car pull into the parking lot. He looked up for a moment and saw a man that he knew was like him.

Evil.

His father always called it a "talent" of their kind, to be able to see when others like them were around. William could never see the good in anyone, until he met Hanna. She shone in her own way, but the man who stood in the parking lot was the opposite of good. William couldn't see his aura, but every few seconds, he could see the monster within. As a child, it had been terrifying to see flashes of twisted faces, but he grew accustomed to them, especially within his own family. This man barely looked human when the wickedness flashed.

"Did you hear me?" the lumber yard boss asked, shaking William from his fixation. "It'll be a few days before a shipment will arrive, so if you want me to put an order in, I need to know now."

"Of course," he said, fighting to concentrate on the man's words. "Of course, order it. I'll have a check to you by Friday."

An old black sedan screeched into the parking lot, grabbing his attention. He couldn't see the driver, but the man with the twisted face quickly looked around before getting in the car. Without hesitation, William stood up, determined to follow them. If there were others like him in town, Peirce certainly didn't know, which made William even more suspicious.

"Whoa, wait a minute," the lumber yard boss said, standing up. "I'll need a check today if I'm going to put the order in."

"Fine," William said quickly. He pulled out a check from his work folder and barely signed it. He handed the blank check off without even asking for a price and rushed out to his truck. It wasn't long before he was on the road, following the direction the car had taken.

After twenty minutes of driving, William had almost given up on trying to find the car, until he saw it parked on the side of the road. The smoke coming from the exhaust pipe meant it was still running and just as he realized it, two people ran from out of the woods and straight to the car. William readied to follow as they pulled out into the road, but a sudden explosion somewhere beyond the woods sounded and caught him off guard.

He cursed loudly and pulled over as the black sedan drove away. Whatever that explosion had been, he knew it wasn't good.

Getting out of his truck, he smelled smoke and saw a black cloud above the tree line. He ran through the woods as fast as he could, arriving at a clearing where the football field sat behind the burning high school.

He cursed again as he ran toward the building.

To be completely honest with himself, he hadn't even considered that Hanna was in the school. He reached a metal door at the far right end of the building and burned himself when he put his hand on the knob. The fire burned fiercely on the other side as he quickly pulled his hand back. It was then that he realized she must be inside somewhere. She was a senior in high school. Why hadn't he thought of that?

A new wave of panic set in as he searched for another entrance. What if she was hurt? What if she was injured somewhere inside, surrounded by fire, flames licking at her as if she were fuel? His chest compressed at the thought. They hardly knew each other, and yet he couldn't stand the thought of her helpless.

He came across a fire window, outlined in red with a pull bar on both sides designed to be pulled out or pushed in. He grabbed it and pulled it down hard.

A gust of dark smoke hit him in the face and his eyes instantly began to water. He crawled inside, unable to see much in the dense blackness that filled the room. He pushed several chairs out of his way before he found the open door that led to the hallway. When he saw that no one was in the vicinity, he felt a little surge of hope. Maybe Hanna had been in the other end of the school when it happened and she was safe, surrounded somewhere by her friends and classmates. But all the wishful thinking in the world wouldn't settle the gnawing feeling in his gut.

He ran up the hall, pushing through doors, searching rooms to make sure no one was around. He called out, hoping no one would answer, and when no one did, he made his way back to the classroom he came in through. With his sleeve bunched up in his hand to block the smoke, he hurried back, but tripped suddenly, landing on the ground with a hard thud.

Turning around, he squinted through the smoke to see a body, slumped against the wall. Hanna lay unconscious, with a look on her face that suggested she was dreaming.

"HANNA!" he yelled, scrambling across to her. "HANNA! Wake up!"

A faint moan was all he could get from her as he pulled her up into his arms and carried her into the room he'd entered from. With a little difficulty, he was able to get her out of the building and carry her to the bleachers on the football field. He put her down and gave her mouth-to-mouth resuscitation, calling out her name in between breaths.

The sinking feeling of dread filled every part of his body as his fear for her turned to anger. Why hadn't someone tried to pull her to safety? Had she stayed behind, looking for a thrill? Where was Peirce, and why wasn't he aware that there was someone, at least two others, like them in town? Everyone in their world knew damn well that bad guys weren't capable of doing the right thing. Why was it William saving Hanna and no one else?

And why had he?

William jumped when he heard a faint scratching at the truck's door. He looked out the window to see Wyatt watching him with concerned eyes. He got out of the truck, and Wyatt attacked him with his nose, sniffing the soot and smoke that clung to his clothes. He caught the faint scent of Hanna and growled in a way that William knew too well.

"I'm fine," he said as he walked toward the front deck. "You wouldn't believe the day I've had."

Wyatt walked next to him and William scratched his ears, his thoughts still on Hanna. He'd kissed her, which had been stupid. It was impulsive and arrogant on his part. She almost died, and he'd chosen that moment to take advantage of her. As many times as he silently cursed himself for doing so, he couldn't stop the satisfaction of it from creeping into his mind.

So what if he had kissed her? He *was* the type of guy to take advantage, wasn't he? If he'd asked himself that question before coming to New Hope, he wouldn't have hesitated with answering yes, but now, as he flipped between guilt and fulfillment, he wasn't so sure anymore.

He let out a groan of frustration. *Why is this so difficult?* He blamed Peirce, since he held him responsible for Hanna's naivety about her situation, and yet William couldn't tell her everything either. She'd think he was some maniac. How could he possibly explain their world to someone who had never heard about it? And that damn kiss . . . he should be avoiding her at all costs, since he knew better than anyone the danger of getting involved, but he couldn't help it. He was drawn to her, like a moth to a flame.

He'd lived in darkness his whole life, with a cursed shadow hanging over him, knowing what he was capable of and what others thought of him and his kind, while Hanna was a shining bit of good in an otherwise shadow-filled world.

But I should avoid her, he finally decided with conviction. She would only be in more trouble if he were around, whether it was with Peirce or those two men who caused the explosion at the high school. He was sure that he would bring her down into the darkness with him, and he didn't want that for her. Yet, if Peirce wasn't aware of the other dangers that lurked in New Hope, what choice did he have?

He looked down at Wyatt as they went into the house.

"Wyatt," he said as the wolf turned to look at him instantly. "Would you go to her? Keep an eye on her for a few nights? Try and go unnoticed, okay?"

Whatever magic or coincidence that connected William to the wolf worked as Wyatt turned back toward the door, scratching at it. William opened the door and watched the wolf disappear into the woods, glad, not for the first time, that he had Wyatt. All his life he had heard about his family's relationship with the wolves, but sometimes, it was hard to believe, even for him. William thought of them as extremely intelligent pets, instead of the spirit animals his father and grandfather claimed them to be. Still, there were some things in their world that just didn't need an explanation, or at least didn't needed to be completely understood.

Shutting the door, he was glad to offer Hanna some sort of protection. If he couldn't be next to her, he could at least have her followed by Wyatt while he planned his next move: to call Peirce himself and have a word with him. If he didn't know that others like them were in town, there was something seriously wrong, and he intended to find out.

CHAPTER THIRTEEN

School was cancelled for the rest of the week, and New Hope was abuzz with gossip about the arson. Hanna had already heard the whispers at work and during Gram's endless phone calls—everyone suspected William had something to do with it. Owen told Gram that he needed to speak with Hanna, but thankfully, he was too busy to find enough time to do so.

She'd been dreading talking with him for the past two days. Had he spoken to William since the fire and found out that he rescued her? Most likely. If she told Owen what happened, it would definitely place William at the school during the explosion, and confirm everyone else's suspicions in the process. She knew Owen was already convinced that William was guilty and once he had a thought in his head, he stuck to it. Hanna just couldn't believe it.

Hanna heard the phone ring upstairs as she put on her moccasin boots. She paused a moment, waiting to see if Gram would call her up. It was almost two-thirty and Carly had texted her half a dozen times already, wondering where she was. She needed to be at work by three for the evening shift, and since she'd been grounded from using the car, Hanna had offered her a ride.

After a moment of waiting, she knew the phone call wasn't for her. She grabbed her keys and headed up the stairs.

"Well, everyone is saying that," came Gram's muffled voice through the door as Hanna reached the top stair. "It's 'William Vann this' and 'William Vann that.'" She paused at the mention of William, and cracked open the door an inch to listen.

"Honestly, I don't know what to believe, but it wouldn't surprise me. I heard he had a record." Gram paused. "Yes, Owen told me all about him and his family, and I wouldn't be surprised if his people came up." Another pause. "Well, of course. When you're in that tax bracket, anything can be swept under the rug."

Hanna felt her cheeks warm as the pang of injustice rose within her chest. It was just like Owen to get Gram on his side. She was holding on to her decision to not see William again, but it was infuriating how everyone thought he was some villain when she knew he wasn't. Of course, she didn't have any other proof, but it just seemed unfair that everyone had already convicted him without all the details.

She opened the door and looked directly at Gram, whose voice suddenly dropped to a whisper. It was getting harder and harder to stick with her decision. The whispering reminded her that she'd been treated like this for years, as if she were fragile and unstable.

"I'll have to call you back. Yes, you too. Goodbye," Gram said, hanging up the phone. When she looked back at Hanna, her face was set. "Going somewhere?"

"Carly needs a ride to work," she answered, a chill in her voice. "Who was that?"

"No one important."

"It sounded important."

"Why? Eavesdropping, were you?"

Hanna glared back at her. She usually never argued with Gram, but she could feel a fight bubbling up.

"Everyone's wrong about him. Owen doesn't know everything, okay?"

"He knows more than you think," she retorted. "And I'd mind that attitude, young lady. It isn't helping your friend any to suddenly become enemies with your family."

"I'm not becoming enemies with anyone. It's just that Owen doesn't know him like I do."

Gram didn't say anything, but she raised her eyebrows and shook her head. Hanna rolled her eyes and left. *This is all*

Owen's fault, she thought as she walked to her car. He didn't even know all the facts. Whatever William or his family had done in the past, one fact remained: he had saved her life twice, and she couldn't turn on him so easily.

When she got into the car, her phone went off with another text from Carly, asking what was taking her so long. She bit the inside of her cheek. Hanna was already in a mood, and she didn't want to blow up at Carly. Stubbornly convincing herself that it wasn't Carly's fault she was mad, she put the car in reverse and left the driveway.

By the time she got to Carly's, she had received another text. She honked the horn and pulled her phone out of her pocket to see what overly dramatic text Carly had written in the fifteen minutes it took to drive to her house. *Honestly, Hanna thought, that girl needs to learn some patience.*

Looking at her phone, she was suddenly breathless. The text wasn't from Carly, it came from William. Her remaining conviction to never talk to him again went out the window. She thanked God that she'd never said it out loud, otherwise she'd have felt compelled to stick to her guns. The text read:

"HELL OF A TOWN YOU GOT HERE."

She read it twice more. What did he mean by that, and how should she respond, considering their last words had been strangely raw and unbridled?

And that kiss! She had thought about it every day since it happened and still didn't know how to react. Was she nervous? Happy? Frightened? Her heart felt like it was doing spins in her chest like a skater on ice. She wanted to know what he thought, but there was too much to ask in a simple text.

She debated how to respond. He probably meant that everyone was coming at him like farmers with pitchforks. She quickly texted back before Carly got to the car.

"IS IT THAT BAD?"

"Hey," Carly said as she opened the door. "Where've you been? I have to be there in twenty minutes."

"My bad," she said quickly, putting her phone back in her pocket.

"Why are you smiling?"

"I am?" She looked in the rearview mirror as she backed out and sure enough, there was a big, dumb smile on her face. She tried to smother it. "I mean, I don't know. It's just nice to be out of the house. Gram's been on my nerves lately. We're kind of fighting."

"Really? You and your Gram never fight."

"I know, right? But this whole arson thing has gotten her all worried, and Owen has her believing that William had something to do with it."

"Oh."

She waited for her to say something else, because Carly always had something else to say, but she remained quiet, looking straight ahead. Hanna shot her a quick look before focusing on the road ahead.

"You don't believe the rumors, right?" she asked suspiciously.

Carly didn't answer.

"Carly—"

"I don't know," she said quickly, not looking over. "It's not completely unbelievable. I mean, he has a record, and it's kind of right up his alley to restore buildings. That's his job. Plus, who else is there? Who do you know in New Hope that would do something like that?"

Hanna stared in disbelief. Was everyone out of their mind?

"You don't know everyone in this town," she said, trying to keep her voice from rising. "Or their thoughts. It could have been some pyro kid in school who thought it would be cool to play with fire between classes or something. Or it could have been an accident in the auto class."

"I thought they ruled out that it was an accident."

"Oh, right, because humans never make mistakes."

"Listen, Hanna. I'm just saying it's kind of weird that the school went up in flames the same time some guy, with a record, shows up in town. And what about those burglaries?"

It had been in the paper yesterday that a string of violent burglaries had been happening around town. She thought it was pretty convenient of the police to make that information public just a day after the explosion.

Anger surged through her. "He didn't do it," she said quietly. "It's impossible."

"Whatever," Carly said as she looked out the window.

They didn't speak for the rest of the ride to J R Barbeque, and barely said goodbye to each other when she got out of the car. Five minutes after she dropped Carly off, she got a text from her saying that she didn't need a ride home. It was just as well, as Hanna wasn't in the mood to pick her up after work. Her phone buzzed with another text from William.

"NOTHING I CAN'T HANDLE."

She was glad he thought so, because if she were the prime suspect of an arson, she'd feel pretty overwhelmed, especially in a small town like this.

Instead of going home, she decided to run a few errands, since she was out. Maybe some mindless chores would help soothe her bad mood. She went to the post office to grab her mail and found a key in the mailbox, which meant there was a package waiting for her at the desk. She went up to the old man who worked behind the linoleum counter. He was talking to a heavyset woman with curly gray hair.

"I heard the father had something to do with those murders a few years back," the large woman said as the elderly man took Hanna's key and walked to the wall lined with large, square lockers. "You remember, don't you? A few years back?"

"I remember hearing something about it," the old man said as he opened a locker in the corner. "Didn't someone go to jail for that though?"

"Oh, come on, Freddy. The police were probably paid off by the family. Things like that happen all the time in my murder mysteries. Conspiracies. It's just about the only thing rich folk know how to do."

Hanna bit her tongue. *Do people really have nothing better to talk about?* Her phone vibrated in her pocket. She pulled out her phone and her heart skipped a beat. It was another text from William.

"WHERE ARE YOU?"

"Sounds like a bunch of nonsense to me," the old man said as he set Hanna's package on the counter. "I think folk around here are just making a bunch of something out of nothing." He nodded at Hanna. "Have a good day, miss."

"You too," she said as she grabbed the package, glad at least one person other than herself wasn't so easily persuaded.

As she walked back to her car, she debated telling William where she was. It wasn't that she didn't want to see him. She was already sitting in her car, halfway through a text telling him where she was, when she stopped herself from finishing it. A dull voice in the back of her mind was telling her to leave it be, to ignore him just as Owen had told her to, but why? William had never been anything but honest with her, as far as she knew. She'd been on the outs with nearly everyone she'd ever been close with recently, and to be honest, it bothered her. It was difficult not being able to talk openly with Owen, or even Carly, now that she seemed to be just as convinced as everyone else that William had something to do with the fire.

For a moment, she wondered why it had to be him that had saved her and not some nice, regular guy that didn't have any mysterious hang-ups. Why couldn't he just be normal? Why did everything have to be so difficult?

As if the universe heard her silent query, she was suddenly thrust forward, followed by the loud sound of metal hitting metal. Something had hit her car.

"Damn it," she grunted through clenched teeth as she looked in her rearview mirror. It was just her luck to be hit by someone while she was parked.

Getting out of the car, she kept her angry face on display. Whoever had just run into her was going to get the full force of her mood.

"Hanna!" Troy said as he got out of the car. "Oh my God! I'm so sorry. Are you okay?"

"You've got to be kidding me," she said under her breath. Could this day get any worse? "Didn't you see me?"

"I was talking on the phone," he said as another person got out of the car. She was a middle-aged woman and had the same dirty-blonde hair as Troy. "I'm so sorry."

"Troy! This is why!" the woman said. "If I've told you once, I've told you a thousand times, do not talk on the phone while you're driving—"

"I would have seen her if you weren't screaming at me to get off the phone, Mom."

"You would have seen her if you weren't on that damn phone in the first place!" His mother tore her eyes away from the dented station wagon's bumper to look at her. Hanna saw several emotions pass over the woman's face before she spoke. "Oh, Hanna. It's you."

"Hi, Mrs. Denton," she said, wondering why every adult who knew her gave her the same look. It was like pity mixed with fear. Not knowing what else to say in this situation she added, "How are you?"

"Fine," was all she said before turning to Troy, who looked dumbfounded. "This is coming out of your money, Troy. You hear me? Your father and I aren't paying for this."

"Okay, Mom, Jeez," he said, turning to Hanna. "I'm real sorry. Do you think you'll be able to get home?"

"Yeah, I'll be fine. Do you want my insurance or something?"

"Oh, right," he said as he patted himself down. "Um, I don't have a pen or paper. Can I get it from you later?"

She didn't like that sound of that. "Actually, I'm really busy," she said quietly. "Mrs. Denton? Do you have a pen?"

"Yes, of course," she said, looking at Troy. "Really, Troy, this isn't the time or place to try and make a date with one of your friends."

Troy's face turned several shades of red while his mother rummaged through her purse for a pen. It was probably not the best choice of wording on his mother's part, but Hanna felt guilty nonetheless.

Why couldn't she just like Troy? But she had her answer even before she had finished the idea. The thought of trying to force herself to like someone like him seemed futile. He was just lacking. Cute by all means, but his looks didn't make up for the doltish way he acted when he was around her. It might have been flattering to some girls when a guy acted all goofy around them, but Hanna just found it vexing.

Without offering for her son to do it, Mrs. Denton scribbled down Troy's insurance and handed Hanna an extra piece of paper to write down hers. She did it as fast as she could and quickly went back to her car. She cringed when the metal scraped again as Troy pulled away from her car, and pulled out her phone to answer William's text.

"LEAVING THE POST OFFICE. YOU?"

She pulled out of the parking lot and drove back toward J R Barbeque, driving about a mile past it to a strip mall that served as the dividing line of New Hope and Port Huron. There was a garage in the mall that could estimate the damage to her car, and she wanted to know as soon as possible. She didn't need another thing to worry about.

A man named Sal took a look at the damaged bumper. She thought he maybe had a younger brother who was in her class, since he looked so familiar, but she didn't ask. Her phone had vibrated again, and she was quick to read it.

"HOME, DOING PAPERWORK."

She texted back:

"SOUNDS LIKE FUN."

She took a seat inside the office of the garage, since Sal said it might take a few minutes to look under the body of her car. The office smelled of gasoline, but the seats were clean, as was the office itself.

"HARDLY. I WAS AT THE DINER, BUT GOT THE FEELING I WASN'T WELCOME."

She frowned.

"Yeah. Apparently you're suspect number one. Guess that makes you famous."

Maybe if she joked with him, he wouldn't be so glum. She had a feeling he was in need of a friendly conversation and hoped joking would cheer him up.

"Used to it."

That wasn't the answer she wanted.

"Referring to your bad rap?"

Maybe if she baited him . . .

"Yes. Still think I'm innocent?"

A loaded question, but a fair one to ask.

"Yes."

Simple, but honest, she thought.

"Really? Or are you just trying to cheer me up?"

She couldn't help but smile. It was as if he knew her inside and out.

"REALLY."

"Miss Loch?" Sal said as he came into the office. She quickly put her phone in her pocket and stood up. "It doesn't look too bad. Made a nice dent in your bumper, but nothing under it is damaged. You're looking at about a three hundred dollar job."

She tried not to wince. At least she wasn't going to be paying for it, but that was still a lot of money to her.

"Okay, cool. Thanks for looking at it."

The sun had begun to set during her twenty minute drive back home, and she let her mind wander, not grabbing onto a single thought for too long. It was nice, not thinking too hard about anything, even for the short time it took to get back to town. She turned down Main Street and passed the diner. She was halfway through town when she decided she should turn back to grab her paycheck.

She had cut into an turnout when she suddenly saw a dog in her headlights. Slamming on the brakes, she felt her car hit the animal, though not as hard as she would have had she not hit her brakes in time.

This day was just getting worse and worse.

CHAPTER FOURTEEN

Hanna got out of the car, walking cautiously to the front. It looked like a dog at first, but she remembered the wolf from a few nights ago and how Gram had almost hit a "dog" as well. She loved them, but wolves were dangerous wild animals, and if it wasn't dead or seriously injured, she could be in trouble. Her headlights gave off enough light to shine on the shoulder of the ill-lit road. She looked around the hood of her car. At first, she thought maybe she'd missed it, but that didn't make sense. She'd definitely felt her car hit something.

She moved around the whole front of her car, but nothing was there. Confused, but grateful that she hadn't killed an animal and her front bumper didn't have damage to match the rear, she started to get back in her car when she heard a noise.

She scanned the woods lining the road. It was hard to see anything, especially since the headlights were so bright in contrast with the dark roadside. She heard a rustling and followed the sound.

"Hello?" she said, hoping it wasn't someone's pet. "Please don't be dead, whatever you are."

She came around the front of the car again and froze. The wolf stood, teeth bared, eyes locked on her.

"Okay," she said, trying to stay calm. "Glad you aren't dead." *Stop talking to it, idiot,* she thought when it growled at her. She inched backward, hoping to get back in her car, but every step she took, it did as well.

She screamed when someone grabbed her arm and forced her to turn around.

"William!" *Come on,* she thought. She liked when he was around, but these coincidences were getting to be a little much.

He stepped around her, his eyes strangely alight. "Go on," he said in a quiet but firm voice. He waved a hand at the wolf, who was no longer growling. "Get out of here." The wolf whined once, but turned and melted into the shadows.

Hanna just gawked at him. "What is it, like your pet?"

He grimaced. "Something like that."

She shook her head, about to say more, when the headlights of another car shone over them. A sedan pulled off the road, facing her car head on. The door opened and someone leaned out.

"Are you okay, miss?" an older male voice asked, though she couldn't see his face.

"Yes, I'm fine," she said, wishing him away.

"Are you sure?" he asked. "If it's a flat tire or something, I can help."

"No, that's okay," she assured him. "I'm just about to leave. Thank you!"

"Oh, okay," the older man said, getting back in the car. He pulled away slowly, watching them carefully. They probably looked suspicious, but she didn't care.

Turning back to William, she planted her hands on her hips and stared him straight in the eye. "All right, enough. I need some explanations. Now. Why do you keep showing up wherever—"

"I was walking," he interrupted.

She made an exasperated noise. "Not just tonight. What were you doing at the school earlier? Why were you there when that truck almost hit me? Why did you come to Michigan in the first place?" She could have kept going—she was on a bit of a roll—but stopped herself.

"Can you give me a ride?"

She blinked. "Um, sure."

They got in the car, and she pulled back onto the road. After a minute of driving, she was going to ask where he wanted her to drive him, but he sighed.

"Do you know the story of the Big Bad Wolf?"

She laughed, surprised. "Actually, I was just reading it the other day in English class."

He stared out his window. "Once upon a time . . ." He paused, shaking his head. "The real story isn't anything like the fairy tale."

She kept her eyes straight, trying to look calm. "What's the real story?" she finally asked.

"The real story is the girl and her grandmother were murdered, not saved by some random guy in the woods. They were brutally murdered. By my ancestor."

"Oh," she said softly. She tried to wrap her head around what he was saying. Even though Owen had somewhat explained their background to her, it seemed even more bizarre hearing it from someone else. She had hoped that maybe Owen was insane. She was eerily calm about the whole thing, however, which only made her worry she was crazy to believe both of them.

"So, you're the descendant of a wolf in a fairy tale," she said, sounding more cynical than she meant to.

"Not exactly . . ." He sighed again. "Wolves have been a part of my family's history since the beginning. The real story of the Big Bad Wolf is about a lost boy who wandered off from his family in a dark forest overseas some three hundred years ago.

"He was found by a wild pack of wolves that adopted him as one of their own. He lived with these wolves for years, until a great drought came and nearly killed everything in the vast wilderness where they lived. Even the wolf pack diminished until there were only a few left. The boy, who was now a man, came across a grandmother and her granddaughter searching for food. Frightened by the man, they ran, and he took after them, deciding that they were prey."

"Oh my God," Hanna whispered as she covered her mouth with her hand.

"He killed them, and as the wolves howled to celebrate, the villagers nearby came to investigate. They caught him and the wolves covered in the victims' blood as they ate. From there, the villagers imprisoned the whole pack and starved the wolves for weeks, until they were so hungry they would eat anything or anyone, including one of their own.

"After they ripped him to shreds, they gained their strength back. They attacked everyone in the village and ate them all to avenge their pack member. But it wasn't enough. They mourned him, until one day, they smelled his scent in the air. As fast as they could run, they came to a little castle where his biological family lived. It's said that the leader of the pack explained the incident to the nobleman telepathically. The nobleman was moved by the wolf's story and distraught over the fate of his long-lost son. He invited the wolves to stay indefinitely, and they did. To this day, wherever we are, they follow."

"That's awful." It was a lot to process, but she felt strangely comfortable knowing it. "Is that why you think you're no good?"

"I am no good, Hanna, and I'm not the only one," he answered.

"What do you mean?"

"All of those stories. Every one of them is based on an actual event and real people. Real people who had families and still have families to this day."

"So, your family is full of murderers," she stated with a shrug. Owen told her as much. Then a sudden thought crept into her mind, sending a chill down her spine. "Are you . . . I mean, have you ever . . ."

"No, no," he said quickly, and she was glad she hadn't said it out loud. "It's hard to explain." He sounded exasperated, as if he was trying to make something as clear as possible. "If you think of every character in a single story, from a waitress just mentioned on a single page to the main protagonist, you'd have a million more words if you were going to tell everything about each, right?"

She nodded in agreement.

"Well, what about that waitress mentioned on just a few pages? What's her story? Where is she from?"

"I don't know," she said.

"And you're not supposed to know, because she isn't part of the main plot. But she had a family, and no matter how many generations pass, she's somewhat of an immortal, forever a waitress during the one night that she was a tiny part in story."

She could tell that William had obviously thought about this for a long time.

"What are you saying, William?" she asked.

"I'm saying I come from a long line of bad people, Hanna. And I know with everything that happened the other day, you probably suspect that my family is to blame. I know Peirce thinks that, but it's not true," he said. "But I do believe that something's going on, and it has to do with you and your story."

She was quiet for a moment. What was her story? Was she really comfortable believing in real-life fairy tales? A tiny part of her whispered "yes," because somewhere deep down, it clicked. She'd often felt like she lived on the fringe of reality, but perhaps she was looking at it the wrong way. Maybe reality lived on the fringe of her, and she was from another world entirely. Could this be why William had singled her out?

"Who from my story would do this?"

He was reluctant to answer, and Hanna couldn't help but feel like he was avoiding her eyes when he looked away.

"I don't know."

"How do you know when you meet someone . . . like us?" It felt odd to say "us," and yet, it also felt right.

"What do you see when you look at me?" he asked, looking back at her.

An incredibly gorgeous guy who has eyes like . . . stop it!

"I don't know what you mean."

"I mean, do you notice anything different around me?"

She glanced at him. There was that weird glow she thought she saw sometimes . . .

"I thought my eyes were bad."

He smiled and her heart skipped. *Gorgeous,* she thought again.

"We have a bit of an aura around us. Sometimes it's obvious, while other times it's really just instinct. I don't really know why or how, but it's one of the quirks, I guess. Yours is almost blinding sometimes."

She felt her cheeks redden. "Oh."

"Can you see it when you look at Peirce?" he asked.

"Can you?" she asked, surprised that he'd asked as she pulled into her driveway, realizing he never said where he wanted to go.

"Speak of the devil," William said.

In her driveway were her grandparents, Owen's flashing cop cruiser, and Owen, who was holding a flashlight. He pointed it up at the windshield as Hanna put the car into park.

"Shit," she said, hitting her steering wheel with the palm of her hand. She looked over at William and he gave her another apologetic smile, brushing a finger on her jaw gently.

"I'll take the blame for this," he said as he leaned over and, right in front of them, kissed her.

Even though she knew she was a dead girl, she let her eyes close as she felt her stomach flip. He kissed her hard, and for the life of her, she couldn't hold herself back. She reached to put her hands up, to touch him, but he held them down. This time, she broke away, after hearing Gram's muffled voice of shock.

"What was that for?" she asked, breathing heavily.

"That was just me being selfish. We didn't get to talk about that yet."

He was the first person in her life to make her feel like *that*. Her skin tingled, and she felt uncomfortably hot, yet invigorated. To hell with everyone if they thought she'd stay away from him. He was completely unbelievable—though he had an unfortunate sense of timing—but she'd be damned if she was going to stay away.

"William—"

"Sorry for telling you all this," he said quickly as he opened the door. Owen stood at her side of the car. "I wish we had more time to talk."

"Not likely after this," she answered as Owen opened her door.

"Hanna!" Owen was nearly yelling. "What the hell are you doing?"

She saw the worry on Gram's face and the anger that was boiling just below the surface of Owen's, but she grew angry too. This was getting to be ridiculous.

"Don't," she warned as she got out and closed the car door.

"'Don't' nothing," Owen challenged. "What are you doing with *him*?" He pointed at William. "He's a suspect."

"Owen—" she began, about to defend William, who broke in.

"Not her fault, Officer," William said, coming around to her side of the car.

"I wasn't talking to you!" Owen said, his finger dangerously close to William's face.

Hanna was surprised when William's tone changed to confrontational.

"Put your finger down," he nearly growled. Apparently, he'd had enough of trying to be civil.

The tension went from palpable to suffocating as Owen turned his full attention on William. They were less than three strides apart, and she knew if she didn't get between them, there would be a fight.

"What the hell do you think you're doing?" Owen said in a deadly voice. They were about the same height and though Owen was leaner, William was more muscular. Owen kept his index finger pointed in William's face. "I told you to stay away from her."

"And I told you to get your hand out of my face," William bit back, swatting Owen's hand away.

It happened in an instant, so quickly that Hanna barely heard Gram's yelp in shock.

"That's enough!" Grandpa said, moving to break them up. Gram held him back with a hand on his arm, shaking her head as Owen and William grappled, each one trying to get the upper hand on the other. William looked as though he was restraining himself, and he wore a strange, almost sadistic smile on his face. After a few moments, Owen had him face down on the hood of Hanna's car.

"Owen, stop it!" she shouted.

"Stay out of this," he shot back as he began to recite William his Miranda Rights. "William Vann, you have the right to remain silent—"

"This is bullshit!" she yelled at him.

"Anything you say can and will be used against you in a court of law—"

"Hanna, come inside," Gram called.

"If you can't afford a lawyer, one will be appointed to you—"

Hanna marched up to Owen just as he was putting on the handcuffs. Grabbing his arm, she tried to pull him off, but he flung his arm back in a single motion and escaped her grasp like a snake through a hole.

"Hanna, back off," he ordered.

"He didn't do anything," she argued as Owen pulled William up. Blood trickled from the corner of William's mouth, but that looked to be his only injury.

"He attacked an officer," Owen said. He pushed William forward and walked him to the cop car.

"You provoked him!"

"Don't make excuses for criminals, Hanna," Owen said, opening the back door to his cruiser. "Why are you taking his side over family?"

"Because my family is acting like an ass!" she shouted.

"It's all right, Hanna," William said, his eyes locked with hers. "Let him do his job." Owen tried to push him down, but he fought to stand. He turned his head slightly so Owen could hear him add, "Missing the white horse and all, huh?"

"Shut it," Owen said as Hanna tried to make sense of everything that was happening.

"Real nice situation you got up here, Peirce," William said, lowering his voice, almost so low that Hanna couldn't hear. "There are darker things out there than me, and you're too worried about an old grudge—"

Owen curled his hand and gave him a quick jab in the side.

"Are you out of your mind?" Hanna yelled.

"It's all right," William coughed. "*Charming*, isn't he?"

Owen put his hand on William's head and lowered him down into the cruiser.

"What do you mean?" she said as Owen closed the door. "Owen, damn you, wait!"

He walked to the driver's side door and opened it, Hanna at his heels. "Owen, please don't do this."

"You don't get it, Hanna," he said, looking back at her grandparents before looking at her. "Vann's dangerous."

"No, he's not," she tried, but he continued.

"Yes, he is," he said, his voice lowered. "He's wanted in a string of burglaries that have been happening in the area.

One was pretty violent and the homeowner is in the hospital, in a coma."

She just stared at him, shocked that he would resort to lying just to make his point.

"Liar," she said, her voice barely audible.

"I'm not lying, kid," he said in his big brother voice. "An eyewitness pointed him out of the book. And he's got a record."

She shook her head. "He's not bad, Owen," she said. "I know he's not. And what did he mean by grudge?"

"Leave it alone," he said as he got into his car.

She watched numbly as the cruiser drove away, watching the dirt in her driveway kick up in the taillights of the car. She stood there for a while, not moving, her mind blank.

What had just happened?

She jumped when she felt a hand land on her shoulder. She turned and saw Grandpa, looking at her sadly.

"I'm sorry, kid," he said, but she didn't fully believe him. "He's just a bad apple."

"No," she said, turning out of his hold and heading for the house. "He's not."

As she walked into the house, she welcomed the howling outside, knowing now that the lone wolf gave her a connection to William.

CHAPTER FIFTEEN

School resumed for Monday's classes, with the Vo-Tech section closed off with yellow caution tape. As the week passed, the news spread like wildfire that the violent burglar and arson suspect had been apprehended by the police, though his name hadn't been released. At work on Friday, Hanna waited on two very well-dressed men with briefcases and serious faces. While refilling their coffee, she overheard William's name and almost dropped the coffee pot on their papers. Hanging around the coffee station to eavesdrop—because what was she going to do, not listen in?—she learned they were William's lawyers, and apparently, they took their jobs very seriously.

They'd been able to keep his name out of the paper due to defamation of character. These weren't average lawyers, she realized. They were the lawyers of Vann Construction and probably two of the best lawyers in the country, at the least the best in South Carolina.

She refused to speak to Owen; the incident at her house last Friday had been her only contact with him all week. She'd also been banned from seeing William, and it was frustrating not being able to talk to him. She wanted to know how he was doing, and she was dying to ask him more about her story. What he had meant when he said "old grudge"? There were a million other things she was sure she could only ask him. Gram and Grandpa nearly had heart attacks when she mentioned going to see him at the police station. That's when she decided to do the next best thing: Google him.

Melanie had given her the idea weeks ago, but she'd felt wrong doing it at the time. She didn't want to be one of those crazy girls who spied on guys. *But*, she reasoned, *Owen did say he had a record, and if he's dangerous, I should know about it, right? That's why the internet was invented: so people can creep on other people and make sure the people they're creeping on aren't creeps themselves.*

Flimsy excuse as it was, it helped keep her guilt at bay, and soon she was typing "Vann Construction, William Vann" into the search engine.

A slew of links, all on the Vann family and Vann Construction appeared. She found their home page, customer review pages, Charleston business owners, charities' sites, society pages, and more. She'd only hoped to find a messily made website, but it looked as though Melanie had been right. They were rich, and pretty well-known in Charleston, South Carolina.

Their home page featured their company logo—an outline of a wolf tastefully drawn between the words "Vann" and "Construction"—and a tab of current projects. Beneath a picture of what looked to be an extremely old theatre was a picture of New Hope High School, with a yellow banner across the picture that said "In Review."

She clicked it, surprised, and up popped a brief summary of the location, the structure, and the materials that would be used. The words "In Review" appeared at the bottom of the paragraph again and she guessed it had to do with the investigation.

She clicked on the "Meet the Company" tab and up popped a page with five headshots and a short description about each person. The first was an elderly man who had a salt-and-pepper beard and bright blue eyes, but there was also a hard look to him. He was Peter Vann, the retired founder of the original Vann Construction. Beneath him was the current president and CEO of the company, Jacob Vann. He was a large, strong-looking man with dark hair, who looked just about as mean and dangerous as a puppy dog. He smiled in his picture, his familiar gray eyes shining and his five o'clock shadow well-trimmed.

William's father, she presumed.

Beneath his photo was a picture of William, who looked like he was trying to find a balance between looking as serious as his grandfather and as welcoming as his father. She didn't know how long she looked at his picture, but since his bio only said that he was the eldest son and currently on location, she didn't learn much.

The next picture was a dated photo of a young woman in a police uniform, maybe age twenty-five. Her name was Annabelle, and her eyes looked almost identical to William's. Underneath her photo was simply the year of her birth followed by the year of her death. She was too old to be William's sister, but the resemblance was uncanny. Hanna felt a pang of sympathy and stared at the picture for a long time. Annabelle was seated between the United States flag and, to her surprise, the State Flag of Michigan.

The last photo was a picture of a woman in her early fifties, William's mother. She had dark blonde hair and dark eyes. She was beautiful, and Hanna felt a little jealous. She hadn't seen her own parents in almost a year. She was surprised she knew that off the top of her head. She rarely thought about the time that passed between seeing her parents.

Shaking her head, she continued to search through the site.

She looked at the picture of William's father again, remembering the conversation she overheard at the diner where he was mentioned. She typed his name followed by "murder" and "Michigan," but she only found a few references from more than ten years ago. Each stated that Jacob Vann had been called into questioning regarding the deaths of an elderly couple, though the police were still looking into the matter.

She couldn't find much more about the Vanns, besides a list of charities and a few pages on their staff. The wolf logo was rather amusing to her, but besides that, they didn't look like anything out of the ordinary—just normal.

But they *weren't* normal, if William was to be believed. And she did believe him. He was unlike anyone she had ever known. When she was around him, she felt like a charged battery. He made her feel alive, nervous, and almost every other emotion under the sun all at the same time. He was beautiful in so many ways; she couldn't believe he thought he was wicked. She wanted more than anything to show him that he wasn't—not that she would be able to, now that he was in jail.

Her cell phone rang and she jumped. Closing out the Vann home page, she grabbed her cell.

"Hello?"

"Hey, it's me," Carly said. "What are you doing this weekend?"

Hanna had the weekend off from work. "Nothing. Why?"

"Do you want to go to Ann Arbor with me to visit Morgan?" she asked quickly. "My mom is freaking out because she thinks Morgan isn't responsible or something like that—"

"I thought your mom was crazy about Morgan?" Hanna interjected. "I thought she was her favorite niece?"

"She was, until Aunt Josie told her that she's living with some random guy."

Hanna fell silent for a second. "And you want me to go with you to Ann Arbor to stay over at Morgan's house, with—and I quote—'some random guy?'"

"One, he's her old roommate's brother, and two, he's gay."

"Oh," she said. "Then why doesn't Morgan just tell your mom that?"

"I don't know. She's trying to be a rebel or something. She's so college cliché," Carly said in an exaggerated voice. "Anyway, my mom said that she'd feel better if one of my friends went, and it's cool with Morgan if you come. Do you want to go?"

"Yeah, sure," Hanna said without much thought.

"Mom! *Hanna's-going-with-me-to-see-Morgan*!" Carly yelled in the distance. "Thanks Hanna. See you tomorrow!"

"No problem," she said, but Carly had already hung up.

She was glad for the weekend plans. She loved Ann Arbor and needed a distraction. Between everything with William and the school burning, she needed to get away and clear her head. Otherwise, she would have been cooped up in the house, looking up the Vann family and driving herself crazy.

She picked up Carly the next afternoon, and they promised her mother a zillion times that they'd be safe and would call when they got to Morgan's. It was a few hours' drive, but long enough for Carly to distract Hanna with her relationship drama and all the gossip circulating in New Hope that didn't have to do with the school burning down or the "capture" of the arsonist.

After Carly got tired of waiting around for Troy to notice her, she went on a date with his best friend, Carl. Hanna pointed out that Carl was her name without the "y" and that it was fitting if they started dating, since she loved herself so much.

"It was only one date. Don't you remember me telling you this?" Carly asked as they entered the city limits. "I told you that we went on a date Wednesday night."

"I must have forgot," Hanna replied, not sure if Carly really had ever told her that.

Carly continued with the story, explaining that Troy became jealous when he found out that she wasn't chasing after him anymore, which was why he'd asked her out on Thursday.

Happy for her, yet disappointed in herself for not knowing her best friend was dating someone, she tried to find an excuse. Besides her own relationship problems, there was none. They reached the downtown district where Morgan lived, found a parking spot, and walked a few blocks to student housing. Carly tapped in Morgan's call number on the number pad and waited.

"Hello?" a male voice answered.

"Um, hi," Carly said. "Is Morgan home?"

"Yeah. MORGAN!" the voice yelled as Hanna and Carly cringed. "YOUR COUSIN'S HERE!"

"Jeez," Hanna said as the buzzer rang and the door unlocked. "He had to shout into the speaker?"

"Relax, Hanna," Carly said as they walked into the building. "Tonight will be fun."

She looked at Carly out of the corner of her eye. She wondered if she'd really needed to take someone with her to Ann Arbor, or if she'd made it up. Had Carly thought she needed a break from all the drama?

"Hey!" Morgan yelled when she opened the door. She threw her arms around Carly. "I'm so happy you could come! Hi, Hanna!" Morgan hugged Hanna next. "I haven't seen you in forever!"

"Hey, Morgan," she said, smiling.

Morgan was two years older and had a very bubbly personality. She was a sweet girl, and though a lot of people thought she was fake, she wasn't. Morgan was just that kind of cheerleader girl, always armed with a compliment and a smile. Hanna found it amusing to see her interact with people, because the majority of them were caught off guard by her cheerfulness. It was also a little disheartening, because she never realized how closed-off people could be until Morgan was around.

They walked into the apartment, stopping dead in their tracks when they saw a six foot tall, raven-haired woman standing in front of a mirror hanging from the living room wall. She was the most muscular woman Hanna had ever seen, wearing far too much makeup and a silver sequined dress with a hem well above her knee.

"Hey," she said in a deep voice that made them jump.

Carly covered her mouth, and Hanna's jaw dropped.

"This is Kyle," Morgan said. "He's a drag queen."

"Obviously," he said, putting on lip gloss. He finished and gave them a wink. "Hey, girls."

"Hi," Carly said, laughter bubbling in her throat.

"Nice to meet you," Hanna said, her eyes wide. She'd never seen a drag queen in real life.

"All right," Morgan said. "Don't you have a show to go to, Kyle?"

"It's Kristine when I'm dressed like this, and yes, I'm late," he said, grabbing a leopard print faux fur coat. "I'll see you later. Tell Dave I said hi."

Kyle/Kristine hurried out of the apartment, running carefully so he didn't trip in his heels. When he was gone, Carly burst out laughing while Hanna just looked at Morgan.

"Well, that's something you don't see every day," she said.

"Uh, try every Saturday. He has a show that he and his friends do at a club near the Kerrytown district. That's not where we're going," Morgan assured them. "We're going to an abandoned garage down on Washington Street."

"Why?" Carly asked, still laughing.

"Because it's where Dave's band is playing tonight."

Hanna and Carly changed and were doing their makeup by the time Morgan was ready to walk out the door. It was just after seven o'clock when Hanna finished doing her hair and wandered into the living room to look at the view.

The city was beautiful at night. She loved coming to Ann Arbor with Gram and Grandpa when she was younger, and she remembered thinking the fairy doors scattered around the downtown district were real, not just part of a city-wide art project.

They decided to walk to the Broken Pony, the abandoned garage where Morgan's boyfriend, Dave, would be playing. It was just a few blocks away from where Morgan lived. Hanna didn't really get the name, but decided it was some kind of hipster thing.

Upon entering the Broken Pony, her assumption was confirmed. College hipsters and pseudo-intellectuals were everywhere, and she couldn't help but feel a little self-conscious as she moved through the crowd. She felt like she was being watched. Music played so loudly it was difficult to hear Carly, who basically had to scream in her ear.

"What?" she yelled after Carly tried to tell her something.

"I said this place is packed!" Carly yelled back as they followed Morgan, who cut through the maze of people like she'd done it a thousand times before.

Is this what college is like? Hanna wondered as they made their way to a large stage flanked by massive speakers at the back of the club. Stagehands moved around, setting up instruments and acoustics.

"They'll be going on first!" Morgan yelled. "Do you guys want anything to drink?"

"No, thanks!" Hanna yelled. Carly just shook her head.

Morgan disappeared back into the crowd, leaving them at the base of the stage. Carly kept elbowing her, nodding her head at several people who were bizarrely dressed. There was a guy with a red mohawk who wore a leather vest and torn up jeans talking to a girl who had far too many piercings in her face. Behind them was a guy who looked like he was almost seven feet tall, with tattoos covering his arms and neck. It was a much different crowd than New Hope, and Hanna thought it funny that a girl like Morgan, who was so prim and proper, hung out in a place like this.

Her thoughts reverted to William in an instant, and she began an inner debate over the way people were perceived and who they actually were. *If everyone in the world was blind, it would probably be a kinder place.*

While having this inner revelation, the lights high above in the rafters started to flicker and the crowd roared to life. A surge of people moved forward, and they had no choice but to move too. Morgan hadn't returned yet, but the energy was electrifying. They found themselves pressed up against a railing that had been set up to separate the crowd from the stage. Four massive men with bald heads and beards came walking out into the space between. Their arms were folded, and each looked meaner than the last.

The lights above went off, and Hanna was amazed when the already deafening cheering got louder. She remembered studying mob mentality during the French Revolution in History and couldn't help but compare it to this, even though they were two completely different situations. Still, if she ever needed to describe the feeling, she could do so now, after being in this massive crowd.

The mood lighting from overhead began to flash yellow and blue, and the crowd pushed forward, nearly crushing them against the rail. Hanna started to feel uncomfortable. There were too many people around her, and the air grew thick and heavy.

Several people walked on stage just as Morgan grabbed her shoulder, shaking her slightly to let her know she was back. Morgan screamed as the band began to play and Carly shouted too, enjoying the vibe. The music was too loud and messy for Hanna's tastes, but she played along, hollering just as much as the others while the band played.

The crowd swayed back and forth, pulsing. It was exhilarating, even though she wasn't a big fan of the music. Metalheads began to dance wildly, looking more like seizure victims while more bodies began to get tossed around in a mosh pit somewhere behind them. Carly jumped up and down while Hanna held on to the fence, standing her ground so she wasn't crushed. Suddenly, hands grabbed her around the waist and pulled her back. Her eyes went wide as everything she saw sharpened. Again, hands grabbed at her, trying to force her back, but Hanna held on to the metal fence, trying vainly to kick backward. She looked to her right, hoping to see Carly, but her friend was gone.

She looked back and saw the bottom of Carly's shoes. She was crowd surfing.

"Carly!" she yelled, but it was no use.

She couldn't hear herself think. Making the decision to try and get to a less crowded spot, she let go the railing and was almost instantly picked up. Though she tried to fight it, she was hoisted into the air and passed overhead by the sea of people. It wasn't what she expected it to feel like, but she still wanted to get down. She didn't trust anyone holding her up.

Quicker than she thought, she was passed forward and screamed when she felt a sudden drop and a pair of large hands catch her. One of the bouncers set her down gently. She stood in the area between the stage and the crowd.

"Go to the door!" the bouncer yelled, pointing down the narrow walkway to a door that said "Exit" above it. "You have to go out and back around to the front of the building!"

She didn't argue, even though she thought it was a little ridiculous to have to leave the building just to come back in. She tried to wait for Carly to be picked out of the crowd by one of the bouncers, but left quickly when she saw they were getting angry with her for waiting around.

As she walked, she saw a million faces, yelling and singing along with the awful music. It was definitely a different experience. A face caught her eye and stopped her dead.

A man in his late twenties stared at her with pure hatred. He looked familiar, but the amount of disdain in his gaze physically sent chills down her spine. She felt a snap of pain split through her head like lightning. The pain made her dizzy, and she jumped when one of the bouncers touched her shoulder.

"Come on!" the bouncer yelled. "Keep the area clear!"

She nodded, desperately trying to ignore the shooting pain in her head. She turned back to face the man, but he'd gone, lost in an ocean of nameless people. She shook herself, wondering if her mind was playing tricks on her as she continued to walk toward the door.

Reaching the exit, she followed a tall brunette girl out of the building and into the cold night. It was refreshing to breathe the cool air, but she was still shaken. Why had that face looked so familiar? And why couldn't she shake the feeling that she was being watched?

"Hey!" Carly's voice called from behind her. Hanna turned and saw Carly and Morgan coming toward her. "That was wild, right?"

"Yeah," Hanna said, deciding not to share her worries about the angry-looking man.

"Let's do it again!" Morgan said.

"Sure," she agreed. Her headache began to subside as she followed them to the front of the garage.

She didn't try to push through the crowd with them this time. She was too aware of everyone and kept her distance for the rest of the show. When Morgan and Carly circled around to find her, she finally convinced them to head back to the apartment. She didn't want to worry Carly and so, kept the headache to herself.

Hanna made her bed on the couch, while Carly pulled out the futon and quickly fell asleep. The pushing and shoving had tired her out, and as Hanna lay wide awake, she wished she'd joined in.

She sighed. She missed the howling from outside her house. William's wolf. As soon as her thoughts found William, they wouldn't leave him, and she suddenly wanted to ask him what he thought about the fierce-looking man she'd seen. She bet his lawyers wouldn't advise him to talk to the deputy's cousin.

Rolling over onto her side, she wondered if he thought about her as much as she thought about him. Sometimes, she felt like every other thought had something to do with him. It was like being under a spell.

Her thoughts drifted to Owen and how angry she was at him, and her grandparents, for acting as though he'd done a brave thing by arresting William. The whole incident upset her. Somehow she was able to sleep, though, and dreamed about a dark house with several windows, where she sat all alone.

CHAPTER SIXTEEN

*B*y the beginning of May, all charges against William were dropped, much to everyone's surprise and Owen's fury. There wasn't any evidence against him for the fire and there were no motives or fingerprints connecting him to the violent burglaries.

Hanna tried calling him, but wasn't surprised when he didn't answer. She left a simple message on his voicemail, asking him to call her back, but she wasn't holding out hope that he would. Her heart couldn't help but hurting a little, and even though her fury at Owen was running out of steam, she blamed him anyway. He'd probably threatened to kill William if he ever talked to her again.

Work on rebuilding the Vo-Tech wing began and Vann Construction won the job. Of course, this made everyone in New Hope extremely suspicious and convinced most of the older people in town that William was the arsonist. The majority of the female student body at New Hope High School had fallen in love with him, especially since he and his crew could be seen frequenting the halls and parking lot throughout the school day. She thought about trying to talk to him the first day he was on campus, but decided against it. She didn't want to make any trouble for him, especially since she probably liked him more than she should. Apparently, so did every other girl in her school.

She felt particularly annoyed when she saw Melanie flirting with him during lunch on Friday. He'd come into the cafeteria to grab a few sodas for his crew, and the entire lunch room quieted as everyone turned to look. He walked around, unfazed, hardly giving anyone in the cafeteria the time of day. Hanna continued to watch him as the rest of students turned back to their meals and conversations. She grew curious when Melanie approached him, and cringed when she flipped her hair and he smiled.

Stupid girls with flippable hair, she thought. She ran her fingers through her own hair and almost choked when William paused and turned to look her way. His eyes scanned over the crowded tables and stopped when they found her. She looked away and began moving her mouth, much to Carly's confusion.

"What are you doing?" Carly asked, her mouth half-full with egg salad.

"Pretending to talk to you," she answered.

"Why?"

"Because William's looking over here and I don't want him to think that I don't have anything better to do than stare at him." Carly looked across the room. "No, don't look!"

"Jeez," Carly said. "Can Melanie be more of a flirt?"

"Stop staring," Hanna said through clenched teeth.

"Why? She obviously wants people to stare. Look at the shirt she's wearing."

"Carly, you're terrible," she chided.

"No, I'm not. I just say what everyone's thinking," she said, eyebrows raised knowingly. "Okay, he's gone."

Hanna looked up at the lunch room door and sure enough, William had gone and Melanie, with a smug smile on her face, rejoined her friends at their table. They were all girls and were basically shrieking with excitement when she sat down.

Hanna wondered what they'd talked about and then quickly hated herself for being jealous. Why should she be jealous? Melanie had gorgeous hair and beautiful features and a great sense of fashion, but guys didn't like that, right? It was too obvious. William wouldn't like a girl like her. Would he?

"Hanna, you have nothing to worry about," Carly said, finishing her sandwich. "She's a bimbo."

"A beautiful bimbo," she said grumpily. "And weren't you just worried about her? With Troy and all?"

"Jeez, Hanna, look at you," Carly said with a knowing grin, ignoring her question. "You're sulking."

"Am not," she lied.

"Yes, you are. Look at your face," Carly said, rummaging through her bag. She pulled out a compact mirror and flipped it open. "See? You look about ready to pop, you're so red."

"Leave me alone, Carly," she snapped, standing up. She didn't want to hear how pathetic she looked. She knew Carly was just trying to help, but she wasn't in the mood.

"Whoa, don't snap at me just because he's ignoring you," Carly said defensively as she stood up too.

Hanna didn't wait for her. She knew she was being mean, but she didn't want to talk to Carly, or anyone, about William. She just wanted to talk to William. He didn't seem to care much about flirting with someone right in front of her, not that she had any right to be upset about it.

We aren't dating, she reminded herself. But he *had* kissed her . . . or had she taken that as more than she should have? She should just ignore him.

Out of sight, out of mind . . . right?

The whole weekend, Hanna avoided Carly and the apology she owed her. She would apologize eventually, just not right away.

She brooded over Melanie and William, as much as she tried not to. Finally, to get out of the house Sunday afternoon, she went to get gas at the Quick Check and had just finished paying when she heard his voice. Turning around, she saw him, in a heated argument with someone on his cell phone.

"Hanna," he said, noticing her and hanging up his phone. He'd never returned her phone call, and she couldn't help but feel slighted. She stopped at the door and turned around. "Hey."

"Hi," she said quietly, looking over her shoulder.

William's reputation had gone downhill since the fire and most people in town had ostracized him as much as possible. Even she had some reservations, like the fact that he had kissed her *twice* and then ignored her. The guy working behind the counter gave them a dirty look.

"How have you been?" he asked, his voice dropping.

"Fine," she said, a little sarcastically. He looked a bit hurt by her tone, and she felt a flash of annoyance. He could flirt with Melanie right in front of her, but she wasn't allowed to say anything? "How are you?" she asked, unable to keep the hurt from her voice.

He looked genuinely disheartened as he shook his head. "I'm sorry, Hanna."

They stepped aside to let a customer out.

"Sorry for what?"

"Everything, I guess. I think coming here was a mistake," he said, looking at the cashier and the customer. Hanna looked too and saw that they were both whispering and giving him the evil eye.

"Got something to say?" she all but barked in their direction.

They both looked offended, but when she turned back to William, he was grinning.

"You shouldn't do that," he said lowly. "I shouldn't be talking to you."

"Shouldn't, shouldn't, shouldn't," she said, rolling her eyes. She was getting tired of this. *Why even say hi then?* she wondered. "I have to go."

He nodded as she walked past him, the little bell ringing above the door as she left. She was frustrated. Why would he say he was sorry? It wasn't his fault that the school burned down, and it wasn't his fault that everyone in town was suspicious of him. Then again, it really didn't bother her that he said he was sorry. It was the fact that he'd said he should never have come to New Hope.

Just as she was about to get into her car, she heard the door open and the little bell ring again.

"Wait," he said, walking toward her like he was on a mission.

She started to tell him to leave her alone when he put his hand up to her cheek and pulled her toward him. His mouth touched hers and like a flash of lightning, all of her senses honed in on him. He kissed her like he was desperate, but for what reason, she couldn't understand.

Before she realized it, he'd pulled away, breathing slightly heavier than before.

"What . . ."

"I'm sorry for causing all this trouble for you and for this town," he said fiercely. "But I'm not sorry for coming here."

"I—"

"And I need you to know that. You're the first good thing I've seen in a long time, and I don't think you can understand what that is like for me. I only ever see the worst in people, but you're like something different entirely, and I don't even know how to take it. I know that's confusing, but I don't want you to think I'm not grateful."

"Grateful for what?"

"For you," he said, pushing a strand of her wild hair out of her face. "Regardless of the little time we might know each other, I'm grateful for meeting you."

She nodded, unable to speak. She looked around, worried that someone had seen them kiss. William noticed and his brow creased.

"I'm not sorry for that either," he said.

"Me neither," she finally said.

"Good, because I have to tell you something."

"What?"

"You're not safe."

"William, if this is about your family—"

"It's not, but listen to me. Someone caused that fire with the intention of hurting a lot of people, and I think it was directed at you. Someone wants you dead."

She stared at him.

"Who?"

"I don't know for certain, but I'm going to find out. Just be careful." He paused, looking down at the little space between them. "I don't think I could stand anything happening to you." He looked up and her heart skipped a beat. "I can't explain it."

She shook her head, agreeing with him. She couldn't explain it either, but there was a spark between them, a tie that held them together; whether it was their own personal feelings, or the fact that they were descendants of storybook characters, she didn't know. All she knew was that it was real, and it felt more formidable than anything she had ever experienced.

"I have to go," he said and kissed her gently on the cheek. She couldn't help but lean into him. "Watch yourself."

"I will," she said as he turned to walk away. He was almost across the parking lot when she opened her mouth. "William!"

He turned.

"Yes?"

"It's a little misleading when you ignore my phone calls and flirt with other girls," she said, feeling like a moron as soon as the words left her lips.

William grinned. "Jealous?"

"No."

"Good," he said as he turned to walk back to his truck.

Hanna watched him drive away as she leaned against her car. She couldn't wipe the ridiculous smile off her face and wondered if maybe she shouldn't have let him kiss her. *Yeah, right,* she thought, climbing into her car.

Still, she noticed her mood had done a complete one-eighty, and she even called Carly to apologize when she got home.

After school on Thursday, Hanna went to work to find Angie training Anne, who had been hired earlier that week. She still wore a bandage wrapped around the burn on her left arm. Hanna wanted to ask her about it, but thought it was better not to intrude.

She was clearing a table, fighting off a headache that'd been bothering her since she got to work, when the door opened. She turned too quickly and knocked two glasses of water on the floor. Looking up, she barely saw the two familiar-looking men in the doorway before her head felt like it exploded.

Dropping an empty plate, she blacked out before she hit the ground.

She sat in the dark room again, but the morning sun wasn't shining through the windows like it had before. The only light that could be seen was from an old oil lamp that sat in the corner of the room. Hanna wore the same purple corduroys as before, but now she could hear voices, whispers coming from somewhere, hidden by the shadows.

"Kill her," a male voice said, so softly she was surprised she heard him. "She saw."

"I'll do it," a young female voice said.

"Stop it, Maryanne," another male voice said. "You're becoming too infatuated with this sort of thing."

"I never get to kill anyone," the female complained.

"One day," the first voice soothed. "One day."

Suddenly, a loud bang sounded and she shut her eyes. The echo pounded in her head like a drum, vibrating throughout her skull.

"Hanna," a muffled voice called.

She didn't want to listen. All she wanted was for the vibrations to stop.

"Hanna, wake up," the voice said again, stronger this time.

The echoing faded. She felt cold, tired, and afraid as she floated in the darkness. She desperately held on to the floating feeling, as if she were only a conscious thought and nothing more.

"Did you call the ambulance?" someone asked.

"About twenty minutes ago."

That's not right, she thought as she reluctantly began to surface from her subconscious state. It only felt like a few seconds. Then, just like before, she snapped back into her body and her eyes opened.

Angie was leaning over her, the trees from the skyline dancing behind her head. They were outside? She saw not only her boss, George, but also William, talking on his cell phone.

"Oh, sweet pea! She's alive!" Angie yelled, pulling Hanna up by her shoulders and hugging her. "George! She's awake!"

"Hanna," William said, coming to her side while George cursed in Greek. "Are you all right?"

"What happened?" she asked hazily. Her head hurt beyond belief, and she was drenched in sweat and shivering.

"You blacked out," William said quietly, his hand coming to her forehead. He pushed back her sweat-soaked hair. She felt ill, but leaned into his touch. She felt calmed by it, as if she'd been on edge, waiting for him to touch her again. "Are you all right?"

"My head hurts," she said. "The bang was so loud."

William looked into her eyes, worry written all over his face.

"What bang?" he asked. "When you hit your head?"

"No. It sounded like a gunshot," she said.

"I'm going to call your grandparents, hun!" Angie said, hurrying back inside and looking back at George, who mumbled in Greek. "George! Get the girl her coat."

"Oh, yes," he said, looking a little dazed. He hurried inside after Angie, leaving Hanna alone with William.

"They called the ambulance, didn't they?" Hanna asked, suddenly worried. She didn't want to go to the hospital. "I'm fine, really. I don't need to go to the hospital." She tried to stand, but he held her still.

"Please, don't move," he asked, though it sounded more like an order. "You hit your head pretty hard."

"I'm fine," she said as his hand moved cautiously over the back of her head. She flinched when he touched a sore spot.

"See?" he said, looking relieved. "Damn, Hanna. You just can't keep out of trouble, can you?" She started to argue the fact that it wasn't her fault she kept blacking out, but William's other hand came over her mouth. "Hold on, let me finish." He took a deep breath, and she didn't know why she was holding hers as he cupped her cheek in his hand. "Do you know how scary it is to see you passed out, lying on the ground?"

Hanna felt the heat rising in her cheeks.

"Oh, is it scary for you? Because I find it relaxing."

"Don't be difficult."

"Difficult?" she said. "This wasn't my fault. I don't black out on purpose."

"I know. I know you don't, but damn if you don't freak people out when it happens," William said, as the corners of his mouth pulled into a grin. "I was coming to see you, actually, but when I got here, they were carrying you out the back door."

"They shouldn't move someone who's had a fall," she said, remembering her first-aid training in gym class. *Why did I say that of all things?* she groaned.

He didn't seem to mind how she chose to answer his confession. "No, I suppose not, but you tend to put people on edge, I guess." He moved his hand down the side of her face and Hanna realized that he hadn't stopped touching her. "What happened?"

She inhaled and exhaled slowly, trying to remember. It was nice to have someone to talk to about her blackouts; someone who seemed to understand without question.

"I was cleaning a couple of tables," she began, looking down at the dirt parking lot. "Then the door opened, I think . . . yeah, and a couple of guys came in . . ." Her brow scrunched as her head pounded. It was as if her own brain didn't want her to remember. "That's it. I woke up here."

She looked at William and braced herself for what she was about to say next.

"I think someone tried to kill me."

Even though a chill went down her spine when she said it out loud, she tried to smile. How crazy must she sound? And why did she feel the need to tell him, of all people?

"What do you mean?" he asked evenly, his eyes never wavering from hers.

"When I blacked out, I was in a dark room, and it was cold. Maybe it's just a dream, but I remember those purple pants." She knew she wasn't making sense. She tried to keep a light tone, worried she might throw up. "They were talking about killing me."

"Who was?"

"I don't know. There was a guy and a girl, maybe two guys, I can't remember," she said, the pounding in her head getting worse. She put her hands to her head. "This damn headache!"

"That's enough," he said as he gingerly helped her up. "Don't hurt yourself."

"It's so annoying," she said in frustration as she got to her feet. William still hadn't let go of her, holding her by the elbow now. "I can hear them, I just can't see them. Everything's dark."

Just then, the back door of the diner opened and Anne came out. She wore a strange expression, but Hanna figured it was because she'd scared her with another blackout.

"Um, Hanna?" Anne said. "Officer Peirce is here. He wants to see you."

"Shit," Hanna muttered under her breath, though William was close enough to hear. Anne turned and went inside. "He's going to have a conniption."

"What do you want to do?" he asked.

She wanted to leave. She didn't want to have to answer any of Owen's questions, not to mention that he would probably freak out if he saw William there. She didn't want to deal with the ambulances or the hospitals, because she knew in her heart it didn't have anything to do with medical things. She had hoped in the beginning that it was something rational, something that medicine could answer and fix, because to think of it in any other way was too frightening. She'd always suspected her blackouts were related to her lost memory, but since she could never understand her memory, she'd tried to find another excuse for them.

"I want to leave," she said after a short pause. "I don't want to deal with anyone."

"Then come on," he said, nodding toward his truck as his hand slid from her elbow down to her hand.

"No, William, you'll get in trouble," she said, trying to pull her hand out of his. "Owen will probably arrest you again."

"I'm not worried about Owen. I'm worried about you."

Hanna's stomach did a flip. She tried to brush off her excitement as he helped her into his truck. He seemed reluctant to let her go, even to walk around to the other side. As they pulled out of the parking lot, Owen exited the back door of the diner.

"He's going to flip out," she said as she looked back to see him. "He'll have the whole New Hope police department looking for us."

"So we'll leave New Hope for a little while," William said. "Where do you want to go?"

She looked at him. She wanted to go as far away as possible, but she knew it wouldn't do her any good. Gram and Grandpa would panic, and Owen would probably shoot William on sight when he found them. The feud between Owen and William seemed palpable and serious.

"I should go home," she said reluctantly, even though it was the last place she wanted to go.

"Yeah," he agreed after a moment, much to her dislike. "You should."

They passed the *Thanks for Visiting New Hope* sign a few minutes later, driving in silence for most of the way. She tried not to worry about the hell storm that awaited her when she got home. Owen had probably informed Gram and Grandpa that she'd had another episode, and who knows what sort of trouble she'd be in since she left after an ambulance had been called. She hated ambulances. She hated the smell, the noises, the gadgets that hung on the walls, gauging a person's life. She'd hated them ever since—

It came out of nowhere and hit her so hard that she couldn't breathe. Her head felt like it would explode.

"Hanna?" William said, with worry in his voice. "Are you okay?"

She sucked in sharp, little breaths as her heart raced. It felt like she was having a panic attack, but instead of the warm feeling all over her body, it was just in her head.

"What's wrong?" William asked loudly, trying to watch her and the road at the same time.

"I was in an ambulance," she said between breaths. "I was in an ambulance."

"When?"

"When I was younger," she said as tears began to roll down her cheeks. She didn't know why she was crying, but she felt as though a rush of air had slammed into her. "I was in an ambulance when I was younger. Before I came to New Hope."

William pulled over to the side of the road. The fear and excitement was so powerful she felt overwhelmed. He put the truck into park and looked at her.

"You remember?"

"Only that I was in an ambulance," she said, until another memory hit her. "Because of the dark house! I was going to the hospital because of the house I was in. They wanted to kill me."

"Who? Who wanted to kill you?"

"They did," she said, confused. "I don't know who they are." She rubbed her temples, trying to sort the images out.

"I think I do," William said quietly.

She looked at him as her thoughts and memories faded. "You do?" she asked slowly. "How would you know?"

She felt ill as she recognized the guilt all over his face. It finally dawned on her that maybe everyone had been right about William Vann. He was dangerous, and here she was, in his truck on the side of the road, surrounded by woods and alone with him.

Panic set in as she went to unbuckle her seat belt.

"Hanna," he said, reaching for her. She pulled away.

"Don't touch me," she said nervously as she fumbled with her seat belt. *Why are seat belts so difficult to unbuckle?*

"Hanna, stop," he said.

"Don't," she said again. "Just don't."

"Let me explain," he said as she finally unhooked the buckle. She reached for the door. "Hanna, when you were eight, I was twelve and living down south. I didn't have anything to do with your kidnapping."

Her hand froze on the door handle. *What did he just say?* She turned her head and saw he was up against his door, almost as if to show her he wouldn't grab her. She relaxed slightly, but the word rang in her ears like a siren.

"Kidnapping?" she repeated. "What kidnapping?"

William shook his head. "I can't believe you don't know," he said, aggravation in his voice. "You don't remember anything about it, and no one has helped you to?"

She felt a flash of annoyance. Of course she didn't remember anything about a kidnapping! Suddenly, it happened again. The wind felt like it was knocked out of her as her head throbbed. Memories filled her mind, hatching and expanding like those little dinosaur toys that expand when they're put into water.

"I was kidnapped," she said. "They took me because I saw them kill that old woman and her husband." She started shaking. "I was playing in the woods, and it was getting late. My mom told me to be inside before it got dark, but I got lost in the woods."

William could have been listening or on the other side of the world, and she didn't know or care. In that moment, she was eight years old again.

"I was lost, and I couldn't get home. I started to cry, but I kept walking, hoping that someone would find me. I found a driveway and . . ." She shook her head. "There was a man with a gun on the porch, pressed against the front of the house . . .

he was waiting . . . then the old man ran out and he shot him in the back. I just stood there. I couldn't move.

"The man with the gun looked at me and smiled. The old woman came running out and was followed by another gunman, who waited to shoot her until she reached the car on the other side of the lawn." She paused and looked over at William. It was like it happened yesterday, and yet, the rest escaped her. "The rest is blurry. The next thing I remember is the dark room and them talking. Then there was a bang, and after that, I was in the ambulance."

Her tears fell like tiny anvils. She shook uncontrollably and knew she would lose it any minute. William looked positively wild, yet there was pain in his eyes; she realized he was emotionally invested in what had happened to her, even if she didn't understand why.

"Hanna," William said gently. "I think I should take you home."

She didn't answer at first. He'd helped her find her memories—she was sure that he'd led her to unlocking them. The pictures in her mind were so graphic and clear, she almost didn't want them for the fear that came with them.

"Okay," she said finally, nodding. "I'm sorry—"

"No," he said, reaching for her. He held her hand. "Don't ever be sorry. What happened wasn't your fault." He spoke fiercely, as if he'd argued the fact hundreds of times.

He held her hand the entire ride home, and she wished she'd never have to let go. When they reached her house, the lights were on, but Owen's cruiser was nowhere to be seen. William got out of the truck and walked around to the other side to help her down. She was still shaken, and she hoped he wouldn't leave just yet.

"You have to go inside alone, Hanna," he said. "It's getting dark."

She looked up at the sunset behind the trees. She knew she'd have to face her grandparents alone.

"I know," she said miserably.

"I won't be far," he said, leaning down and pressing his lips to hers.

It wasn't a passionate kiss, but the comfort it brought her left only one word in her mind: love. She wanted to tell him she loved him, but knew it wasn't the time or the place.

He held her closely for several moments before finally letting go. Then, as if on cue, a howl sounded around them. She looked at William with questioning eyes.

"I still don't understand the whole wolf thing. How can it follow you like it does?" she whispered.

"It's like a curse," he said quietly. "He's a constant reminder of who I am, but that's how I take it. My father believes that they're more like our guardians, says there's magic there, but it's kind of hard to believe in magic these days. I've always just thought of it as a dark bond."

"Would he ever hurt someone you cared about?" she asked, not sure why she wanted to know.

"Never," he promised before pushing her gently toward the house.

She reluctantly let go of his hand and walked to the house. She could feel him watching her as she walked up the front steps and turned around before opening the front door. He stood there, arms loosely folded, waiting for her to get inside. She gave a little wave before she turned to open the door and went inside.

CHAPTER SEVENTEEN

Hanna walked into the kitchen and found Gram and Grandpa, looking worried. They both leapt to their feet when they saw her. She braced herself for an onslaught of inquiries.

"Hey," she said, wiping away the nearly dried tears that clung to her cheeks.

"Hanna!" Gram said, grabbing her and hugging her tightly. "Do you have any idea how worried we've been? No, I don't think you do. You seem to think you can just walk around town, getting into cars with strangers, not telling anyone where you're going or what you're doing. It's like you want something bad to happen to you!"

She felt the flames of injustice tingle at the back of her neck. She wasn't about to be scolded, not after they'd lied to her for ten years about why she didn't have any memories.

"You've really disappointed us," Grandpa said. "Why are you acting so careless?"

"Disappointed?" she repeated in disbelief. "You want to talk about being disappointed? About being careless?" She was unable to keep the words in, and her voice cracked with emotion. "How is that I've lived in this house for ten years and neither of you ever mentioned that I was kidnapped?"

Their faces paled in shock.

"What? Was I never supposed to know?"

"You remember?" Gram said in a hushed voice, as if saying it louder was risky. "How?"

She didn't want to say. She didn't want to tell them anything.

"I remember," she said, without explaining. "But I don't understand. Why would you keep something like that from me?"

"Hanna, dear," Grandpa started. "It was for your own protection."

"Protection from what?"

They looked frightened. Gram started wiping tears away. Hanna wished that William had come inside. She felt queasy, as if the truth was poison and her grandparents had fed her the tainted apple.

"Hanna," Gram sobbed. "When they found you, you refused to talk." Grandpa almost interrupted, so used to keeping the secret, but he quieted down when she shot him a look. "You didn't talk for so long, and no doctor knew why. You kept blacking out and waking up, but there was no change. They said you were in shock, but it seemed impossible to be in shock for months . . ."

"Months?" she repeated.

Gram nodded, unable to continue.

"Until one day, you just blacked out," Grandpa said. "We were all so scared. Ever since the kidnapping, your parents were wracked with guilt and felt like no matter what they did, it only hurt you more."

"That was the first day of third grade," Hanna said, suddenly remembering. "I had to go to the doctor's after school."

"That's right," Grandpa continued. "You woke up and didn't remember anything. You were talking again, and smiling as if the past several months never happened. You were a regular, happy kid who was excited and a little nervous about starting school. But that was the last black out you ever had, until a few weeks ago." He shook his head sadly. "Your parents blamed themselves. It's why they left. They were so worried you couldn't be happy with them. We all agreed never to bring it up—if you didn't remember, what was the point of bringing all the pain to the surface again?"

"Almost everyone in New Hope knew you had been kidnapped," Gram finally said, calming down. "But I don't think anyone was ever willing to ask you directly about it. Once everyone heard you'd forgotten, so did they, for the most part."

Hanna felt betrayed. It sounded like Mom and Dad had left so they didn't have to deal with her, and Gram and Grandpa had lied to her every day for nearly ten years to avoid the problem. It also explained why she'd never understood the way people acted around her. Bitterness stabbed at her as her anger flared.

"So, that's it? That's why no one ever told me? Because everyone was too scared to deal with it?"

"Hanna—" Grandpa tried.

"No," she said loudly, cutting him off. "No, I don't want to hear it. You both had no right to keep it from me. Mom and Dad had no right." She laughed bitterly. "I can't believe this. Everyone in the damn town knew, and no one told me. I had to find out on my own."

"That Vann guy started this," Gram said to Grandpa.

"Don't you dare blame William!" Hanna nearly shouted.

"Honey," Gram began. "William isn't . . . he isn't the best sort."

"Why? Because of who his ancestors are?"

They both stared at her in shock.

"Yeah," she continued. "I know about our history, too. William's the only one who's been honest with me about anything. It's funny; the only person who cared enough to help me understand is the guy you all insist is no good." She rolled her eyes, despite herself. "Even *he* thinks it. Well, you're all wrong. Did you forget he saved my life?"

Gram looked surprised. "He told you he wasn't good?"

"Yeah, and he's wrong. And so are you."

She turned toward the basement door, but thought better of it. She headed for the front door instead.

"I'm getting some fresh air," she snapped.

"Hanna, don't leave like this," Gram said, following her. "Don't be mad."

"I'm not mad," she said, turning around before she reached the door. "I'm *disappointed*," she said, throwing their word back at them. They looked hurt, and she felt a twinge of guilt, but she wouldn't apologize. "Just leave me alone."

She left quickly, unsure if she'd be able to control herself any longer. Her emotions were reeling. All the years of numbness vanished. Everything she should have felt for the last ten years came rushing over her, and it was too much.

She hoped William would still be standing in her driveway, but he was gone. She remembered her car was still at the diner and cursed. Aggravated, she kept walking, not willing to go back inside. She felt suffocated in there. She'd just walk to her car. Town was only a few miles away and she needed the time to cool off. She heard the howling start in the woods around her. Unlike her first encounters with him, she now welcomed the idea of the wolf showing himself.

Her steps slowed as she gradually calmed down, but her thoughts still tumbled over one truth to the next. That was why her parents had left? They ran away from their guilt, and she was forced to grow up without them, without any knowledge of what happened to her. Was she psychologically damaged? Had she been pitied by everyone since then? Had everyone in New Hope felt awkward around her? Was that why she felt like such an outsider?

Paranoia took over. Why was Carly her friend? How many of her classmates knew about what happened to her? Were people only nice to her in hopes of finding out some bizarre detail of her twisted history?

Her heart pounded as panic settled in her stomach. Was this what it was going to be like, remembering from now on? She felt sick, like her head and heart were going in separate directions, but trying to get to the same conclusion.

And who were these people who kidnapped her? Why could she remember their voices now and nothing else? Why had it been William who told her and not someone else?

William . . .

She stopped walking as she thought of him. Why did he care so much when she finally remembered? She shook her head. What was it about him that made her feel so comforted and frightened at the same time? Even if he was related to a psychopath that lived once upon a time, it didn't make *him* evil. The burden of it made him bitter, but not bad. They both had baggage, and it made her smile to think of it. He

235

had a good heart; she didn't care if they were from different worlds. She loved him.

A light rain began to fall as she turned off her road and walked down Route 17 toward town. It seemed to get colder the closer spring got, and she was glad she was still wearing her winter jacket, even though it was May.

The raindrops vanished as they hit the pavement, and it calmed her to feel them disappear on her head. The lights of cars kept shining and passing by. She was almost near the main road in town when a set of headlights shone behind her, but didn't pass.

She kept walking until she heard a car door open and slam shut. She stopped.

"Hello?" a male voice called.

She turned around, squinting. A large bear of a man was silhouetted in the truck's lights.

"Yes?" she said, trying to shield her eyes from the lights. Had the guy left his high beams on?

"Are you okay?"

"I'm fine, thanks," she said, turning to continue her walk. Her head ached from squinting at the bright lights.

"You shouldn't be walking on the side of a busy road like this in the dark," the guy said loudly. "Do you need a ride somewhere?"

The hairs on the back of her neck stood up and her stomach turned unpleasantly. She saw every raindrop and heard every leaf rustle around her. She could smell the crispness in the air.

Get out of here, her inner voice warned.

"No," she said awkwardly. "Thanks."

"Aw, come on," he said. "It's dangerous out here."

Hanna felt her heart drop as another car door opened. He was right. It was dangerous out here, and not because she was walking alone. *They* were dangerous, and for the first time in her life, she had the good sense to run from the feeling.

She bolted down the road as fast as she could in her flats. Unfortunately, her shoes didn't have very good traction and the wet road was slick. She heard the two doors slam behind her as the engine roared to life. Her heart pounded in her ears and she tried to think of how far it was to the diner. She tried to cut across the street, but the truck came from behind and sped past her. For a second, she thought it would just keep going, but the driver slammed on his brakes and the truck stopped abruptly.

Hanna began to panic when the driver and the passenger got out. Not having a choice, she booked across the road. She almost made it, but suddenly, she was grabbed by the collar of her coat. She heard her phone fall from her pocket and sound like it smashed to pieces.

"GET OFF ME!" she shouted as loud as she could, flailing like a wild animal.

Whoever had a hold of her dragged her back across the street. She fought as hard as she could, screaming at the top of her lungs.

"Shut up!" the large man bellowed, tightening his grip as he hauled her quickly toward the truck.

"I don't know about this," a female voice sounded from somewhere.

"Shut up, Maryanne," said a male voice.

Hanna kicked and swung her fists around, trying to hit the man who dragged her, but he was too strong and she was getting tired. The other man held the back door open and she was pushed into the back seat.

"LET ME GO!" she screamed before they got duct tape on her mouth. They tied her hands, the second man sitting on her legs in the backseat.

She tried to squirm, but it was too hard to move beneath the weight of him while the female held her shoulders down. By the time the large man who'd grabbed her got into the driver's seat, she'd gotten a look at his face. Her eyes went wide and her nostrils flared as she recognized the angry-faced man from Ann Arbor. Her head felt like it would shatter.

"Knock her out," the driver said, seeing her eyes on him.

"Bill—"

"I said do it!" he growled.

She tried to look at the ones holding her face down against the seat, but the man grabbed a gun from his side and brought it down with a solid *thunk*.

She caught a glimpse and thought she recognized the girl before everything went black.

CHAPTER EIGHTEEN

*W*illiam pulled into the police station, surprising himself that he'd decided to come. His lawyers would have a million things to say if they knew that he'd decided to talk to Peirce, but none of that mattered now. After dropping Hanna off at her house, he knew things were about to get ugly, and he needed to talk to Peirce one-on-one.

He quickly got out of his truck and walked up to the heavy glass doors, pulling his coat tightly around him. There wasn't much wind tonight, but the temperature was below anything his Southern skin had ever dealt with. He found it comforting, though, the way the cold made him more alert.

The florescent lights inside made him squint as he walked up to the desk where an older woman sat. She gave him a slight look before doing a double take and standing up with fear in her eyes. He was used to this look.

"Vann?" she said, her voice a high-pitched squeak. "What do you want?"

He held his hands up to show no ill intentions.

"I want to speak with Officer Peirce," he said slowly. "That's all. I need to talk to him."

"Stay right there," she commanded weakly as she hurried around the desk and down the hallway.

Moments later, Peirce walked out of his office, trailed by the elderly woman and an older man, who William knew as the police chief. He stood perfectly still, eyes locked with Peirce's grim face as he stalked toward him.

"What?" Peirce said as he came toward him.

"I need to talk to you," he said, noticing the elderly woman cowering behind him. She may have been frightened, but he knew she and the police chief shouldn't hear what he had to say. "In private."

"Regarding?" he said angrily. "Maybe about how you took Hanna for a joy ride when she needed to go to the hospital earlier?"

"I didn't take her on a joy ride."

"Oh, no? Your lawyers may have me tied up with paperwork up to my neck, but don't think I won't arrest you again—"

"I didn't come here to argue with you. I came to talk."

"About what?"

Idiot, he thought. He was going to make this difficult. *Fine by me.*

"About Goldilocks and the three bears," he said loudly, certain that the old woman and Peirce's boss would think he was crazy.

Peirce cursed. "My office," he said, turning back down the hallway.

"You sure, Peirce?" the police chief asked.

Peirce's silence was his answer as William followed. The police chief gave him a dirty look while the secretary returned to her desk swiftly. William couldn't help but grin at her. Regardless of him being good, bad, or whatever the hell he was, he *did* enjoy making people uncomfortable.

He followed Peirce into a decent-sized room with wood paneling and filing cabinets. Two chairs sat on one side of a small desk, while another sat opposite, facing the door. Peirce didn't sit. He leaned on the side of the desk, shaking his head, obviously displeased. William noticed several pictures on his desk. They all looked like relatives—real relatives—of Peirce. The man obviously didn't appreciate his lingering stares.

"What do you want, Vann?" he bit out. "I'm busy."

"Hanna remembers," William said quickly, ignoring Peirce's sudden head jerk. "We were driving and talking and ambulances came up in the conversation. Suddenly, she started rambling. She remembers the kidnapping."

Peirce let out an exasperated breath.

"You son of a bitch," he said lowly, turning on him. "Do you know what you've done?"

"Don't blame this on me. She was going to remember one day, but that's not why I'm here. I want to know if you looked into the release of Billy Hertz. Did you find anything? Or about his brother?"

"Now, why would I tell you?"

Like a spark to a match, his temper ignited. He took one threatening step toward Peirce.

"Don't act like they don't mean anything to me," he said through gritted teeth. "You know damn well that I'm involved in this and whether you like it or not, they're going to come back for her."

Peirce let out a humorless laugh.

"Billy Hertz has been released for three months. Why would he wait that long to come back for Hanna? His brother has been off the radar since he was released six months ago. Their sister died in a house fire. Why come back at all, since Hanna can't remember anything?"

"You think they know about her blocked memory?" William asked, surprised that Peirce was so nearsighted. "And even if they did, what does it matter to them? They're murderers, man, don't you understand that? They'd do anything to cover up their tracks, especially with a grudge against Hanna after being locked up for her kidnapping. They're going to come after her."

"Is that how you people work?" Peirce said, pushing off his desk as he took a seat. "Kill anything that gets in your way?"

He shook his head in disbelief.

"You damned fool. You can't get over the fact that I'm friends with her."

"You shouldn't be here," Peirce said loudly. "You're all alike. A magnet to others like you. It would probably be your fault if Billy Hertz was in the area, which he isn't—"

"What about those string of burglaries? What about what I told you after the fire?"

"You don't even know what he looks like."

"I know what I saw."

"And what was that exactly? A bad guy?" Peirce shook his head. "I bet it was like looking into a mirror."

William slammed his fist on the desk.

"You stupid son of a bitch," he growled, his fury flowing out of him. "They killed a member of my family. How the hell do you think I could be like them?"

"Because you are," Peirce said, though William could see the conflict in his eyes. William and Billy were both from bad families, but when one did evil to another, there was nothing but bad blood, and Peirce knew it. All out war. "Or is this a revenge thing? Using Hanna as a pawn?"

"You're so damned focused on me you haven't even paid attention to anything else. Hanna's in danger, I know it. I can feel it, and the longer we sit here arguing about this, the longer she's out there, without any protection."

"She has all the protection she needs."

William shook his head.

"You and that hero complex," he said bitterly. "You shouldn't be here either. You know better than to mess with her fate."

That got a rise out of Peirce. He placed his hands on the desk and slowly rose from his seat.

"I know it was you that night, with Roderick," he said vehemently. "It had Vann written all over it."

William wouldn't let him take the focus from Hanna, especially when he still believed that Roderick had stolen something very precious from the Peirce family out of pure malice. To this day, William didn't know what he had helped steal, but he knew Roderick. He came from a long line of cheats and liars, but if there was anything Roderick was, it was loyal to his friends. Whatever it was he'd stolen from Peirce, it was for the right reasons.

"Roderick is the least of my worries," he said. "Hanna's in danger. We need to find the Hertz brothers."

"*We* don't need to do anything," Peirce said, as he walked around the desk. "You need to get out of here. I'll take care of Hanna."

"What are you going to do?"

"I'll send a squad car over there to patrol the perimeters—"

A sudden knock at the door cut him off.

"Office Peirce?" the secretary's muffled voice said through the door.

"Yes?"

"A phone call for you, line three."

"Not right now."

"It's Loretta. She said Hanna's gone out for a walk and hasn't come back. It's been over an hour."

Tension snapped through Peirce's body, and William felt his insides freeze. Peirce turned and grabbed the phone.

"Hello?" He paused. "Calm down, when did she leave?" He looked at his watch, and then at the clock above the door. "Did she say where she was going? Did you try to call her cell? The line's dead. Yes. Yes, I'll go out and . . . yes, I'll call you a soon as possible."

He hung up the phone. William was already halfway out the door. "Where do you think you're going?" Peirce called after him.

"I'm going out to find her," he said over his shoulder.

"No, you're not."

William turned on his heel and Peirce nearly knocked into him.

"I'm going no matter what you say, understand?" he said fiercely. "And if you try to stop me, I'll break your damn arm."

"Is that a threat?"

"Yeah, it is," he said.

He was out the door and halfway to his car when a howl echoed in the distance. He paused, trying to hear what direction it came from.

"What the hell is that?" Peirce called out from the doors. Several other cops followed him. He waved them back as he walked toward William, lowering his voice. "Friend of yours?"

"She's in trouble," he said with steely conviction. "I swear, if anything happens to her, I'm coming after you."

"You're staying away from this."

"Wyatt knows where she is," William said quickly, annoyed that he had to confess it.

"Who's Wyatt?"

"The wolf you're hearing. He knows where she is, and she's in danger. You won't be able to find her without me." He took a step toward him. "It's the Hertz brothers. I know it."

Peirce's face contorted, visibly weighing the pros and cons of his words. They didn't have much time. Suddenly, a light seemed to go off, and Peirce turned to the officers behind him.

"Rodriguez! Pull Hanna Loch's file. I need a list of the locations where the Hertzes took her during her four-day absence." The officer named Rodriguez turned and ran back into the station as Peirce turned to face William. "Are you one hundred percent sure about this?"

"Yes."

"You better be," he said, distrustfully. "You'll ride with me. And if, by the grace of something bigger than me this turns out all right, I want you to disappear. You know that Hanna and you could never work. You can't be that dense not to realize it."

Peirce's words mimicked the same thoughts he'd been having for weeks, but to hear them out loud felt like a sucker punch to the gut. Pierce was right. Even if everything did work out in the end, he and Hanna could never be together. Regardless of the whole mess they were in, facts were facts, and he knew them religiously. There was only ever a battle between good and evil, never peace.

It dug at him to admit it, but he nodded stiffly.

"If she's still alive after this, I'll disappear," he said tightly, looking at Peirce. "I know better than to expect anything else."

For a second, William thought he saw a flash of sympathy pass over Peirce's face before he nodded grimly and turned toward his cruiser. He followed quickly, pulling out his phone to call his father. He was flying in tonight and was probably at the house by now. If they were going to find the Hertz brothers, his father should know.

After all, they had killed his sister, William's aunt.

CHAPTER NINETEEN

Images and sensations flashed in Hanna's mind. The dim moonlight through the clouds. The faint patter of raindrops from tree branches. The feeling of being half-carried, half-dragged, her legs pricked by dead bramble. She would see or hear just for a moment before blackness took over again, and she was neither here nor there, until the gaps between the pictures shortened.

The next time she opened her eyes, she was sitting in a chair, hands tied behind her back, just like when she was a girl. She thought she was dreaming again, but when she looked down, she saw she wasn't wearing her purple corduroy pants. She wore her gray slacks and the white button-down shirt she'd worn to work.

This wasn't a dream . . . it was a real life nightmare.

She scanned her surroundings. The room in which she sat was dimly lit and looked to be a hundred years old. It was dirty and cold, with broken furniture pieces and garbage scattered on the floor. A few LED lanterns were placed on the floor and one large oil lantern sat atop a dingy table in the corner.

No light shone through the broken windows to her right, but she knew the sunrise could be seen through them. She'd seen it happen before, and she hoped that she would be able to see it again. The smell in the stale air was wintery and rotting, like wet wood and death, and the entire atmosphere reeked with decay.

The pain in her head was blinding, but she tried to ignore it. It wouldn't help her situation if her attackers thought she was weak.

She remembered their faces. Had she really seen who she thought in the truck? A movement in the left-hand corner startled her. A rat sifted through an old bag of chips thrown in the corner. She was focused on the rat, hoping it wouldn't come toward her, when a voice suddenly sounded from the dark.

"How are you, Hanna?" it asked, strange and soft, like a child's.

"Anne," Hanna whispered. So she had seen her. "Get me out of here."

"My name's Maryanne," she said. Hanna was unnerved by the unshakable calm in her voice. She stepped out of the archway that led into what looked to be an old, empty kitchen. It was too dark to tell for certain if the others were in the next room.

She wore a black, high-collared button-down shirt that hid her bandaged arm. Little ruffles ran up the front of it and dark jeans were tucked into her knee-high black boots. She tilted her head, her long brown hair cascading down her back, her eyes unblinking. "You don't remember me?"

Hanna was still for a moment before shaking her head slowly, unsure of what to say or how to respond. Did she mean from school? She didn't want to upset her—something about her seemed unhinged. As she came closer, Hanna could see her eyes were wide, a crazed gleam flashing behind them. A memory of those same eyes hit her, looking at her from that same spot in the room. She'd been here before, with Maryanne.

"You tricked me," Hanna whispered before she blacked out again.

She was lost and running through the woods, calling out for Mom. It felt like she'd been gone for hours. Finally, she found a field with a red barn and a driveway leading to a white house. There was an old blue car and a white truck parked in front. She

saw a man on the porch with a gun, and then an old man came out, running.

The gunman held his arm out straight and suddenl,y the air rang out with an ear-splitting noise.

She grabbed her ears as several crows flew out of the old oak tree standing next to the house. Her eyes followed the birds until another shot rang out. She looked back and saw an old woman fall to the ground.

She didn't know what to do. She couldn't move or speak. She just looked at the old woman, who lay still.

The wind blew and the dust from the road swirled around her as the gunman pointed at her. He said something over his shoulder.

Frozen still, she just stared at him.

The door of the house opened and another man came out, gripping the back of an older girl's neck and pushing her in front of him. She wore a beautiful blue dress and her hair looked like it had been curled. The man walked her down the front steps roughly and held the barrel of a gun to her head. Hanna could see she was crying.

They walked to the edge of the lawn. She was still too petrified to move when the gunman suddenly let go of his victim, pushing her to the ground. He turned and began to walk back to the house. The girl coughed and cried in the dusty road, looking at Hanna like she was her savior. Letting her good nature take over, Hanna reached for her.

"Come on," she said, her voice small.

Suddenly, the girl grabbed Hanna's hand, pulling her down to the ground. The girl wrestled to hold her as the gunmen came running. Hanna tried to scream, but something hit her head, and she passed out.

Hanna opened her eyes, unsure if she was reliving the past or truly awake.

"Pay attention when I'm talking to you!" Maryanne said shrilly.

"You tricked me," Hanna said, her head still reeling with the moment she'd just relived. "I thought you were in trouble."

"I didn't trick you," Maryanne spat. "You were just stupid."

"Why did you take me?"

"Because you would have told on us," Maryanne said, as if speaking to a child. She shook her head and made a clicking noise with her tongue and teeth. "No, no, no. We couldn't have that. You would have sent us to jail."

"You went to jail," Hanna said, puzzle pieces slowly fitting together. "The police found me here."

"They sent Billy away," Maryanne said, her voice eerily soft. "Billy was the oldest, and the worst. He was the one that shot the cop who showed up last time. Bjorn was seventeen and confused, so they sent him to juvenile detention. And me? I was just fifteen and in the wrong place at the wrong time. I couldn't be held responsible for my older brothers' actions. I went into foster care."

"What do you want with me?" Hanna asked, breathing heavily. "I never did anything to you—"

"Never did anything?" Maryanne said, her eyes wide. She dropped the little girl act she'd perfected while impersonating a high-schooler, her voice now deep and deadly. "You ruined our lives. We were going to get away scot-free, and then you showed up. You shouldn't have been there." She let out a humorless, shrieking laugh that sent chills down Hanna's spine. "So here we are."

"Why now? After all this time?"

"Because Billy finally got out," Maryanne said, crouching down to the floor so she could look up at her. She smiled and her voice changed back to sweet. "Isn't that great?"

She's insane. "Yes," she agreed, playing along. "He's been away for a long time, I guess."

"Almost ten years," Anne said, nodding. "But it's all right. We're a family again. Bjorn found me living with a foster family in Detroit when I was seventeen, and he was able to burn the house down so we could get away. We've been waiting all these years for Billy, and now that we have him back, we can finally kill you." A bizarre smile unfolded on her face. "And then there won't be anyone in our way anymore."

Hanna tried not to react to the idea of her impending death. She had to keep talking to Anne, or Maryanne, or whoever she was, not only to distract herself, but hopefully to keep her from doing something irreversible.

"Why am I in your way?" Hanna said. "I didn't even remember you or Billy or Bjorn until earlier tonight."

That wasn't the best thing to say. Maryanne's face switched from pleasant to blank.

"You didn't remember us?" she said, her voice deep again. "I remembered you. I remembered you every day. Every day. EVERY DAY!" she yelled, standing up to kick a broken chair across the room.

"Maryanne!" a male voice called as he entered the room. It was the younger one, Bjorn. "Be quiet!"

"She doesn't remember us, Bjorn! She said she doesn't remember us!" Maryanne whined, pointing an accusing finger at her. "She doesn't remember that she ruined our lives!"

"Maryanne, calm down," Bjorn said as he grabbed her by the shoulders. He shook her violently. "Your mouth is going to get us caught."

"But—"

"Do you want Billy sent away again?" Bjorn threatened. "Do you want to be sent away? Because, if you keep screaming like this . . ."

"I'm sorry, Bjorn, I didn't mean to scream," she said, her voice turning to a loud whisper, eyes wide like a cat's. Her emotions seemed to switch with the wind. Hanna could barely tell if she was smiling or frowning, her face was so twisted with raw paranoia. "But she doesn't remember that this is all her fault and that's why she needs to die."

For the first time since the car, Bjorn looked at Hanna. His eyes weren't crazed like Maryanne's, but full of fury and hatred, the same eyes she had seen at the diner the day Troy asked her to prom. Hanna looked away, hoping that she hadn't aggravated him further by simply staring at him. He looked like the slightest annoyance would set him off.

"You don't have to explain to her why she has to die, Maryanne," he said to his sister. "She'll be dead soon, and we can get out of here."

Maryanne nodded as he let her go, her hands coming together almost prayer-like. She continued to nod while walking around the room, seemingly lost in her thoughts. Hanna watched her until the eldest brother entered the room.

"She okay?" Billy asked, nodding at his sister.

"She'll be fine. She's just riled up by this one," Bjorn said, kicking an old soda can in Hanna's direction. "Apparently, the brat didn't remember us, and it upset Maryanne."

"Oh, she remembers us," Billy said, unholstering a gun from his hip. He sauntered up to Hanna in a way that reminded her of the cowboys in Grandpa's favorite Western movies, but not nearly as entertaining. She thought of Grandpa and wondered how long it had been since she began the walk to her car. Hopefully, it had been a few hours and someone realized she was missing by now.

All of her thoughts were pushed to the back of her mind when Billy pressed the gun to her cheek. It was cold steel, but she only felt the pressure of it. Everything in the house was cold. She stared back into his dark eyes.

"Don't you?" Billy said. His breath smelled of stale cigarettes. His hair hung out of his beanie hat like snakes out of a tree, filthy and long. He cocked the gun and Hanna inhaled sharply, her eyes unblinking. "I bet I can jog your memory."

Billy pointed the gun over his head in one swift motion and pulled the trigger. She shook as pieces of rotted roof fell on top of them.

"Damn it, Billy!" Bjorn yelled. "You're going to get us caught!"

"We're not getting caught," Billy snapped as Maryanne stopped pacing to watch. "Stop your worrying." He turned his focus back on Hanna. "You remember me now?"

Like a floodgate opening, every memory she'd ever blocked came rushing back. She remembered the house her parents had, her bedroom before she moved. She saw flashes of her mom and dad arguing, and heard them blame each other for her kidnapping and persistent silence. She remembered having to sit down with them and be told she was going to live with Gram and Grandpa. She recalled sitting in doctors' offices, being asked questions and giving no answers. She remembered everything about her kidnapping, every word the three siblings said in front of her the first time they took her—how they killed the farmer for his money, and shot his wife because she was hiding and tried to run.

She squeezed her eyes shut and all the pictures clicked together.

The noise woke her. They were fighting, yelling at one another as Billy waved his gun around. The gun went off and she heard the wall splinter behind her. A howling outside echoed through the house, magnifying after the shot rang out. They all jumped and Maryanne screamed as the window shattered, a huge black shape landing on the floor between them.

The wolf snarled viciously when Billy pointed his gun at it, and it took three shots from both him and Bjorn before its massive body sank to the ground. Hanna stared, stunned, as the others started yelling again, pointing wildly at the dead wolf.

An instant later, the door kicked in and a young woman with long dark hair and dressed in a police uniform entered, her pistol aimed at Bjorn. Hanna wanted to warn her to run, that Billy was out of her line of vision with his gun, but the shots rang out before she could. Her clear grey eyes found Hanna's and swept over the wolf's body as she stumbled . . .

Hanna forced away the memory of the woman's body falling over her, not wanting to remember how she died. The memory that someone had died to save her from this exact same predicament made her nauseous.

"Why is she crying?" Bjorn asked as tears ran down Hanna's cheeks.

"Because she's afraid to die," Billy said. "Isn't that right, princess?"

She inhaled sharply and exhaled slowly, refusing to let them see her fear. Her eyes fixed boldly on Billy's face. If she was going to die, she wouldn't let them take any pleasure in killing her, especially if she didn't have anything else left to lose.

"I'm not afraid to die," she said, making her voice strong. "And I'm not afraid of you."

"Oh, no?" Billy said, cocking his head to the side. He lifted the gun again, twirling it around a loose piece of her hair. "And what makes you so brave?"

"I'm not brave," she said quietly as she recited her last prayers in her head. "But I was never aware of any of you. I never knew you existed." She glanced at Maryanne, who was nearly shaking with fury. "You weren't anything until you came looking for me. You're still nothing to me now, but not remembering was always a sort of torture." Hanna forced a smile. "Now, I actually have peace."

"What?" Maryanne screamed, looking frantic.

"Not knowing was terrifying, but now that I know what frightened me, I'm not afraid of you anymore."

"Billy," Maryanne began, pulling at his arm. "I want her to be tortured. I want her to feel what it's been like. I want her to feel pain."

"Knock it off, Maryanne," Billy said, ripping his arm out of her hands.

"No!" she argued. "I want to make her suffer!"

Psycho, Hanna thought.

"Bjorn, grab her," Billy said as Maryanne clawed at him. Bjorn stepped forward, restraining her.

"Get off me, Bjorn!" she yelled. "I want to do it! I want to kill her!"

"Damn it, Maryanne, be quiet!" Bjorn said, struggling to hold on to her. "She's going to act like this for days if you don't let her kill this girl, Billy."

"That's enough," Billy said, cocking his gun again and pointing it directly into Hanna's face. Maryanne screamed with jealousy. "You're going to die now."

Hanna tried not to react, while Maryanne's screams echoed off the walls. She closed her eyes and let her thoughts take over. She thought of her parents and grandparents, of Carly and her old car, school, and friends.

Of William . . .

Would William be her last thought? She didn't know why, but she wanted to smile. It seemed so unfair that her short life would end here that it was almost funny, in a dark sort of way. Ever since William came into her life, it had been the sort of perfect chaos that only happened in fairy tales. She hoped he would find someone and live the rest of his life happily, without a thought of the girl who died once upon a time . . .

Just then, Maryanne's screams quieted as a loud howl sounded throughout the room, as if a wolf stood in the shack with them. Hanna could barely believe what she was hearing, but as the howl ended—in that beautiful, sorrowful way that howls end—she knew she wasn't dead yet.

"What the hell is it with these things?" Bjorn yelled.

Hanna opened her eyes and found herself looking down the barrel of a handgun. She looked up at Billy, whose attention was focused on the broken window behind him. She knew he'd pull the trigger any second, so she swung her body as hard as she could. Her chair tipped, and she slammed painfully to the floor. The gun went off, but the bullet didn't hit her. She closed her eyes and lay still as another shot went off, sending more bits of rotted ceiling and wall falling on top of her.

When she opened her eyes, her heart soared as she saw the wolf, yet it quickly plummeted when she remembered how the scene had last played out. She found the grisly sight of Bjorn twitching in a pool of dark blood as the wolf turned on Billy. Shots, snarls, shouts, and snapping teeth encircled her as she tried to free her hands from behind her back. She hoped a stray bullet wouldn't find her. Turning awkwardly, she struggled with her bindings, finally loosening them, and saw Billy flail on the ground as the massive gray wolf bit into the flesh of his neck.

Billy roared with pain as they wrestled and speckles of warm blood hit her cheek. His gun went flying into the air, landing somewhere beside them.

Maryanne's screams were deafening, and Hanna couldn't tear her eyes away from the bloody scene. Within seconds, the fight had gone out of Billy's body while the wolf held him down in its jaws. It resembled a scene from a nature show, and she silently compared the wolf to a lion and Billy to an antelope.

With a final jerk of its head, the wolf ended Billy's life right in front of her, discarding his victim like a rag doll.

"No!" Maryanne screamed over and over. She crouched over Billy's body, crying and wailing like a banshee.

The wolf didn't seem concerned with her and padded over to Hanna's side. She buried her hands in his coat and tried to calm herself, but she shook uncontrollably. His fur felt warm and sticky, and when she looked down, she saw her hands were red with blood.

"Oh, no," she whispered, tears springing to her eyes.

Suddenly, there was shouting coming from outside. Lights shone through the cracked old walls and windows, which Hanna found blinding after so long in the dimness.

"You!" Maryanne hissed suddenly, grabbing Hanna's attention. She reached for something on the ground behind Billy's body and Hanna's stomach dropped. "You ruined everything!"

Once again, she was looking at Billy's gun. The wolf growled menacingly, but his sides heaved in pain. Hanna buried her face in his fur.

"Don't worry," she whispered to it. "It will be over soon."

She heard a shot and wondered if the girl had missed her. Then, Maryanne screamed and when Hanna looked up, she saw her rolling on the ground, clutching her side, the gun dropped and forgotten. The door slammed open and an officer ran in, his gun finding the two dead men first before training in on Maryanne.

"Owen!" Hanna nearly sobbed.

CHAPTER TWENTY

The noise of police swarming the shack was nearly deafening, and it didn't help that Maryanne screamed like a lunatic while they tried to restrain her. Hanna sat motionless—she couldn't manage much else.

"Hanna!"

The wolf growled when Owen came near and an officer behind him pointed his gun.

"Don't touch him!" she yelled, throwing her arms around the wolf protectively.

"Stand down!" Owen shouted. "Hanna," he said, his voice soft. "Are you all right? I need to get you outside."

Hanna didn't move. She was determined not to leave the wolf. "Hanna, I need you to get up and come with me."

"No," she said fiercely.

She heard footsteps coming closer and turned her head a fraction to see the police still had their weapons drawn, despite Owen's order to stand down.

"Tell them to get out of here!" she yelled.

Owen waved a hand at them and they grudgingly lowered their weapons. "Give us a minute," he said, glancing at Maryanne. "Get *her* out of here."

They dragged the still thrashing girl out of the house. It was eerily quiet without the walls echoing her screams.

"Hanna—"

"No one is touching him," she said, her voice cold and set with unwavering grit.

"Hanna, if he's hurt, then he has to get help." He stretched out a hand. "You have to come with me so William can get him out of here."

She didn't believe him. "William is here? I want to see him."

Owen sighed, moving to the open door and leaning out, his arm beckoning. A moment later, William rushed through the door, his eyes frantic.

"He saved me!" she cried, the tears falling. "I'm so sorry, William. He's hurt . . ."

"It's all right." William wrapped a soothing arm around her as he kneeled next to them. The wolf whined and pressed his head to William's chest. "Wyatt will be all right."

"Is that his name?" she asked and William nodded.

They stayed quiet a moment, Hanna's arms still wrapped around Wyatt and William's arms embracing them both.

"Hanna," Owen said. "Come with me. They'll be okay."

Numbly, Hanna agreed, and Owen helped her to her feet. He barked orders at the other officers as they exited the shack. Police cars, ambulances, and even ATVs were all squeezed into the small dirt driveway. She guessed from the dark and the dewy chill that it was probably four o'clock in the morning. Several cops were dusting Billy's truck for fingerprints. She walked by slowly, watching them as she was directed to an ambulance. Someone had draped a wool blanket around her shoulders, but she was in such a dreamlike state that she'd barely noticed. Owen left her at an ambulance with the promise he would check on William and the wolf and be right back.

As she watched dozens of police officers walk back and forth outside, she felt another surge of guilt. Everyone was here for her. Her lip began to shake and she bit it hard enough to bleed. She didn't want to think about it. She didn't want to be awake.

Unfortunately, it didn't look as if she'd get a chance to sleep anytime soon. Instead, a man she recognized as Detective Morris handed her a cup of coffee and began asking her questions, about what she'd done the night before and why she left her house without a car. He asked her every question and made sure he covered every detail.

The sky changed from impenetrable darkness to a deep gray overcast. She looked around and noticed it was still raining. She tried to focus on Detective Morris's questions, but it was difficult, especially when she saw the gurneys being pushed into the shack.

"He killed him," she said softly, interrupting Detective Morris's questioning.

"Who is 'he,' and who was killed?" he asked, flipping past several pages of his notepad.

"Billy Hertz. He killed the farmer and his wife the first time they took me. I saw him and his brother gun them both down, but I just never remembered. I blocked it all out. That's why they kidnapped me in the first place, and why they came back for me last night. They wanted to make sure I never linked them to the murders. It was bad enough they were convicted in my kidnapping."

Detective Morris was speechless. Luckily, another voice grabbed their attention and broke the silence.

"Sir, we need to take her to a hospital," a female officer said. "Her grandparents are waiting."

"I'm not finished questioning her," Morris said. "Damn it, where's Peirce?"

"Here, sir," Owen said, showing up at the detective's side. "What do you need?"

"Ride with her and finish the questioning," he said, turning to her. "You understand that we have to go over it all now while everything is fresh in your mind, correct?"

"Yes, Detective," she said.

"Good. Peirce? Get her out of here."

Owen nodded and helped her into the ambulance. She hesitated at first because she hated ambulances, not to mention that she didn't want someone checking her for bruises while riding on bumpy roads. After some negotiating, it was decided that her physical could wait until she got to the hospital and Owen would sit in the back with her, without anyone else. The medical examiner seemed slighted by this, but climbed out of the back without much protest.

When the doors closed and they were finally alone, the ambulance lurched forward. The glow around Owen, though faint, was still visible, and Hanna gazed in awe of it. Although, now that she thought of it, hadn't Owen always looked slightly different from everyone else in New Hope? Sure, he was good-looking and charming, but Hanna had always assumed he looked different because he came from the city and was worldly. Now, looking at him, she realized he'd always had a glow surrounding him.

"Owen," she said slowly. "You're glowing."

He smirked and shook his head, as if trying to shake off the glow itself.

"Why do we have these auras? And how come I'm just noticing them?"

"Well, before me, you blocked out ever seeing them. I think you might have pushed them off as a light trick or cloudy contacts. The thing is, I don't really know. There's a myth our kind uses to explain them, but it's too unbelievable."

"Try me," she said.

Owen smiled.

"All right. There were once three sisters, one of whom is known by many different names, but we call her the Godmother."

"As in—"

"Don't say it," he interrupted quickly. "The story goes that these sisters were practitioners of the occult. The middle sister had a son, and she named the elder sister his Godmother. The other sister was not pleased with this decision, growing so angry that she swore vengeance on the elder sister who had stolen a title she saw as rightfully hers.

"For years, the two fought as their wrath and magical abilities grew. As the nephew became a young man, he began to collect stories from the nearby towns and countries that surrounded their homeland. The Godmother chose to embellish these tales with a new character, a woman with the power to overcome evil. Well, that didn't sit well with the other sister, who added a character who couldn't be taken down by anyone. The Godmother cast a spell to make all characters visible by an unnatural glow, a halo, to warn the heroes of these stories. The good would shine with brilliant colors, while the bad would glow with ominous light. And so, as it was in the stories, it was in real life. The two sisters had immersed so much of themselves in their nephew's stories that they became the stories, and it rendered them immortal."

"So, somewhere in the world, there are two sisters still battling it out?"

"Not in this world, the normal world, but somewhere in our world, in some far corner behind the shadows lives the Godmother, and you better believe that on the opposite side of the world lives the Other." Owen smiled then and shook his head. "But that's just an old wives' tale."

"But aren't we?" she asked and his smile faltered. "Who are you, Owen?"

"Owen Peirce, deputy of the New Hope Police Department, Michigan," he recited. "But that's not the me you're referring to, is it?"

"Owen, my head feels like it's splitting in two. Please," she said, closing her eyes as she pinched the bridge of her nose. "Who are you?"

"Prince Charming," he said, wincing. "At least, I'm the great-great-grandson of Prince Charming."

Hanna looked at him, her mouth hanging open with surprise.

"I know, it's ridiculous, but that's where I get the glow."

"Is that what William meant when you two were fighting? About the white horse and being charming?"

"Yes."

"But what did he mean about an old grudge?"

"A friend of mine betrayed me and my family several years ago, and William was involved," Owen said. "There's been bad blood between us ever since."

The glow around Owen was much different than William's. His was almost blinding now, and she bet it was because, in a way, he'd just saved a damsel in distress. She almost smiled.

"William asked me before if I noticed your glow. I can't believe I never realized." She paused. "Can everyone see it?"

"No. The only people who notice it are others like us," he said. "Gram can see it, barely. That's why you can. Because your relation is through her ancestry."

She'd suspected for a while who she was related to from the old stories, but hadn't said it out loud. It seemed beyond real, and she didn't want to believe it for the simple reason that she didn't want to be any more of a freak than she already was.

"You have to know by now, Hanna," Owen said, his eyes on her.

"I know," she said softly. "But it's so bizarre. I mean, what are we? We glow, I'm living a nightmare, William's . . ." she trailed off. The thought of William and his bleeding wolf hurt her heart and tears welled up in her eyes. "I mean, there doesn't seem to be any rhyme or reason to any of it."

"I know, kid," Owen said. "It seems like it doesn't make sense but, generally, we tend to have similar qualities and experiences as our ancestors."

"How do you know all this, Owen?"

He fell silent for a moment, bringing his hands together in thought. He looked deeply conflicted and she was worried about what he might say.

"Hanna, I wasn't adopted by your aunt and uncle," he confessed slowly. He took a deep breath and exhaled while she watched, wide-eyed. "We're descendants of folktale characters, right? Well, my family was aware of this, and it was something we knew and talked about on a regular basis. We were comfortable, even proud of our identities and the fact that the past didn't dictate our futures. We were, again, comfortable. Why wouldn't we be? We were related to one of the most wealthy, happy, and beloved characters that ever existed. We never really had to deal with the ugly side of it, because everyone was *comfortable*."

By the third time he said comfortable, Hanna got the feeling he was anything but.

"I grew up accepting these things as a reality, but for those who didn't, it's hard to believe, especially in the world today. Magical kingdoms and fairies who tell tales don't exist anymore, but we're still here, telling the same stories over and over again."

She was quiet a moment, thinking. "So, just because William's ancestors were murderers, you thought he was as well? But you just saw the real murderers."

Owen looked ashamed and at the same time convinced he was right. "It's what I've always been told, Hanna," he said.

"What do you mean? What's so wrong about the Vanns?"

"William's father, while not ever found guilty of any crimes, is still a crooked businessman. I've been raised to hate the Vanns and others like them. My friend grew up from a similar story, and I ignored the warnings. He turned out as evil as the rest of them." She saw a pained expression pass over his face at the mention of his former friend. "It's not like I want William to be the bad guy. I just know he's capable."

A thought occurred to her. "How did you find me?"

He avoided her gaze.

"Owen."

He looked back at her and sighed. "I knew William's family was connected with wolves. He came to the station, and when we found out you'd been taken, he said his wolf would take us there. The animal traveled faster than us—he could cut through the forest—but William knew where he was every minute."

She glared at him reproachfully. "And you *still* think he's evil?"

"I'm sorry, all right?" he said, throwing up his hands. "You're right. If you hadn't met William, if your stories hadn't combined, then you'd be six feet under right now and not riding in this ambulance."

He leaned in, suddenly very serious. "Listen to me, kid. Regardless of all that's happened with William, he is still a member of a very dark family. I don't want to tell you how to live your life, but I think you'd be risking a lot by continuing to see him."

"But the Hertzes are gone. My story is over," she said, shaking her head. "I don't have to worry about any more interference ruining my life."

"These stories don't control our destinies, Hanna, but they do mold them. I was supposed to fall in love with a girl whose great-great-grandmother lost a glass shoe a few hundred years ago," he said. "But it's not going to turn out that way."

A shadow of a smile passed over Owen's face and for the first time in all her time of knowing him, she realized she didn't know him at all. She *wanted* to know his whole story.

"But see?" he said. "Your life can't be dictated by once upon a time. If you love a mysterious wolf-man, then you can't help that. But, will his story will accept *you*?"

She managed a smile in return.

"Who lives like that? Not doing things because of what might happen?" Her words echoed Carly's thoughts from that day in the mall. "Where did they go? William and Wyatt, I mean," she asked. Surely all those officers wouldn't have let William just leave with a giant wolf at his heels.

"They'll be all right. William's family arrived yesterday to oversee the rest of the Vo-Tech project. I'm sure their wolves aren't far behind. Mr. Vann will make sure William and his wolf get to where they need to be."

Hanna leaned against the wall of the ambulance, relieved. She was silent the rest of the way, lost in thought. William had probably read every story ever told about evil wolves, and besides a handful of mythologies, they were mostly portrayed in a bad light. But after something like tonight, how could he still think he was bad? He could never be anything but a prince to her now.

After arriving at the hospital, several EMTs and nurses crowded around Hanna as Owen moved away quietly, talking into his phone. She protested a wheelchair at first, finally conceding at Owen's pleading look. She thought about the friend he mentioned. If William wasn't bad, perhaps there were others. Maybe his friend's story wasn't over yet.

"Owen!" she called as she was wheeled toward the hospital doors.

"Yeah, kid?" he said, looking up at her, his phone still up to his ear.

"What was your friend's name?" she asked. "The one who betrayed you?"

"Roderick," he said, a look of confusion on his face. "Why?"

"Maybe he needs a second chance," she said as the glass doors closed.

The hospital staff made sure she had no internal bleeding or head injuries and set her up in her own room. Gram and Grandpa were shown in minutes later, both near collapsing with relief at the sight of her. She was surprised to learn that her parents were coming—they'd already landed in Los Angeles—but she kept it to herself. She was glad they were coming, even if it had taken a near fatal kidnapping.

A nurse came in and gave her a sedative. "To help you rest," she explained with a smile before leaving.

She slept without dreaming and could have stayed that way for years. When she groggily opened her eyes, the room was dark and still, with only the faint beeping of the machines and hallway lights disturbing her sleep. She tried to change her position, stopping when she felt eyes on her.

Slowly, she looked around the room and noticed that she was, in fact, being watched. She grabbed the bedside control and turned on her overhead light. A tall, middle-aged man in a suit grinned at her, his eyes bright, and she knew him instantly from his picture.

"Hello," he said after several uncomfortable seconds of silence. "I'm Mr. Vann."

CHAPTER TWENTY-ONE

Hanna didn't say anything as she looked at William's father. He was dressed in a beautiful black suit and crisp white shirt that seemed to glow beneath the black tie that hung around his neck. He held a thin black briefcase, making him look impeccable and expensive. She was embarrassed that she was only dressed in a paper gown. Was there ever a better example of being on opposite ends of the spectrum?

"So, you're the one in Goldilocks's line that has our William so wound up."

It wasn't a question. She didn't know if she was shocked by seeing him or just on edge due to the last twenty-four hours, but she tensed up when he took a step forward. He noticed, stopping and tilting his head.

"You're not afraid of me, are you?" he asked with his Southern accent, a hint of a smile playing at the corner of his mouth.

A minute stretched as she assessed him. "No," she said finally, relaxing. "I'm just surprised to see you."

He nodded and took a seat in a plastic chair next to her bed.

"So you know who I am? I doubt William showed you my picture," he said, still smiling. "I'm guessing you did some investigative computer work. Isn't that right?"

She blushed and nodded.

"I thought so. No need to be worried. It's smart to snoop on people you don't know, especially if you're in the position where you have to trust them."

"I don't trust you," she said quietly. His smile faltered a little, but his eyes seemed to shine.

"Clever girl," he said, his voice calm. "I'm not a trustworthy man." That made her smile, albeit a little nervously, until he finished saying, "I am, however, a businessman."

She shifted her body, sitting up straight in her bed.

"Why are you here, Mr. Vann?"

"Ah, getting down to the point, just the way I like it. Yes, Miss Loch, let's talk business. My son, William, isn't an average sort of young man."

"I know," she said.

"Yes, I know you know, and that isn't exactly protocol, but we'll get to that later." He pulled his black leather case onto his lap and opened it up. "I have several papers for you to read over and sign. A confidentiality agreement. I don't expect you to open your mouth about it, being from quite a special line yourself, but it's a precaution I insist we take. Do you understand?" He handed her several pages.

"I'm not telling anyone anything about any of this," she said, not taking the papers. "They'll send me away for being crazy."

"Yes, they will," he agreed, not a hint of amusement in his voice. "But that doesn't concern me."

He didn't seem to be trying to frighten or worry her, but he was doing it anyway. He shook the papers in his hand until she took them.

"Where's William?" Hanna asked, changing the subject. "And Wyatt? Are they all right?"

"They're fine," Mr. Vann said, not divulging any more than that. "I'd like to know what happened last night."

"Do you have a few hours?" Hanna asked in a snarky tone. She was tired and something about Mr. Vann rubbed her the wrong way.

"I have all the time in the world," he said, smirking.

She sighed and began the story of how she'd blacked out at work the day before and how William had been there. She told him what they'd spoken about, what she'd learned from her grandparents, and how she'd decided to walk to her car.

Her headache returned while she told him about her struggle with her captors, but she wasn't surprised. It was the first time she had told the whole story from beginning to end, without omitting anything about William, and she knew it wouldn't be the last.

When she got to the part where she saw the wolf behind Billy, she paused and looked at Mr. Vann.

"What is it?" he asked.

"This wasn't the first time I was kidnapped, but I'm sure you knew, didn't you?"

He nodded slowly.

"There was a wolf last time, too. And a policewoman, with eyes like William's," she said quietly, looking at her hands. "It ended differently then."

He sighed, nodding. "She was my sister, Annabelle," he said, his voice pained. "She was a detective for the Michigan State Police when the amber alert went out for you, a newly minted detective with a strong vendetta against crimes involving children." A shadow of a smile passed over Mr. Vann's face. "She was William's godmother. In our world, that's a very serious honor. Godparents are our protectors, our wish granters, our greatest confidants . . . . When we made her William's godmother, she took the honor very seriously.

"She was a wonderful sister, a tremendous woman. I think it was because of her love and bond with William that she decided to work on cases that involved children. Of course, it could have been the fact that our great-grandfather had murdered a child and her grandmother." He paused and Hanna felt sick as he spoke so nonchalantly about it. "History tends to repeat itself in our world, but I guess you know that better than I."

"That's the most awful thing I've ever heard," she said.

"Yes," he said, a strange look passing over his face. "I agree. But whatever Annabelle's reasoning, she thought she could be the godmother every child should have and wanted desperately to save every one of them."

She realized she was twirling her necklace around her finger absentmindedly, and let it fall.

"Annabelle was a different breed. She was a fighter, never completely comfortable with our history. Especially after making her William's godmother . . . something about the title made her a little self-righteous."

He smiled. "She was always a bit of an outcast when it came to the family. She thought working in law enforcement might make up for the stigma that went along with the Vann name. That's why she moved here to our lake house. The only thing people knew about us up here was our construction company. No one knew about our family, and she wanted to be in a place where she could make a new life, one separate from the one she had always known. She wanted the world to know that we weren't the monsters the old stories portrayed us to be." He sighed again, looking at her. "I tried to tell her the world wouldn't care, that she should be proud of who she was and stay away from others in different stories." He smirked. "I tried to tell William much the same. It seems neither of them listened."

"You seem comfortable with who you are, Mr. Vann," she said, concerned by the thought that William's family had told him to stay away from her as much as hers had.

"I am," he answered, and she believed he'd never had any qualm with his family's history.

"So Annabelle heard the amber alert and tracked me?" she said, trying to fill in the blanks.

"Tracked you down to the very same shack you were found in tonight, I believe," he said, giving her a strange look. She felt a wave of guilt slam into her. This man's only sister had died to save her. She felt sick with sorrow. He probably thought his sister had died in vain—and really, hadn't she? He'd lost a sister and almost a son for her stupidity. He probably hated her.

"She had beautiful eyes," she said softly, unable to push away the memory of them staring at her as the woman died.

"Yes," he said, nodding. "Yes, she had remarkable eyes, identical to William's."

"Billy shot her," she blurted out. She wanted him to know for some reason, perhaps to lighten the burden of her own guilt.

He nodded. "Billy Hertz shot her dead," he said quietly. He gestured to her necklace. "I don't know how you got that. It was Annabelle's favorite necklace. William actually picked it out for her."

"It was in my things when I left the hospital the first time," she said, holding the little locket in her hand. Hanna tried to take it off, but the little lobster claw clasp kept slipping in her fingers. "You should have it."

"No, no, Miss Loch," he said, putting his hand up to stop her. "I'm glad you have it. It's nothing but a shiny piece of metal to me, but it meant something to her, and to you, I suspect. You should keep it."

No wonder William seemed strange when he first saw it. In fact, every time William had acted bizarrely seemed to make perfect sense now—all the times he'd seemed so upset when she was in danger. His aunt had died to give her a life and she did stupid things like stand in front of speeding trucks and trains.

"Did she know I was like you?" she asked. "From the old stories?"

"I'm sure she could see your aura. It's quite bright, you know," he said, looking her over. "People with our background tend to migrate to the same places. Some of the Belles think we Beasts have meetings or something to keep tabs on them, not unlike their Annual Ball, but that's not it. We like to know where others like us are, regardless of their stories. Although, I'm sure even if we didn't know, there'd be some mystical force keeping us in close proximity with one another. But that's all I'll say on the matter. You'd likely not believe me if I told you, anyway."

"Annual Ball?"

"Yes, though you wouldn't be invited. They're a stuck-up bunch, those descendants of princes and princesses. They have a soirée every year, to keep in touch with other stuck-ups. 'The Good,' they call themselves. The good for nothings, if you ask me. It is odd that you wouldn't at least know about it, but," he paused, leaning in, "in your case, Goldilocks wasn't exactly one of the Good."

Hanna didn't like the way he said that. She frowned, making a face as if she had a sour candy in her mouth.

"Why did William come here?" she asked, not looking up. She didn't want to see any of his expressions in case he had to lie to her. "Why now?"

"He came because of you, I think," he said honestly. "We'd heard Billy Hertz had been released from jail, and he believed that Billy would go after the girl Annabelle saved, especially because of who the Hertzes are. They're very much like their ancestors."

Her head shot up.

"Just three siblings and the girl that got away . . . funny how we turn out, isn't it, Miss Loch?" She was uncomfortable when he smiled, his teeth showing. "But William, I think, wanted to see you, to know who you were and see if you were worth it."

Mr. Vann closed his briefcase and stood up. "You can read over those papers, if you like, and sign them later."

She felt oddly out of place in his presence.

"It was interesting meeting you, Miss Loch." He turned to leave and was almost out the door when she called him back.

"Mr. Vann," she said quickly. "I'm sorry you lost your sister."

"Why would you be sorry?" he asked, turning back to look at her. "It wasn't your fault."

"But she was looking for me."

"And she found you. She did her job."

"But was I worth it?" she asked softly. She certainly didn't feel worthy enough.

"You were worth it to her. I think that's all that matters now," he said, and disappeared into the hallway.

She was glad he left before the tears fell down her cheeks. Gratitude, anger, sadness, guilt, and more seemed to swarm her as she cried alone in her hospital room. Why had William ever wanted to meet her? Her life had been worth it to Annabelle, but now that he knew her, did William agree? Or did he wish his favorite aunt and godmother was alive, with her dead instead?

She cried harder now, shaking with every sob. She had to get out. She got out of bed and pulled on the pair of jeans and shirt Gram had brought her from home. The door handle of her room twisted before she turned it, and she stepped back in surprise when it opened.

"I thought you'd be asleep . . ." William said. He noticed her tear-stained cheeks. "What's wrong?" He took a step toward her, but she backed away.

"No, I can't," she choked out, wiping more tears from her cheeks. She took a deep breath and looked at him. "I met your dad."

"What did he say?" William almost growled, his eyes flashing. "Did he upset you?"

She suddenly wondered if he even liked his father. Was it any of her business?

"No, I'm just . . . he just told me about Annabelle," she said, looking at the ground. "I remember her."

The silence hung in the air like a knife about to drop and cut her to pieces. Daring to look up, she winced at the blank expression on his face.

"Detective Vann was my aunt," he said after a few moments. "She was my godmother, too."

"I'm so sorry," she cried, unable to hold back fresh tears. "I didn't know. I didn't know about any of it until yesterday."

She sobbed as she stood there, hugging her shoulders for fear she might fall if something didn't hold her up. She'd torn a family apart and she couldn't bare it. It was all her fault. Everything that had happened was her fault, and she hated herself for it.

She jumped when she felt William's arms wrap around her, holding her tightly as she tried to shake him away. She didn't deserve the comfort she felt in his arms.

"It's not your fault, Hanna," he whispered into her ear as he held her. "You were just a kid—"

"I shouldn't have wandered off." She wept into his shoulder as she voiced everything that made her feel guilty. "I shouldn't have gotten lost. If I had just stayed put—"

"Hanna," he said, holding her at a distance. His beautiful eyes looked into hers, but she couldn't bring herself to look at him. He brought his hand up to her chin and tilted her head to meet his eyes. "Hanna, none of what happened was your fault."

"You must hate me," she stuttered.

"Hate you?" he said, the words spoken as if they were a foreign language. "I could never hate you."

"But I—"

"But nothing. Me hate you? It's impossible. I don't think you could ever do anything for me to hate you." He paused and leaned his forehead onto hers. "You're brilliant, you know that? You're resilient, despite everything that's happened to you. Your honesty and courage . . . it's amazing. You're amazing."

Her tears stopped as she looked at him.

"What happened ten years ago can't be changed, and the only thing you can do now is live the best life you can. Go to college, go travel the world, go anywhere and do anything and everything you want. Don't ever feel guilty about being a survivor." He paused, his eyes closed as she held her breath. "Most people couldn't dream of doing what you've done, Hanna. You're a fighter, and you deserve a long, happy life. Move on from this . . ."

She felt her insides turn. Why did he sound like he was saying goodbye?

"William—" she tried, but he stopped her from speaking with a gentle touch of his hand.

"You'll be fine," he said quietly.

"William, why are you saying this?"

"Because you need to hear it."

He pressed his mouth to hers. It was a deep kiss that filled her with want and passion. He held her tightly. She couldn't make sense of him saying goodbye. Just as she thought he would never let go, he released her roughly.

She stood there, watching him as he breathed heavily, unwilling to look at her.

"William—"

"You'll move on from this, Hanna," he said, still refusing to look at her.

"What if I don't want to move on from this?" she asked, moving toward him. "What if I want to be a part of this world?"

He *did* want her, she could feel it. So why was he doing this? She waited for him to answer for what seemed like ages. He finally turned to look at her.

"Forget it, Hanna," he said with steely conviction.

She watched as he turned to go.

"Enough," she said defiantly. "You can't just tell me to forget about all of this, about you. You're what I want, and it's not going to change."

"It won't work."

"I don't think I could love someone who isn't you," she said, determined to make him see. "You will *never* be evil to me, and I don't *want* to love someone who isn't you."

His hand stilled on the door and the moments stretched for what seemed like hours before he spoke. "Goodbye, Hanna," he said, not looking at her.

She bit her lip to stop herself from making a pitiful noise as she felt her heart break. The door had almost closed behind him when she found her voice again. "I love you," she said softly. The door clicked shut, but she needed to say it. "I'm afraid I always will."

She fell back into her bed, trying not to cry, unwilling to let herself shed anymore tears.

She closed her eyes and tried to block everything out without much success. Toying with her necklace, Hanna didn't know how long she stared into oblivion before her eyelids eventually closed and sleep stole over her.

CHAPTER TWENTY-TWO

After several more days in the hospital, Hanna was finally cleared to return home, much to her family's excitement. Her parents had arrived in New Hope the day after the kidnapping and she was a little uncomfortable at how much Mom cried. Dad chatted nervously about everything they'd gone through ten years earlier with her first kidnapping, so much so that it started to annoy her.

Carly was waiting at the house when she came home via police car, courtesy of Owen. He and Gram spoke a lot during her stay in the hospital. Slowly, she began to understand who they were and why Owen had been asked to come and watch over her, especially after Billy Hertz made parole.

With Billy and Bjorn Hertz both dead, Maryanne had a mental breakdown—though Hanna didn't think she'd been very stable to begin with—and was taken to the Western State Psychiatric Hospital to be evaluated. Owen reassured Hanna that she would never see Maryanne again, since she would be found incompetent to stand trial, but she didn't care. She never wanted to think of Maryanne Hertz or her brothers again.

She smiled and talked to everyone who was at her house for her homecoming. Family, friends from school, neighbors, and work friends all came to welcome her home, and while she'd doubted their intentions before, she was touched now. She truly felt loved and accepted by a community that had come together to make her childhood as normal as possible. She even got choked up when she first stepped into the house, which was decorated with white and yellow balloons and streamers. It was a wonderful party, but her joy to be alive and home, surrounded by friends and family, was only half of her. The other half had already gone.

She hadn't heard from William or his father since she'd seen them in the hospital. It was as if they'd just disappeared, and no one seemed interested in talking about it since the police discovered that Maryanne had planned the school's explosion. The Hertzes were who everyone was talking about these days—the Vanns had simply slipped into obscurity.

"So?" Carly said quietly as they sat on the back porch. The party had died down considerably, and the warmth of the spring sun was beginning to wane. "Are you going to go to prom?"

Carly was smiling her "I've-got-something-to-tell-you" smile.

"No, are you?" she played along.

"Yes," she said proudly. "Troy asked me."

"Lucky you," she replied, not about to tell her best friend that her boyfriend had asked her to prom first. "But I don't think I'm up to it."

"Are you sure? I think some normal high school activity would be good for you."

She smiled, grateful to have such a good friend.

"You could probably go stag if you don't want to go with anyone. Plus, we're going to the lake afterward for the weekend. It'll be fun."

"I'm sure it will be," she said. The thought of seeing her entire class looking at her while she walked into prom made her a little uneasy. "But I'll be fine."

"Well, let me know if you change your mind," Carly said, standing up. "It starts at eight next Friday night, so you have some time to decide."

Hanna stood up and hugged Carly.

"Thanks, Carly," she said. "I'll definitely come over and see your dress before you go."

"All right. Bye, girl," Carly said as she made her way back into the house.

"Bye," she said, sitting back down.

Lost in her thoughts, she didn't hear the sliding door open and close behind her. Owen appeared at her side and she looked up, startled.

"Hey, kid," he said, taking Carly's empty seat. "How are you feeling?"

"Okay," she answered.

"How is it seeing your parents?" he asked, nodding inside the house.

Hanna turned around and saw her mother chatting with Mrs. Hines while her father spoke with Grandpa. They seemed more relaxed than she ever remembered seeing them.

"They want me to go with them this summer, on an expedition off the coast of South Africa," she admitted. "Something about the feeding habits of the great white shark."

"That sounds like it could be interesting," Owen said. "Are you going to go?"

"I don't know," she said absentmindedly.

"You seemed preoccupied," he said cautiously.

"Have you heard anything from William?" she asked.

Owen looked at his hands.

"They left," he said quietly. "His father and his lawyers left town a few days ago. The crew is still here, working on the school, but I haven't heard from William or seen him around. I think he went back to South Carolina."

She nodded, not sure how to feel. William seemed as determined to avoid her as she was to be with him. *Take a hint,* she thought sarcastically.

"I guess that makes sense," she said quietly.

"I'm sorry, kid," he said. "I know you really liked him."

"I love him," she said honestly, not really sure why she felt the need to tell Owen. Maybe she thought he would understand better than anyone, especially since William was like them. "Pathetic, right?"

Owen sighed heavily and reached for her hand.

"Maybe a summer off the coast of South Africa would do you some good, kid," he began. "Clear your head; get out of this place."

"Yeah, probably," she said. "It would be nice to get away before college started."

"Do you know where you're going yet?"

She didn't want to tell him that she'd been accepted to a college in Charleston, even though she hadn't decided yet.

"No, not yet," she said.

"Well, you better get on that," he said, standing up. "I've got to go, though. I'm doing the graveyard shift tonight."

As he turned to leave, she stood up and hugged him.

"Thank you, Owen," she said. "For everything."

"No problem," he said with a playful smirk as he opened the sliding glass door.

Soon after he left, the rest of the guests departed. It wasn't long after that before she retreated to her bedroom and got ready for bed. As she turned off the lights and got under the covers, she heard the door to her bedroom open and footsteps. She turned her light back on and saw her grandmother cautiously walking down the stairs, holding something behind her back.

"Hi Gram, what's up?" she asked, fighting a yawn. It had been a very exhausting day and sleep was steadily taking over.

"Oh, I just wanted to give you something, sweetheart," she said, pulling a small book from behind her back. She handed it to Hanna, who recognized it as the little journal she'd found in the attic. "I thought you might like to have this."

"Is that . . . is that how all of it began?" Hanna asked.

"It's the very first telling of our story, written well over two hundred years ago, by our ancestor, Ingrid."

She handed it to Hanna.

"So you did take it from the attic that day. Why?"

"I was afraid that it might spark a memory." Gram sighed and took a seat on Hanna's bed. "It was so terrifying after the first time you were kidnapped; we were all so worried that you'd never speak again. We didn't know what was wrong. Then, when you finally came around and couldn't remember any of it, well, we all just thought it was best to keep you in the dark. I had hoped to teach you all about our family history for years until then. I'm quite proud of it, and I wanted you to be too, but I was too afraid. We all were . . . . But now that it's finished, I think you ought to have this. It belongs to you."

"Thanks Gram, but I can't read it. It's in another language."

Hanna watched as Gram grinned, a twinkle in her eye that she rarely saw.

"Oh, I think I'd give it another go if I were you," she said as she stood up. "It's not every day you read your own fairy tale."

"Owen hates that word," Hanna said.

"Owen doesn't like to believe it, but there's a bit of magic in us. Even though I'm sure he's seen his fair share of it."

"Magic?"

Gram gave her a wink and headed up the stairs. Hanna looked down at the book and opened it. The words were still foreign, until she noticed them shaking on the fragile page. Within seconds, the little words began to transform and spell out the story.

"Once upon a time . . ." she whispered to herself.

She settled into bed. In the background, she could hear the wooden feet of chairs being scraped against the floor above her as Gram put the kitchen back to its normal state. She eventually drifted to sleep, her new treasure clutched in her arms.

Hanna spent the majority of the next few days with her parents, going shopping and out to eat. It was nice to hang out with them by herself, and for the first time in years, she felt like a normal teenager. They talked about school and work and traveling to South Africa for the summer. It had always been a daydream of hers to be on a boat, living with her parents in some exotic part of the world for months on end.

After eating at J R Barbecue the Friday of prom, they drove back to the house and were barely in the doorway when the phone rang. Gram passed her the phone.

"It's Carly," Gram warned, her eyebrows raised. "She's panicking about her dress."

"Oh, Jeez," she said as she took the phone. "Thanks for the warning." She placed the receiver to her ear. "Hello?"

"Hanna!" Carly yelled into her ear. "I'm freaking out! When are you getting a new cell? I need you here!"

"Okay, okay, I'll be over in a few," she said, hanging up.

"Honey," Mom began. "I don't know if it's such a good idea for you to go out alone."

"It's fine," she said, giving her a smile. "I want to."

"But can't Carly call someone else?" Dad suggested. "Does she really need you?"

"It's prom, Dad, and she's my best friend," she said, reaching for her keys. "It'll be fine. I'll go there, help her out, and come right back. Promise."

They looked less than convinced.

"Of course," Gram said, stepping forward after a moment of silence. "Go, have fun with Carly."

"Thanks," Hanna said.

"We love you," Mom said as she walked out of the house.

"Love you all too," she called behind her, glad to be getting out alone.

It wasn't that she didn't love and appreciate her family, but it was getting a little suffocating, being surrounded by them every minute of every day. She hadn't been out of their sight since her parents arrived at the hospital and that was nearly two weeks ago. She wanted to get back to normal as quickly as possible, and helping Carly calm down from overreacting about something was about as normal as she could imagine.

Of course, she hadn't felt like her old self in months. Ever since William came into her life, she'd only felt half complete unless he was close to her. Now that he was gone, she could only pretend everything was fine, lest someone thought she was depressed. She'd already made it clear that she didn't want to talk to a psychologist about her ordeal.

Upon arriving at Carly's, she found two screaming twins running around the living room while a blurry-eyed Carly held a blue-and-black-striped gown to her chest.

"I can't believe this!" Carly cried. Her eyes lit up in desperate hope as Hanna walked into the living room. "Hanna! Oh my God, can you sew?"

Uh oh.

"Let me see it," she said, sidestepping one of the twins. Carly handed it to her. "Where's the problem?"

"Jake cut the left strap off my dress," she said loudly as her younger brother stopped running around. His bottom lip trembled when Carly shot him a look. "Don't even think your crying is going to bug me."

As if on cue, Jake began to sob and Carly's mother came stomping out of the hallway.

"Carly!" her mother began. "Stop yelling at Jake!"

"It's not my fault that he's a crybaby!" Carly shouted over Jake's wailing. "He just ruined the most significant night of my adolescent life!"

"Stop overreacting," her mother said.

"Hanna!" Carly yelled, making Hanna feel almost like a parent.

"Okay, okay," she said. "Let's go to your room and try and fix it."

Carly relented, and with a thankful look from Carly's mother, they retreated to her bedroom. Once alone, she saw the complete damage of the strap, and since it looked unsalvageable, they decided to cut the rest of the fabric off and make it a single-strap dress. With much tucking and pinning, the dress looked wonderful and even slightly more expensive with the new finishing touch.

Troy arrived at Carly's house an hour later in a limo with the rest of the lacrosse team. Feeling a little out of place,

Hanna waved with Carly's mother and father as the limo drove off into the night. She said goodbye and drove home, trying not to feel terribly sorry for herself since she wasn't going to prom.

As she pulled into the driveway, she noticed the lights of the house were switched off. She guessed that everyone would pretend to be asleep, and she wouldn't have been surprised if Carly's mother called her house to confirm that she was safe and on her way home.

She closed the door to her station wagon and turned to walk up her front steps, but a sound sent chills down to her core and she stopped dead. A wolf's howl, long and low.

"William," she whispered, as she heard feet crunching through the gravel behind her. She turned around and blinked.

There he was, standing alone, as if he had never left, dressed in a pair of jeans and a long-sleeve flannel shirt. He smiled and she felt her stomach flip.

"Hey," he said softly as he stopped a few feet away from her.

"What are you doing here?" she asked.

"I had some unfinished business here," he said, his face showing deep concentration before he broke eye contact with her. "I shouldn't have left like I did. I wasn't ready or willing to accept what you were saying."

Hanna kept her distance. She had felt too exposed the last time they met, and she didn't want to jump first if he was just going to shut her down again.

"So?" she offered.

"So," he said, putting his hands in his pockets. "I want you to know that this might be difficult. At least at first."

"What will be difficult?" she asked, goading him to say it.

He looked at her, a hint of amusement behind his gaze. She folded her arms and stared back at him. She thought he might not answer, until he inhaled and exhaled loudly.

"You're not going to make this easy, are you?"

Hanna raised her brow and waited.

"I want you to know that us being together might be difficult. Again, at first."

Hanna could have screamed she was so happy, but she didn't move. She simply smiled, deciding to play with him a little.

"What makes you think I still want to be difficult with you?"

Whether William knew she was teasing or not, he stepped toward her, so only a few inches separated them. He looked down at her, and she could smell the clean scent of soap on him. She inhaled deeply, admiring the way his dark hair looked so perfectly imperfect.

"Well, do you?"

"I'm going to need a better offer than that," she said, smiling widely now that she saw the contentment in his face.

"Hanna Loch," he began, shaking his head as his mouth curved into a smile. "Would you like to be difficult with me?"

She bit the inside of her bottom lip and looked away for a moment. As if he had to ask.

"Yes, William Vann," she said, looking up at him. "Yes, I would."

She stood on her toes and kissed him, his arms going around her waist as he pulled her up into him. Her heart felt like it would explode with joy. She kissed him like she never had before, and he let her; for the smallest of moments, Hanna truly believed in magic. And she didn't even care how cliché she was being.

When he pulled away, he was breathing heavily and looked a little amazed.

"Do you want to do something tonight?" he offered. "I know it's your prom and all. I wouldn't want you to miss it if it's important to you."

She thought for a moment before looking up and smiling.

"Let's go for a walk," she said, holding out her hand.

"A walk? That's all you want to do?" he said, curling his fingers with hers.

"That's all I want to do," she said.

They walked down her driveway and into the night. She would bring up her acceptance to Charleston later, but for now, all she wanted was to walk quietly into the night with him. And so they did, followed closely by Wyatt . . .

Maybe happily ever after was a real thing after all.

ABOUT MELINDA

Melinda Michaels is the author of *Golden* and currently lives in Milford, Pennsylvania. A self-proclaimed historian with a rare sense of humor, Melinda finds an immense amount of joy in knowing useless facts, exploring historical places and drinking copious amounts of coffee. When she's not writing she can be found researching obscured time periods for her own amusement or refurbishing old furniture.

Melinda loves Philadelphia and visits often to enjoy the city with her husband Andrew. Together they have three rambunctious pets. Archie the Beagle, Winston the Boston Terrier and Beatrice the cat. *Golden* is the first in a Young Adult magic realism series.

ACKNOWLEDGEMENTS

My sincerest appreciation to my husband, **Andrew**, my wonderful family and friends. With special gratitude to the brilliant **Virginia** and to the lovely people at **REUTS Publications**. Thank you all from the bottom of my heart!